Praise for the works of Stac

Devil's Slide

...*Devil's Slide* though, is phenomenally written! Emotional, exquisitely paced, and tense for almost the entirety of the tale, readers are kept on the edges of their seats, never sure how things will turn out.

-Carolyn M., *NetGalley*

Amid Secrets

Amid Secrets, the third novel in the Falling Castles series, is definitely a tale filled with suspense, multiple dilemmas, and lots of twists and turns in the plot. Just about everyone we have met in the first two books of this series ends up in some sort of crisis or life-changing event. In other words, this is another exceptional mystery, intrigue, and romantic thriller by Stacy Lynn Miller.

-Betty H., *NetGalley*

Absolutely brilliant. The whole series has kept me engaged, and on my toes and hooked me in. Great storyline, fantastic characters throughout the book, gripping suspense storyline, cannot fault this author at all.

-Jo R., *NetGalley*

Blind Suspicion

With the first book ending on a cliffhanger, I was very much looking forward to reading this sequel and it was so satisfying. Lynn Miller knows how to keep things interesting, and I'm learning that the different volumes in her series never feel repetitive. ...In summary, drama, romance, and mystery—what's not to like? I hope to see more books in this series.

-Meike V., NetGalley

Honestly? Stacy Lynn Miller is probably one of the better authors I've come across in the last few years. If you want something fresh, gripping, entertaining and keeps you guessing to the end, this author is for you. *Blind Suspicion* is the sequel to *Despite Chaos*, another fantastic read, I recommend you read it first.

-Jo R., NetGalley

This novel is a very enticing and captivating story full of love, drama, loyalty, family dynamics (both good and bad ones), romance, mystery and so many other things...

-Laurie D., NetGalley

Despite Chaos

I honestly do not know what to say! Fantastic story. Everything I've read by Stacy Lynn Miller has been entertaining, engaging, and gripping. *Despite Chaos* is yet another amazing story, it's a must book to own in 2022. It's a 5/5. And with a cliffhanger like that... Can't wait for that sequel.

-Emma S., NetGalley

Stacy Lynn Miller has a great ability to write messy, complicated people that are easy to like. With this first book in the "Falling Castles" series, she does it again with Alexandra Castle and Tyler Falling.

-Colleen C., NetGalley

This is a well-written, slow-burn romance. There's romance, competition, blackmail, embezzlement and jealousy. The story was fast-paced, and I enjoyed every minute of it. The love, support, and understanding of Tyler's husband was astounding. Hands down a great read and I recommend getting a copy.

-Bonnie K., *NetGalley*

Beyond the Smoke

This was really good! This is the third book in Miller's Manhattan Sloane Thriller series and is the best written book of the series. I was caught up in the mystery, it kept me turning the pages, but so did the romance.

-Lex Kent's Reviews, *goodreads*

I loved the first two novels, but I think this one might be the best yet. …I've enjoyed all the mystery, excitement, action, and intrigue in the plots of these books, but I've fallen in love with these characters, and want to know what's happening in their lives. This is the mark of an exceptionally talented author.

-Betty H., *NetGalley*

From the Ashes

I have been looking forward to reading *From the Ashes* by Stacy Lynn Miller since I read her first Manhattan Sloane novel back in April. I fell in love with Sloane, Finn, and all the other characters in this story while reading the first book, and I wanted more, especially since the story didn't completely end with the first novel. I'm happy to say I loved this book as much as the first one.

I highly recommend both novels, though, so get them both. You won't be disappointed.

-Betty H., NetGalley

…Miller is a wonderful storyteller and this story had me sitting on the edge of my seat from start to finish. The first book in the series, *Out of the Flames*, was a 5-star read and *From the Ashes* is the same as it ducks and weaves and thrills and spills all the way to the end. The chemistry between Sloane and Harper is palpable. …Miller certainly knows how to write angst into her characters. This book is a thrill a minute and I can't wait for the next one.

-Lissa G., NetGalley

Out of the Flames

This is the debut novel of Stacy Lynn Miller and it's very, very good. The book is a roller coaster of emotion as you ride the highs and lows with Sloane as she navigates her way through her life which is riddled with guilt, self blame, and eventually love… The story line is really solid.

-Lissa G., NetGalley

If you are looking for a book that is emotional, exciting, hopeful, and entertaining, you came to the right place. There are characters you will love, and characters you will love to hate. And the important thing is that Miller makes you care about them so, yes, you might need the tissues just like I did. I see a lot of potential in Miller and I can't wait to read book two.

-Lex Kent's 2020 Favorites List
Lex Kent's Reviews, goodreads

If you are looking for an adventure novel with mystery, intrigue, romance, and a lot of angst, then look no further.

…I'm really impressed with how well this tale is written. The story itself is excellent, and the characters are well-developed and easy to connect with.

-Betty H., NetGalley

Last Barrel

Other Bella Books by Stacy Lynn Miller

A Manhattan Sloane Thriller
Out of the Flames
From the Ashes
Beyond the Smoke

Falling Castles Series
Despite Chaos
Blind Suspicion
Amid Secrets

Speakeasy Series
Devil's Slide
Whiskey War

About the Author

A late bloomer, Stacy Lynn Miller took up writing after retiring from the Air Force. Her twenty years of toting a gun and police badge, tinkering with computers, and sleuthing for clues as an investigator form the foundation of her Lexi Mills crime thriller series and Manhattan Sloane romantic thriller series. She is visually impaired, a proud stroke survivor, mother of two, tech nerd, chocolate lover, and terrible golfer with a hole-in-one. When you can't find her writing, she'll be golfing or drinking wine (sometimes both) with friends and family in Northern California.

For more information about Stacy, visit her website at stacylynnmiller.com. You can also connect with her on Instagram @stacylynnmiller, X @stacylynnmiller, or Facebook @stacylynnmillerauthor

Last Barrel

Stacy Lynn Miller

BELLA
BOOKS

2024

Bella Books, Inc.
P.O. Box 10543
Tallahassee, FL 32302

First Edition - 2024

Editor: Medora MacDougall
Cover Designer: Heather Honeywell

ISBN: 978-1-64247-520-3

PUBLISHER'S NOTE

Acknowledgments

Thank you, Barbara Gould, my plotting partner in crime, for serving as the best sounding board I could ever ask for.

Thank you, Linda and Jessica Hill, for believing in my work.

Thank you, Medora MacDougall, for bringing out the best in me.

Finally, to my family. Thank you for loving me.

Dedication

To Emeryn, Elizabeth, Kyrien, Kelson, Matthew,
and Llewyn

CHAPTER ONE

June 1933

Dax stuffed her hands deeper into the pockets of her wool peacoat, protecting them from the cold overnight ocean breeze. Her feet bobbed with the Foster House dock as the marina waves continued their steady creep toward the shoreline. She kept her stare focused on the water lit faintly by the moonlight peeking through slow-moving clouds and watched for the skiffs from the Canadian cargo ship.

Her brother-in-law, Hank O'Keefe, stood silently beside her at the railing. Quiet was his natural state unless Dax's sister was nearby, but tonight, he seemed sullen.

"Is something wrong, Hank?" she asked.

"Change is on the horizon."

"The whole country is about to change, but I'm not sure if it will be good for the Beacon Club," Dax said.

They'd both read the *Halfmoon Bay Review* editorial detailing the chances of the Twenty-first Amendment passing after New Jersey became the fifth state to ratify it. The polls in the article came to an earth-shattering conclusion: repeal of Prohibition was a foregone conclusion. It was only a matter of when Dax would buy her last barrel of illegal whiskey.

The last two months had given her a dismal peek into the future if repeal passed. The sale of beer and wine had been legal since President Roosevelt signed the Cullen-Harrison Act in April, just weeks after his inauguration. Within a week, a dress shop down the street converted into a bar, peeling off several of Dax's customers. She predicted a bar would pop up on every corner within six months when the sale of spirits became legal again.

Hank focused on the water in the distance, matching Dax's stare. "Maybe now war vets won't go broke escaping their pain."

"What do you mean?" Dax asked.

"Every speakeasy, including ours, charges an arm and a leg for a drink when most vets are already a limb or two short. Don't get me wrong, I understand why we charge so much. The Canadians charge us twice as much for a barrel as they do north of the border, and we have to pay off the cops and local Prohis. The overhead is high, but we're still making money hand over fist."

"We're the ones taking the risk, Hank. It's not illegal to drink booze, but it is to manufacture, transport, or sell it. If we get arrested, we'll need the money to get us out of jail."

"I know, but vets can't save a penny or catch a break. It's like the horror of that damn war never ends. They're on a carousel and can't get off."

"Is that what happened to you?" Dax asked.

Beyond his distinction as the best American sharpshooter during the Great War, she'd learned little about Hank's life during the three years since he'd come to live with them and they'd officially become family. She'd gotten the impression he'd witnessed unspeakable atrocities.

"It was until I met May." Hank craned his head toward her. Despite the darkness, she saw a glimmer of sadness in his eyes. "I'm lucky. Most don't have a woman like her in their lives."

"Can I ask you something, Hank?" Dax waited for his affirmative nod. "You once told me Grace had taken you in when you were at your lowest. Had you just come back from the war?"

"It was almost two years after I returned." He shifted uncomfortably against the railing. "A drunk behind the wheel of a car had killed my first wife. The nightmares about Caroline's death, the war, and everything I'd done didn't stop, but Grace and Clive were there to make sure I didn't eat my gun."

"Then May came along," Dax said, the corners of her lips drawing up. Her sister often drew out in him a gentle side he rarely showed others.

"When the nightmares stopped, I knew she was my ticket off the carousel."

"And you were her ticket, too. I've never seen her this happy. I'm glad you were there for her when our mother passed away last year." Dax's sister had taken their mother's death much harder than she had. The day her parents sent her away thirteen years ago was when she had mourned their loss. She had considered herself an orphan since.

Several minutes of silence passed before Dax spoke again. "What do you think repeal will mean for the Seaside after it reopens on the Fourth of July?"

The last four months had been brutal on the town. Grace Parsons, the Hollywood star and Rose's ex who took over Frankie Wilkes's properties following his death, closed the Seaside Hotel for repairs after a heavy winter storm that damaged most of the guest rooms. Thankfully, the Foster House had escaped with only minor issues due to Dax's reinforcements over the years. Grace took the closing as an opportunity to redesign the floors, adding adjoining rooms for privacy. Couples could check in as man and wife and pair up as they pleased behind closed doors. The improvement would make the Seaside a safe place for people with different sexual appetites, like Grace, Clive, Rose, and Dax.

"With Grace's Hollywood and political friends coming throughout the year, the hotel should be fine."

"I hope you're right, Hank."

"You don't know Grace like I do. After everything she's done so people like you can come here without fear of being found out, she won't let it die. The world needs more places like the Seaside."

"The world needs more people like you who only judge us based on how we treat others, not who we love."

Soon, the sound of multiple outboard motors cut through the night, signaling the skiffs were approaching rapidly with their load. Being able to shift the deliveries to Friday morning after Governor James Rolph took office in 1931 had been a godsend. Rolph had made it clear he would not enforce the Volstead Act, leaving it up to the federal government to tackle. That meant Captain Burch had only the Coast Guard and Prohibition agents to contend with and Dax could sleep in on her days off. However, she didn't expect these deliveries to last much longer. If repeal passed as the local newspaper had forecasted, smuggling runs under the cloak of darkness and secrecy like this one would become unnecessary with a stroke of a pen. In its wake, Dax expected a fiasco with sourcing legal booze, like she'd encountered with beer and wine. Demand was high and supply was low, requiring a significant outlay for the first month of deliveries. She would have to earmark more funds for the inevitability.

The first motorboat silhouette appeared in the moonlight, then a second and a third. They slowed to angle into their designated slips until all six boats were in position. Men from each boat jumped onto the dock, tying the lines to the mooring bollards. The crews unloaded their illegal cargo like well-oiled machines, stacking the crates and barrels along the wood platforms in twelve minutes. One by one, the teams reboarded, untied their lines, and retreated into the darkness.

When it was time for the sixth boat to take off, the senior man waved Dax over and handed her an envelope. "From Captain Burch. He sends his apologies."

"Thank you," Dax said. She looked at the envelope, finding a wax seal on the back with the captain's mark. *Odd*, she thought. The captain typically communicated through his onshore money man, who collected payment from his customers every other week. This likely meant he was raising his prices again. When beer and wine became legal, Burch said he'd initially lost a third of his customers. His losses continued to climb, and he had to raise prices to justify the cost of continuing the runs. Those who could not afford the increase turned to backwoods stills to fill the gap until repeal passed. Money was getting tighter, but Dax refused to settle. She'd built the Beacon Club's and Seaside's reputations by offering only the best in liquor, entertainment, and experience. She would pay or broker a deal they both could live with.

The senior man also handed Dax a two-foot square box weighing about ten pounds. "The item you requested the captain pick up in Seattle. He said no charge. It's the least he could do for his favorite customer, considering the contents of his letter."

"Please pass along my thanks." Dax grew more concerned about the letter, but whatever was in it would have to wait until she and Hank had safely stowed their shipment inside the basement. "Please tell him we're looking forward to hosting him and his wife for the grand reopening of the Seaside next month."

The last smuggler tipped his cap and pointed toward the envelope in Dax's hand. "The letter will explain." He boarded his skiff, and it disappeared into the marina.

Hank whistled for the waiting drivers from the four speakeasies in neighboring towns to load their new stock into the trucks. This latest batch of drivers and helpers wasn't as friendly as the ones in the past. When Dax first brokered the arrangement with Captain Burch to deliver his cargo at the Foster House dock instead of the beaches north of town, she had a good relationship with the other crews. They no longer had to navigate the dangerous curves around Devil's Slide and were grateful for her intervention. But this new crop had no such history with her. They kept to themselves and trusted no one. And Dax didn't trust them, especially the crew from Redwood City, where Roy Wilkes was running for county sheriff. Wilkes had an ax to grind with her, so she watched them like a hawk.

The smugglers had etched a mark on each barrel and crate, designating which item belonged to which customer to speed loading. The less time they spent at the dock increased the chance of everyone getting away with their cargo. As crews identified their unique marks and ran the items up the gangway to their waiting trucks, Dax kept count. Orders were the same each week, except for holidays. The Fourth of July was a month away, which accounted for Dax's double order for the reopening of the Seaside. It might explain why the Redwood City crew would grab an extra whiskey barrel, but not the two they were taking.

Dax placed her personal box on a covered water barrel and elbowed Hank in the side. "They're at it again." Expecting a fight if she failed to catch them off guard, she pulled her pistol from the back of her waistband and rested it against her thigh.

Hank did the same. He followed her to the back of their truck, where Wilkes's men were lugging a barrel earmarked for the Beacon Club. She waited until they placed it on the ground prior to loading it onto the truck bed. Otherwise, they might drop twelve hundred dollars in future sales.

Dax stepped forward and pressed her gun's muzzle into the man's back. "I think you miscounted again."

The man flew an elbow back, striking Dax on the left cheekbone and sending her tumbling to the ground. While the coppery taste of blood filled her mouth, she tightened her grip on the pistol. With her blinded by pain, it was now three against one—them against Hank. Dax feared it would not be a fair fight.

A scuffle started behind her, followed by three loud thuds. She finally got her bearings and refocused on her surroundings, finding the uneven playing field had tilted in the expected direction. The three men writhed in pain on the ocean-moistened pavement while Hank stood over them, returning his gun to the waist holster beneath his jacket.

"It's never okay to hit a woman." Hank sneered, clenching both hands into fists. "Now, unless you want me to finish this, you'll unload what isn't yours."

Dax righted herself and stood, thankful and also embarrassed for needing Hank to come to her aid. He'd saved her from a more severe beating, but he'd also shown everyone she could not defend herself. Her success depended on the mystique that she was as tough as anyone in the business, but his heroics may have set back her image.

The three rubbed their wounds and rose to their feet. She waited until the Beacon Club's other barrel was safely on the ground before telling them the consequences of their third and final mistake with her. "I warned you when I caught you stealing last month. Now, I'm barring your owner from using this dock. Captain Burch will get my message by tomorrow. Good luck in convincing him to make a separate drop-off somewhere."

The Redwood City men laughed and issued threats of revenge before peeling out of the back parking lot. Hank turned to her. "Roy Wilkes won't be happy."

"Then he shouldn't have sent men who steal."

"This might start another whiskey war."

"We stopped them once. We can do it again." Dax forced her jaw open. The pain dissipated, settling into soreness and forecasting she might have trouble eating for several days. Maybe another war wasn't such a good idea.

"I'm done killing, Dax."

She had no words in return for Hank. He had taken on a small army three years ago, winning the war the Wilkes brothers had started in their thirst for control of Half Moon Bay. No one on Wilkes's side survived that night. Dax didn't know the entire story behind the atrocities Hank witnessed during the Great War, but she knew Grace enlisting him to employ his unique skills to defeat Frankie Wilkes had cost a piece of himself.

She laid a comforting hand on his shoulder. "Thanks for defending me tonight, but I can't look weak again."

"I understand. I'll leave one for you next time." Hank's wink was the closest he'd come to boasting in their years of living and working together. He let his actions speak for him, but this playful side was refreshing, a sign of softening up after two years of marriage.

"Let's hope there is no next time."

"We better hurry and get you back to bed," Hank said. "You have a long day ahead of you."

"That I do. Thanks for offering to manage the club tonight."

"You and Rose deserve a night in the city. Be sure to give Grace and Clive my best."

"Of course."

They sifted through the cargo, storing the Beacon Club stock in the basement and the items bound for the Seaside Club into the company truck. It had twice the power with a V-8 engine and double the hauling capacity of her old Model T pickup. The new Ford flatbed was a beast on four wheels and driving it over Devil's Slide would have been a dream. However, given the agreement with Captain Burch to deliver the liquor to their dock, the purchase had seemed like a waste of money when something less robust would have sufficed. But Grace had insisted on only the best for the Seaside. When finished, the remodeled hotel and club would be the jewel of the West Coast, making Half Moon Bay *the* vacation spot along the Pacific.

Dax drove to the end of the block and pulled to the hotel's loading dock. After three trips to the Seaside's basement, she and Hank secured the load in the newly built hidden vault behind the bar.

The club occupied the same space as before, but the remodeling touched every aspect of the room except one. The stage Dax had built before the whiskey war between her and Frankie Wilkes was a focal point worthy of Grace's vision for a destination more glamorous than Hollywood's Frolic Room. Dax remembered the care she'd put into building it. After discovering how rotted the underbelly had become, she obsessed over designing a platform to last a century for one reason— Rose. Dax could not have the woman she loved performing on anything less sturdy or fetching.

She imagined the grand reopening with movie stars and their friends filling the hotel. During the day, some would picnic at the beaches north of town and others would take small launches around the inner harbor to drink champagne and make love in broad daylight. At night, space at the club would be by reservation only. Servers would scurry around, delivering meals and nonstop liquor while the guests waited for the main attraction.

Crystal lights would adorn the ceiling and walls. Elegant white linens and bone china would decorate the tables. When the clock struck eight, Lester would seat himself behind his piano and announce, "The Seaside Club is proud to bring you the Songstress of the Pacific, Rose Hamilton." The crowd would go wild with applause, and Rose would mesmerize them with song after song until she'd convinced each guest they were going home with her, but Dax would know Rose had eyes only for her.

After returning to the Beacon Club to complete the paperwork associated with the night's shipment, Dax poured two cups of water, sat next to Hank at the bar where she'd placed the special delivery from Captain Burch, and pressed the cold glass against her left cheek to stem the swelling.

"Is that Rose's birthday present?" Hank asked.

"Yep. I'm glad Burch came through in time."

"I'm surprised Edith couldn't get one from the city."

"They sold out in three days. No one for two hundred miles will get another shipment for weeks." Dax could have kicked herself for not jumping at the chance to get one of these babies the day they first arrived in San Francisco. She could say it was because of her working nights, but it would not be accurate. She'd simply forgotten.

"Well, she'll love it," Hank said.

Moments later, she broke the seal on Captain Burch's letter and read it. Considering this week's special election, its contents weren't surprising, but the news nonetheless made her angry.

"Any problems?" Hank asked.

"Nothing we can't handle." Dax returned the letter to its envelope and placed it in her jacket pocket, weighing whether to call Grace. She was the Beacon Club's primary investor and owner of the Seaside, but she'd put Dax in charge of club operations. Dax was confident she could work out something with Burch. She had to. Otherwise, the Beacon and Seaside Clubs might wither until repeal. "Let's hope the election goes the way we want."

"That bad, huh?" Hank said.

"We'll be fine." Dax sounded more optimistic than she felt. But losing everything didn't matter. She and Rose were thirty years old—Rose as of today—and were no strangers to being penniless. Until Grace opened the Beacon Club, neither knew what it was like to walk into a store and not worry about the price of things. Struggling again didn't scare her, not as long as she had Rose.

CHAPTER TWO

Dax carried Rose's gift up the basement stairs, with Hank two steps behind. Surprisingly, streaks of light showed through the gap at the bottom of the door, alerting her that someone was in the Foster House kitchen. The restaurant staff wasn't due to arrive for another two hours to prepare for the breakfast service, so it likely meant one thing.

Dax pushed the kitchen door open at the top, confirming her suspicion. May could not sleep again. Thirty-four hadn't treated her sister well. The doctor had called it early menopause, also known as deficiency disease, but most women called it the change. Frequent bouts of uncontrollable sweating plagued her, making sleeping through the night impossible.

May was dressed, nursing a cup of coffee at the center chopping block and reading Agatha Christie's latest novel, *Peril at End House*. She peered over the top of her book when the door opened fully, rattling the pail on the floor and the mops hanging from the wall hooks. The dark circles under her eyes were particularly prominent, making Dax dread her own change. Hopefully, it would hold off for another decade.

"Good morning." May raised the mug but lowered it quickly when Dax stepped closer. She focused on Dax's face, narrowed her eyes in concern, and put down her book and cup. "What happened to you?"

"Roy Wilkes's men got sticky fingers again."

May winced, touching Dax's cheek. "Let me get you something cold to put on it."

Dax clutched May's arm with her free hand when she rose from her stool. "I already did. I just want to get to bed for a few hours."

Hank came up behind May and kissed her on the forehead. "Can't sleep again?" He inspected the contents of her cup. "Can I get you some tea or warm milk instead? Maybe you can get in another hour."

"I'd rather stay up and get through the breakfast service."

Hank sat on the stool next to May and squeezed her hand. "Then let Sheila take over the lunch service so you can go home and nap."

"But—" May started.

"But nothing." Hank sounded firm. Since they married, he'd watched over May like a guardian yet never imposed his will on her. He treated her like a true partner, unlike her late husband, Logan, who had likened her to a servant, not his wife. Hank was perfect for her, and she was the same for him. They lifted the other from the darkness of their former lives, creating a beautiful one with respect and love at the core.

"You're right, Hank." May returned his concern with a loving squeeze of his hand.

"Maybe it's time to start cutting back."

"I've been telling you that for years." Dax was glad May had finally listened but was frustrated it had taken so long.

"I know, but I felt Grace giving Hank and me the property across the highway as a wedding gift was too much."

"She's family." Hank shook his head like he and May had gone over this a thousand times. "You didn't want Logan's old house even though Grace said she could get it back from the bank for pennies on the dollar."

May waved him off. "I'd rather that monstrosity sit empty. It's no surprise the bank still can't find a buyer for it."

"Well, I'm glad you took Grace's generous gift," Dax said. "I got to remodel it with Hank for you two to live in. It's what a family does for one another. No one is keeping score. You don't have to cook to earn your share because you provide something more important. You're the family glue."

May sighed. "It's not scorekeeping, Dax. It's something more."

Dax placed the box on the chopping block and sat on the third stool. May didn't have to say what had been driving her to get up at four o'clock five days a week and cook for the breakfast and lunch crowd for three years. Dax managed the Beacon Club and the Seaside remodel. Hank managed the dining room during the Half Moon Bay week, and the club on Dax's nights off. Rose provided nightly entertainment, keeping the club and restaurant packed in the evenings. May owned the Foster House outright, but her contribution was cooking. While her new leg brace helped her stand for more extended periods, she still had limitations. If she stopped, she would give up her purpose.

"I understand, May. But you provide so much more to the restaurant than cooking. Sheila is a decent cook who, yes, has her own way of doing things, but you're the heart and soul of the Foster House. You know what people like to eat and how they like it prepared, which is why Ida's Café closed and this place thrived. That was all you."

"Which is why I still need to work."

"Work? Yes. But cook every day? No," Dax said. "We can bring in another cook. Our restaurants need your vision and supervision. If you tire yourself out, we lose the force we desperately need. Without you, the Foster House and Seaside Café would be nothing more than highway stands between Los Angeles and San Francisco."

"I couldn't have said it better," Hank said. "So cut yourself some slack and work out a schedule where you can cook and be your wonderful creative self." He kissed her on the lips.

May's growing smile was a sign Hank and Dax had hit the right tone.

Dax snatched her box from the countertop. "Well, if you're not going back to sleep, I will."

She kissed May on the cheek before exiting the kitchen. Sleep called her from the top of the stairs, making her choose between lying in Rose's arms beneath the covers and making sure she woke up feeling special on her birthday. Despite dragging her feet to the last step, her choice was simple. Dax turned toward the living room to set up Rose's gift so it would be the first thing she saw when she stepped from their room.

After placing the box on the table, she ripped open the top, pulled out this month's most challenging household item to buy in California, and put it on the corner of the desk that was most prominent when entering the room. Dax caressed the precious gift. Even Grace, with all her connections, could not source one in time for Rose's birthday, but Captain Burch had had a wider reach.

She plugged it into a wall outlet she'd installed in the living room last year to accommodate the extra lamps they bought with their new couch and table. When she leaned forward to fiddle with the power knob, a pair of slender arms wrapped around her torso from behind. Dax melted into the warm touch like she did whenever Rose pulled her close. Since the day Rose came back into her life, she'd savored every moment her soft body was against her.

Rose rested her cheek on the side of Dax's shoulder. "Is that what I think it is?"

"You weren't supposed to see it yet," Dax said. "I wanted to put a bow on it."

"It's perfect the way it is." Rose ran a hand across the dark walnut cabinet. "How did you find one? Edith said they were sold out."

"Grace isn't the only one with connections," Dax said with a flavor of self-satisfaction.

After all this time, she should not feel threatened, and she didn't, but Grace was rich, beautiful, worldly, sexy as hell, and Rose's first lover. She was sure about Rose's love for her, yet she felt more accomplished when she did something Grace could not. Rose would say she was being silly, but living up to Rose's experience with Grace would be a lifelong endeavor. Dax could not compete with Grace's money, so buying Rose things had become about knowing her better than anyone else in the world. The cost didn't matter as much as the sentiment.

They kept a radio in the Foster House in the dining room for customers and for May since climbing the stairs was still problematic in her leg brace. However, Rose had mentioned in passing several months earlier that it would be nice to have a radio upstairs in her and Dax's living quarters for romantic evenings alone. After one talk with Hank, Dax knew the exact model to get. The first production run was so popular it had sold out everywhere, but Dax convinced Captain Burch to hunt one down, using his bill collectors up and down the Pacific Coast. He didn't let on the trouble he'd gone through to find one, but Dax suspected he had done some arm twisting.

Rose powered on her new Philco Baby Grand Radio and tuned it to the only all-night radio station from San Francisco. Ethel Waters's latest hit song, one of Rose's current favorites, was playing. "It sounds great." She turned to face Dax and gasped, placing two fingertips on her cheek. "What happened?"

"Wilkes's men tried to steal two of our barrels tonight, but Hank and I took care of it."

"It looks like they took care of you." Rose's expression turned long, filled with sadness and frustration.

"They got off one only good lick, but I barred them from using the dock for their deliveries. Now they'll have to beg Burch to deliver elsewhere or find another supplier."

"This is why I worry about you at night. This business is so dangerous."

Dax caressed the new radio before turning toward Rose. It was the only set on the market capable of tuning in to the local police bands. She placed her hands on Rose's hips, squeezing the soft cotton fabric of her nightgown between her fingers. "I know you've been worried about us in the club late at night. This way, you can monitor the police calls and fall asleep knowing we're okay."

Rose hooked her arms around Dax's neck and swayed to the rhythm of the slow song. "And when you're here, the music can set the mood." She pulled Dax in for a languid kiss, letting it linger too long if she planned to get back to sleep anytime soon. The last vestige of exhaustion left Dax when Rose pressed a knee into her center, using the deliberate up-and-down motion she'd perfected during their years together. The move guaranteed their clothes would find the floor within minutes.

Rose drifted her hands to Dax's double-braided suspenders, hooking her middle fingers under the smooth fabric and trailing them downward while sending her tongue searching. She grazed the top of each breast, making their tips ache with desire. Each strip of woven cotton eased from her shoulders moments before Rose worked on the buttons of Dax's shirt.

When the kiss broke, Rose's eyes brimmed with a familiar smoldering—her prelude to seduction. "I want one more treat for my birthday," she whispered.

She'd perfected the art of making love to her microphone on stage with a hand and drawing in every man and woman in the audience with her eyes. Those unique skills created an irresistible foreplay like a songstress of the sea, pulling weary captains to her voice. The piercing stare was her opening salvo. This morning's was a preview of what should be another unforgettable encounter.

Dax grabbed Rose by the hand to take her to their bed, but Rose resisted. "No, here." The rasp in Rose's voice was her secret weapon. It turned Dax speechless and unable to move unless commanded.

Rose guided her to a sofa cushion. "Lean back." She kneeled at Dax's feet, unsnapped the fly of her work dungarees, and lowered them past her knees. Lingering over her center, she inhaled. "You smell so good."

Every inch ached for Rose's lips. From the first day she'd laid eyes on Rose, her lips held mystery for Dax. She'd wanted to know how soft they would feel against hers and if they tasted of cherry. Their taste changed daily, depending on the Foster House menu, but how they felt remained constant. They were soft, smooth, and moist.

Unable to hold her head up, Dax leaned it back against the top of the sofa. She forced out one word. "Taste."

Rose eased Dax's folds apart. "This is the treat I want."

Soon they lay partially clothed on the sofa, Rose wrapped in Dax's arms and a blanket covering them. Sleep was overtaking Dax quickly, but she had to be the first to say the words today. "Happy birthday, Rose."

"Get some sleep, Dax." Rose squirmed, positioning her head against the crook of Dax's neck. "We have a long night ahead of us."

Sharing Rose with Grace on her birthday wasn't ideal, but making Rose happy was bigger than Dax's insecurities. She would go through fire a thousand times to make it happen.

CHAPTER THREE

Rose woke with her head rising and lowering to the rhythm of Dax's breathing. Safe. Calm. Relaxed. Grateful. Trusting. Loving. Dax's embrace infused every positive emotion she'd experienced in thirty years of living. If she could replicate and bottle the peaceful sensation, she would become the wealthiest person in the world. Everyone would want to experience the pure bliss she felt at this moment.

If not for a call of nature, Rose could have stayed curled up with Dax for hours, but the longer she remained, the more urgent the need became to traipse down the hallway. She slowly lifted Dax's arm and rocked herself to a sitting position. Dax roused, but Rose caressed her abdomen and whispered, "Sleep. I'll be back soon."

When Dax rolled more to her side, Rose stood, pulled the blanket over Dax's shoulder, and kissed her forehead. The faint grin on her face suggested she was equally content. She was the best birthday present of all. Dax filled her heart in a way no other person could. Not even her dead parents or brother made her feel as loved or more sure of herself. Grace had come the closest, but her effect on Rose paled compared to Dax's. With Dax, she felt capable of overcoming any hurdle and enduring any burden.

After showering and dressing, Rose descended the stairs to the business part of the Foster House. The place was packed. It had been every morning since Ida and her husband shuttered their café last year. Her cousin's stubbornness was to blame. Ida had refused to update her menu to meet the changing tastes of her customers. Not even dropping prices had stopped the mass migration to the Foster House.

Instead of going to the kitchen to eat as was her custom when Dax wasn't with her, Rose turned toward the dining room for one more birthday indulgence. The head waitress, Ruth, acknowledged her presence with a firm jut of her chin before gesturing toward an unoccupied table in the center. Rose waved her over, preferring to sit at her and Dax's special booth, even if it meant waiting for it to clear.

Ruth darted closer, her traditional speed during rush hours. "Happy birthday, young lady. What can we get you today?"

"Can you tell me when my regular booth is available?" Rose glanced in its direction, noting three men at the table.

Ruth's expression grew long. "It might be a while. They just arrived, and the kitchen is running a little behind."

"Behind with two cooks?"

Ruth leaned in closer. "May sent Sheila home. It's her time of the month, and she had cramps something awful this morning."

"She's fortunate May is the owner. She has a big heart."

"We're all fortunate," Ruth added a wink. She briefly worked for Ida years ago and witnessed firsthand how not to run a restaurant and treat employees. Unless a staff member was in the hospital, recovering from a horrible accident, Ida never excused a missed shift, nor did she let anyone go home early. Work was work, period, end of story.

"I better lend a hand." Rose rolled up the sleeves of her blouse. She strode to the kitchen door and was extending a hand to push through when it swung open to a server carrying two orders. Rose could not hide her wry smile. Remembering how her cousin treated her when she first moved to Half Moon Bay, she could not help the small indulgence. "Morning, Ida. I hear you broke a glass yesterday. You're lucky May doesn't take the cost from your paycheck."

Ida harrumphed without stopping. When Rose worked for her, she had docked her pay for every broken glass and plate for years, even the ones that were already chipped. Now she was merely thankful for the job. She was good at waiting tables, carried the plates like a professional, and was pleasant enough around the customers. However, when Rose or Dax entered the room, she could not hide her contempt. She would not dare make a scene, but her sneers made it clear she still considered their relationship a sin. The only words she'd said to Rose since May hired her were, "What will it be?" when she took her order.

Rose stepped inside the kitchen, letting her smile linger. It was wrong to needle Ida, but it sure felt good. May was at the stove, grilling multiple orders and wiping the sweat from her brow with a forearm. Hank was at the center block, chopping vegetables, with tears running down his cheeks.

"Life isn't so bad, Hank." Rose chuckled.

"It's these damn onions."

May glanced over her shoulder. "I always knew he was a big crybaby."

"Thank goodness Clive isn't here. I'd never live this down."

"Trust me." May wagged her spatula at her husband. "Your cousin will hear every juicy tidbit if you don't get me those onions in the next five minutes." Extortion wasn't her style, but Rose loved her playfulness.

Rose grabbed an apron from the wall hooks near the back door.

"What do you think you're doing?" May placed both hands on her hips like she'd caught Rose with her hand in the cookie jar.

"Pitching in to get you through the morning rush."

"It's your birthday, Rose. You shouldn't be working."

"You said it. It's my birthday, so I get to do what I want. Right now, I want to help you. It's either Ida or me."

"When hell freezes over." May's sour expression was priceless. She clearly regretted her moment of sympathy when Ida came to her last year. "I may have hired her out of compassion to wait tables, but I won't let her touch one mixing bowl in this kitchen. She would run this place into the ground like she did her own café."

"Maybe it's time to recognize your lapse in judgment and let her go."

May relented. "Life made her hard, Rose. No mother should be forced to give up a child. I may not trust her in the kitchen, but she's an efficient waitress. Unless she does something I can't forgive, she stays."

"You *do* have a big heart, May," Rose said. "I would have let her and Morris starve."

"You say that, but I know you, Rose Hamilton. You would have done the same thing if you were in my shoes."

Rose didn't want to admit it, but May was probably right. It wasn't in her nature to turn away someone in need, but she would never give Ida the satisfaction of knowing it. She winked at May, donned the apron, and went to work for the next hour, cooking orders and refilling the prep station with ingredients.

When the crowd thinned and the last pie for the day was in the oven, Rose sat at the center chopping block with May and Hank to eat brunch. Between bites, Hank read the morning newspaper a customer had left behind at a table.

Rose glanced at the headline on the front page, "New Sheriff in Town." Learning the results of Tuesday's special election had her on pins and needles. She tried to read the details of the article but was at the wrong angle to see them clearly. "Hank, can you flip back to the first page? It says who won the election."

"Yeah." Hank rattled the pages, closed the paper, and laid it between their plates. "It's something I'd rather forget."

Rose focused on the first paragraph and gasped. "Oh no." The race to replace the sheriff who died in a car crash in April should have been a simple choice for voters. However, money and friendly newspapers in Redwood City and San Mateo painting a fantastical history of the challenger to the heir apparent had tipped the scales. Roy Wilkes may have been a war veteran, but he was not the saint the editorials had made him out to be. Rose certainly would not have described him as an altruistic businessman and an integral member of the community. She would have labeled him a greedy, vengeful, and dangerous man who ran an illegal speakeasy in the basement of his restaurant in Redwood City.

In the wake of his threats of revenge for killing his brother, it had become clear Roy Wilkes was behind the attacks on Charlie's Garage and the Foster House the night of the whiskey war. But no one could surface their suspicions without exposing the Beacon Club speakeasy operation to the Prohibition agents. Now Roy Wilkes, someone with an ax to grind, was the chief law enforcement officer in the county.

"Oh no, what?" The instantly recognizable voice came from behind Rose. Dax had entered through the dining room, kissed Rose on her head, and sat on the last available stool.

"Roy Wilkes was elected sheriff. He takes over next week."

May released a weighty sigh, wringing her hands. "I was afraid of this."

"I was too." Rose turned to Dax, envisioning a police raid on Wilkes's first day wearing the badge. He would haul in every club employee, toss them into a cramped cell, and hold them until he was good and ready to let them see a judge. "This changes everything. He'll be gunning for us."

"He'll jail us all unless we shut down the club." May shook her head in disbelief.

"I agree this isn't good," Hank said, "but maybe we still can use the dock as leverage, renegotiate his deliveries in exchange for leaving us alone."

"I'm afraid he's one step ahead of us," Dax said. "The note I got from Burch said if Wilkes won the election, he and other owners would need another location to accept the cargo because Wilkes planned to shut us down permanently by any means necessary."

"That's it," May said. "I want the club closed before he takes office."

"There's no way we're closing the Beacon Club," Dax said. "We can legally sell beer and wine."

"Then I want every last drop of hard liquor out of there."
May stood, placing her palms on the countertop, to stress her
point, a stance she rarely took with family. "I won't chance any
of us going to jail."

"We have a week to figure this out." Dax used a calm tone,
motioning slowly for May to sit. "I'm off to meet with Burch's
man. Hopefully, we can work something out." Dax made a
sandwich with toast and bacon and kissed Rose. "I'll be back in
an hour or two, so be ready for our drive to the city."

"Be careful. This is a dangerous business." Rose had a bad
feeling. Despite what help Burch might provide, she suspected
nothing would stop Wilkes from exacting his revenge.

After Dax left through the back door, the bell rang, signaling
the pies were done in the oven. Rose pulled them out, set one
aside for a special friend, and turned to May. "I'll let the apple
cool and deliver it after I clean up here."

"Can you pick up last week's tin? I had to toss two out this
week."

"Sure thing."

"And tell Charlie that Hank will bring over a batch of fresh
biscuits on Tuesday when he drops off the old truck for an oil
change."

"She'll like that."

Charlie, Dax's former best friend, hadn't stepped inside
the Foster House since the night of the whiskey war, when
her garage, the building her father had built, her life's work,
had been burned down. Rose could not blame her for being
upset but thought her anger would have faded after three years.
Charlie had an enduring capacity to hold a grudge, but Rose
could be equally stubborn and would not stop trying to put a
dent in her bullheadedness.

CHAPTER FOUR

Once up to speed on the highway, Charlie Dawson drifted her right hand from the gear shifter to pet Brutus. He'd squeezed between her and Henry, owner of the local department store and of a truck in need of repair, on the bench seat of her tow truck and raised his head but seemed particularly tired today, which was saying something. He was never the same after being burned in the garage fire; he now spent most of his days sleeping. Even climbing the stairs had become problematic, requiring Charlie to carry him up for the night and down to spend the day with her in the garage.

"We'll be home in a few minutes, boy." Charlie had been his constant companion since that awful night, leaving him for only quick errands. She didn't want to leave him alone for more than an hour, so she even took him along on parts runs into San Mateo or tow truck runs like this one. He tired more quickly, but at least they were together.

"It's good seeing him out and about," Henry said. "Edith and I don't see much of him these days."

"I know." Charlie gave Brutus an extra caress, pushing back her growing melancholy since Brutus opted for the corner of her office last year instead of the sidewalk in front of her garage as his hangout spot. He'd stopped greeting the locals as they passed by on foot, so his world had shrunk to the garage and the inside of Charlie's trucks.

Once at the garage, Henry jumped out and raised the left bay door with a press of a button. Charlie backed in Henry's Model TT as far as she could before applying the parking brake on her truck. It required some effort, but with Henry's help, she lined up his car over the hydraulic lift.

After parking the tow truck in its reserved spot, Charlie lifted Brutus from the bench seat and carried him toward the building. Maybe it was the exertion of pushing a broken-down truck into place, but she struggled more than usual to bear her dog's weight. She wasn't sure how much an English bulldog was supposed to weigh, but she was sure it wasn't this much. "Geez, boy. I should cut back on your portions."

Charlie eased him to the ground when they reached the bay threshold, the maximum distance Brutus was willing to walk these days to get to his bed in the office. She set him up with his blanket in the corner and poured Henry a cup of coffee. "Give me a few minutes. I'll look at her."

Suspecting a major rear axle leak, Charlie raised the truck by the lift to inspect the back end. The axle was covered in oil, which was a bad sign. Most of the oil was on the left side, telling her to start there. The 1925 Model TT was a decent car but notorious for leaks. If it wasn't an axle, it was the transmission or crankcase. Their gaskets wore out quicker than Brutus on walks, so she kept plenty in stock.

After wiping off most of the fluid, she traced the assembly with her fingertips, looking for the leak source. "There you are." Spinning both back wheels to test the mechanics of the axle, she discovered everything was still operating soundly. She stepped to the office, pulled the shop rag dangling from her back pocket, and wiped the oil and grease from her hands.

Henry put down his coffee mug and rose from the chair, wringing his newsboy cap. "What's the verdict?"

"Good news. She only needs a new rear axle gasket. You did the right thing by calling me instead of driving her to the shop once you found the puddle of oil. You saved yourself a lot of money and heartache."

Henry let out a sputtering breath. "That's great, but how much will it cost to replace the gasket?" The anxiety on his face and in his voice was heartbreaking. Money was tight now for most businesses in Half Moon Bay. The only people not feeling the pinch were government officials and those working at the Beacon Club. None of them had to worry about getting enough business to put food on the table or pay the power company or tax bill twice a year. Charlie could not let Henry worry about such things.

"No charge. You and Edith were so kind after my place burned down. Brutus and I would have lived on the streets until Grace Parsons had it rebuilt if you hadn't opened your home to us. It's the least I can do."

"Taking you in was the right thing to do. Edith and I couldn't stand seeing you two suffer. I thank you kindly for your generosity, Charlie, but I can't let you take a loss. At least let me pay you for the parts and materials."

Charlie wiped her hand more thoroughly before shaking Henry's hand. "You got a deal. Two dollars should cover it."

"You're a good friend, Charlie Dawson. When do you think you'll have her done?"

"I have a gasket in the shop, so after I fix a transmission, it should only take two or three hours to replace it. I know Saturday is your big delivery morning, so I'll get her done today even if I have to stay open late."

"Half Moon Bay is lucky to have you. We'll watch for your lights," Henry said. Their department store and second-story residence was across the street and a few buildings up. He and his wife had the perfect view of her garage from their living room. "I'm sure Edith will walk over supper whether or not you're done."

"That would be great. Tell her thank you."

Once Henry left, Charlie closed the bay door and went to work on Doc Hughes's transmission. She should have it done in four or five hours, assuming no one came in with an emergency flat or needed a tow. Within the first hour, she had the parts disassembled and inspected. The wear and tear pattern meant two things. Doc Hughes was grinding the clutch something awful, and Charlie was going to need to replace them all to get the gears shifting like they were supposed to. Though she'd warned the doctor about this possibility, he would not be happy with the bill after she repaired it.

The bell over the front entrance chimed, alerting Charlie and Brutus to the arrival of a customer. He barked while she wiped her hands with a clean rag. "I got it, boy. Go back to sleep." Brutus immediately quieted.

Charlie turned from her workbench toward the door. The smile on the face of the woman entering made her heart beat a little faster. It always did. And whatever treat she'd brought her today, it smelled delicious.

The woman closed the door, turned the lock on the knob, and flipped the sign to read, "Closed for Lunch." She drew the blind for privacy. Her walk was as mesmerizing as her smile, making the rest of the world evaporate for the scant minutes they stole during the day when their schedules allowed.

"I didn't think you could make it today," Charlie said, grateful she had come.

"I never pass up an opportunity to see you."

"That's good to know."

"Are you hungry?"

"For you? Always." Charlie pressed their lips together. She deepened the pressure and let the tingles the kiss generated build until a moan released, breaking their connection.

"You're so good at this."

"I should be. I've been kissing you the same way since we were teenagers." Charlie glanced at the baking tin in Jules's hand. "What did you bring for lunch?"

"Sophie made enchiladas at the boarding house last night. She said I could take the extras for lunch today."

"I like her much better than the old biddy who ran the place before."

"Grace made a wise choice to send Mrs. Prescott packing. Sophie had lived there for years. It made sense to offer her the position." Jules raised the dish a little higher. "I warmed them before I left, but I think they could use a little more heat. Do you want to eat upstairs or downstairs today?"

"Downstairs. Brutus is more tired than usual. We should let him sleep instead of carrying him upstairs to be with us."

Jules peeked inside the office and pursed her lips when Brutus wagged his tail but didn't get up. "I'll be back in ten minutes." She kissed Charlie before ascending the stairs to the residence level.

Charlie washed up in the downstairs bathroom, thinking Jules was the best part of the day for her and Brutus. She visited during her workday meal break and spent the night two or three times a week. It was the most they thought would not raise the eyebrows of the town's nosey busybodies, but it didn't seem enough. She wished for a time when their relationship didn't matter to others or for a circumstance like Dax and Rose had, where they could live under the same roof without being questioned. But without someone like May and Hank in the picture to provide cover, she would have to make the best of her lot.

Minutes later, she exited, drying her hands with a paper towel, and discovered Brutus snoring up a storm on his bed of blankets. A knock on the front door sounded but failed to wake him, another sign he was shutting down.

She padded to the door, expecting to find a grumpy customer who could not wait for her to have an hour to herself for lunch but was met by the second prettiest woman in Half Moon Bay. She opened the door wide enough to not wake the bell and placed an index finger over her lips, signaling for Rose to remain quiet. "Brutus is sleeping."

Rose mouthed, "Oh," raised the pie she was carrying, and whispered, "I thought you would like apple this week."

"I would. Thanks." Charlie waved her inside and closed the door behind her. "I have something for your birthday."

"You shouldn't have."

Charlie accepted the pie and led Rose to the door leading to her office. "Wait here." She tiptoed inside and opened her desk drawer, taking care not to wake Brutus. After retrieving a gift wrapped in tissue paper, she returned to the garage. "Happy birthday, Rose. It's not much, but I saw it and thought of you."

Rose carefully unwrapped the gift, revealing a white satin rose attached to a matching hair ribbon. "It's beautiful, Charlie. Thank you, but it's too much." She gave her a hug and kissed her on the cheek.

"Edith gave me a good deal on it. She said it was part of a broken bridal headband."

"Well, it's amazing. I'll wear it during my performance tomorrow night."

"I'm glad you like it." Charlie had hit a home run with the gift, but she felt oddly glum.

"What's wrong, Charlie? You look sad."

"I miss hearing you sing, that's all. You're really something on stage."

"There's no reason you can't attend one of my performances." Rose placed a hand on her forearm, her expression growing long and sympathetic.

"You know why I can't come."

"You mean won't. I understand why you blame Dax for your place burning down and Brutus getting hurt, but she was doing what she thought was best for all of us."

"There's more to it, Rose. Because of her—" Images of what she had to do that horrible night flashed in her head.

"Because of her, what?" Rose asked. "You and Hank refuse to tell us what happened. What haven't you told us?"

Charlie closed her eyes, trying to block the memories she'd wanted desperately to bury for the last three years, but she failed. Blood was on her hands, and she feared she would never clean her conscience from its stain. She felt trapped, condemned to never be free from it, but could not bring herself to share it again. Once with Jules was more than she could bear.

"Happy birthday, Rose." Jules appeared from around the corner at the base of the stairs, carrying the dish of enchiladas.

She whispered something into Rose's ear but Charlie could not make it out. After placing the plate on Charlie's desk, she returned, giving Rose a proper hug. "I thought you'd be off to San Francisco by now to spend the day shopping before Grace's premiere."

"We're leaving in an hour. Dax has some business to tend to."

"Always business," Charlie mumbled. Dax cared about three things—Rose, her sister, and making money. She had no idea how her single-mindedness had impacted Hank or Charlie.

"What kind of crack was that?" Rose asked. "Dax has worked hard to keep the clubs going. If she hadn't, the Foster House would have closed its doors along with Ida's. This town would have dried up long ago without the guests the Beacon Club and the Seaside attract."

"You don't have to remind me. Since Grace closed the hotel four months ago to remodel, every business in Half Moon Bay but yours barely makes a profit."

"And Grace has helped them make ends meet until the Seaside reopens. She offered to help you too." Rose's defense of Grace sounded like idol worship. Charlie long suspected some feelings still lingered between Rose and Grace, and this all but confirmed it.

"I've taken enough from her. I won't take more." Charlie had accepted the replacement of what she'd lost in the fire since Grace had been the ultimate target. She had expected Grace to rebuild in kind, but she went overboard, compensating for a guilty conscience.

Rose lowered and shook her head. "You're too stubborn for your own good, Charlie Dawson." She looked up, staring into Charlie's eyes. "People like us have to stick together. Blood relations mean nothing for most of us when our families discover what we are, so we make our own families and cling to those who won't judge us. I still consider you family and hate that you won't have anything to do with us. It hurt more than when my parents disowned me. Of all the people in the world, we should have each other's back. I don't expect you to forget, but I ask you to forgive. To open your heart to us again."

"It's not that simple." Guilt, fear, and shame collided in a thunderous explosion in Charlie's head, making it pound relentlessly. She would never be free.

"Then tell me what is making it so complicated."

When Charlie buried her face in her hands, Jules said, "I think it's time for you to go, Rose. Charlie has a lot of work to do today."

Charlie felt something bump against her lower leg and opened her eyes. Brutus had gotten up from his bed, nuzzled against her, and looked at her with sad, drawn-in eyes. Like he'd done many times before, he sensed her pain and had come to comfort her. Charlie kneeled, pulling Brutus in for a long embrace. She held on for eight seconds, one for each year they'd been companions.

"Perhaps you're right," Rose said. "When you get a chance, Jules, can you return the pie tins to the Foster House? We're running low."

"Of course."

Once Rose departed, Jules locked up again.

Charlie remained on her knee, rubbing Brutus behind the ears. "You still have some energy in you. How about a treat, boy?" She reached into her pocket and broke off a piece of her 3 Musketeers bar.

"You're not going to give that to him, are you?" Jules used her dismissive voice, the one really asking, *What the hell are you thinking?*

"Yeah, why?"

"Chocolate is toxic to dogs. It can make him really sick."

Charlie fell to her bottom. The cold from the concrete seeped through her jeans and sent a familiar chill of death through her as a horrid reality formed in her head. "I've been poisoning my dog?" She'd felt terrible about his injuries and started giving him a treat once a week. Then, this spring, she gave him a piece once a day after he strained his back leg climbing the stairs. "I am a killer."

Jules joined her on the floor, rubbing a long shirt sleeve. "You are not a killer, Charlie." She raised a hand under her chin until their eyes met. "This explains why he's been so tired recently. He'll be fine in a few days once it's all out of his system."

Guilt blinded Charlie to any label of herself as other than a killer. Since Dax came into her life, she'd become an instrument of death when every fiber in her body told her that taking a life, no matter how justified, was wrong. She killed Riley King by pushing him over Devil's Slide. She killed Frankie Wilkes by picking up a gun and shooting him. Both these acts gave her nightmares, but the night she killed Frankie was the worst.

Charlie shook off Jules's grasp and wrapped her arms around Brutus, pulling him into her lap to block the rest out. "I almost killed you." She held him for dear life, not feeling this much pain since her parents died during the Spanish Flu epidemic of 1918. It hadn't mattered that they'd disowned her for being caught with a woman the month before. Losing them twice had cut her to the core. "I'm so sorry, Brutus. I'm so sorry."

Jules scooted behind Charlie, throwing a comforting arm around her shoulder. "I know this isn't all about Brutus. You had no choice, Charlie. Frankie had the drop on Hank. If you hadn't picked up the gun when you did, he would have killed Hank and everyone hiding in the pantry."

"But I shot a man in the back of the head." Charlie lifted her hands, remembering what she'd found on them when she wiped her face clean after shooting Frankie from two feet away. "His brains were on my face."

"You shot a man who had already killed Grace's guards. He tried to burn us alive and sent a small army to kill everyone in the Foster House. You stopped him."

"How many times do I have to kill to stop more killing?" Charlie was sure it would not end with Dax around. "I can't do it again, which is why I can never again be friends with Dax."

CHAPTER FIVE

The new company truck took the gentle bends of Highway 1 smoothly, reminding Dax of running her hand down the curves of Rose's legs. Both were hypnotic. Ocean waves crashed along the rocky shoreline to her right, and rows and rows of artichoke and brussels sprouts fields lined her left. She made her final turn onto Pigeon Point Road. Ahead was the magnificent one-hundred-fifteen-foot-tall lighthouse, but she stopped short of it at the keeper's buildings, the meeting location for Burch's man for the last two years.

Stepping from the truck, Dax zipped up her jacket to counter the biting ocean breeze. This part of the California coastline wasn't known for frequent storms this time of year, but when one hit, it typically packed a wallop with high winds and drenching rain. Today's marine layer was light in color, telling Dax it should burn off in another hour, clearing the route for her and Rose to take to San Francisco later today.

Dax noted construction workers reframing a section of the next-door building following last month's fire. No one was injured, but the head lighthouse keeper had lost the living room and a bedroom. The lines looked straight and stud spacing appeared standard. Another man was stacking sheetrock inside the room. She had considered using it as a wall backer for the Seaside remodel because it was faster and cheaper to install, but plaster was more mold-and fire-resistant and provided better soundproofing between the rooms.

Dax waved at a worker as he positioned another stud and asked, "Sixteen on center?" Her question assumed he'd placed the center of the studs every sixteen inches along the base.

He looked up wide-eyed, clearly surprised by her expert knowledge. "On the nose." He added a wink.

Dax tapped the tip of her nose with an index finger, acknowledging his playfulness. She knocked on the door of the first residential building. Moments later, the keeper's wife opened it and ushered Dax inside.

"Hello, Mrs. Monroe."

She gasped, focusing on Dax's bruised eye. "What happened?"

"A minor disagreement." Dax gestured her thumb toward the other building. "I see construction is moving along."

"Yes, yes. Finally. If all goes well, we should move back in by the Fourth of July."

"If they fall behind, please call us at the Foster House. We'd be happy to lend a hand."

"That's very kind of you, Miss Dax."

"If I might make a suggestion, I saw your crew is preparing to use drywall. You might consider plaster since you're so close to the ocean. Less chance of developing mold."

"I'll speak with my husband." Monroe's eyes lit with appreciation. "Can I get you something to drink?"

"No, thank you, I'm fine. Am I early?" Typically, Mr. Burch's man and Dax were right on time, but he wasn't there.

"He's washing up after helping with the framing."

"Ahh." Dax nodded. His sense of community was a trait Dax could leverage during their meeting. "I'd offer to roll up my sleeves, but I have to be in San Francisco in a few hours for a special event."

"Ahh, yes. The movie premiere. Please pass along our best to Miss Parsons."

"I will."

Burch's man appeared in the hallway, drying his hands with a small towel. "Prompt as always."

Dax had dealt with this man since Logan Foster was alive and they brokered their first arrangement with Captain Burch for liquor and the use of the Foster House dock. He'd never given his name, giving the impression of a preference for anonymity, and she'd never asked. As long as the cargo and money flowed back and forth, knowing his name was irrelevant.

"We've built our relationship on trust. I'm not about to change that." Dax handed him an envelope containing the cash for the last two deliveries.

He pocketed the money. "I take it you've read Captain Burch's note and the morning's paper."

"I have, but I also have a proposal the captain should be interested in."

"Please sit." The man gestured toward the small round dining table between the kitchen and living room.

"I understand the position Captain Burch is in. Roy Wilkes is an important customer with more power after being elected sheriff. After taking office, he'll want retribution for his brother. I understand he's preemptively advised Captain Burch to relocate the drop-off location to the original sites at the beaches since he intends to shut us down. But I have a solution to keep all of us in business."

"I'm listening." The man's response and facial expression were unreadable, as usual. He never showed a hint of emotion.

"I can assure you the other speakeasy owners in the area dislike and distrust Wilkes as much as we do. In fact, I caught his men trying to steal a portion of our load last night and said I'd ban them from using the dock for future deliveries. They've tried the same with the other clubs."

"I see," he said. "That explains the shiner."

"Yes, it does, but I'm willing to overlook the indiscretion of his people if Wilkes agrees to keep things the way they are. This will only work if we band together. If Captain Burch threatens to dry up the pipeline of alcohol and the others promise to blackball Wilkes from the resale market if he acts against the Beacon and Seaside, we'll corner him. The captain won't lose any business."

"You've made a sound proposal, Dax, but it assumes Mr. Wilkes will respond rationally. Reasonableness disappears when family is involved, but I will present your idea to the captain tonight."

"Wilkes officially becomes sheriff next Friday, so I ask for a decision before then. And if he decides in my favor, I need him to present the terms to Wilkes before he can wreak havoc."

"I'll make sure he's aware of the urgency."

"Thank you. Consideration is all I can ask." Dax understood her business. The bottom line, not sentiment, would dictate Burch's action.

The man stood, signaling the end of their meeting. He uncharacteristically rested a hand on Dax's arm when she rose. "Be careful, Miss Xander. I fear for your safety." His unprecedented warning and show of affection suggested her chances with Burch were slim, and their best hope was a prompt passage of repeal.

"I will."

The marine layer had burned away before Dax returned the company truck to its reserved spot behind the Foster House, forecasting an easy drive to San Francisco. The back parking lot had opened up, signaling the lunch rush was almost over. Once inside, she returned the truck keys and work jacket to the hook near the back door. May was cleaning the grill, and Hank was washing plates and flatware at the sink, Dax's old job. He craned his head toward her.

"How did it go?" he asked.

"I asked for a coalition to squeeze Wilkes." Dax explained her proposal and impression of an outside chance of Burch agreeing to it.

"Considering Wilkes will have the law on his side next week, your suggestion is our only play. I hope it works. Otherwise, we'll have to stop selling liquor."

"Even if we do, I have a feeling Wilkes will find a way to get revenge. He might squeeze our beer and wine suppliers."

"You're probably right," Hank said.

"Where's Rose?"

May turned around, holding a grill scraper. "Making herself pretty for your big date tonight."

"Then I better catch up. We need to leave in twenty minutes."

Climbing the stairs, Dax heard music when she reached the top. She glanced toward the desk where she'd left the radio earlier this morning, realizing it was gone. Tracing the music to its source, Dax tiptoed to her and Rose's bedroom door, eased it open with her fingertips, and discovered Rose at her vanity dressed in her white silk stage dress, brushing her hair. Dax fell more in love with her with each graceful stroke. They were luckier than most people like them, living in the same room, and Dax never took a day together for granted.

Several moments passed before Rose said, "Are you going to stand there all day watching?"

"I could." Dax walked inside, taking slow, deliberate strides. If Rose wanted to stay and make love for the rest of the day, she would gladly accommodate her.

"But I've never been to a movie premiere. So many movie stars are going to be there."

Dax stopped behind Rose slightly to one side and bent at the knees until their heads were even. She joined her stare into the mirror. "You're as big a star as any one of them, and you're much prettier."

Rose's cheeks blushed with embarrassment. "You're just saying such things because you're my girlfriend."

Dax inched her head close, making sure to not muss her hair. "Is that what we are to each other? Girlfriends? It feels more like we're married."

"I agree." Rose turned, giving Dax a tender kiss on the lips.

"Then it's settled," Dax said. "When it's just us, you're my wife, and I'm yours."

"Did you just propose to me, Darlene Augusta Xander?"

"I guess I did." Dax let a smile grow. The idea of being able to marry Rose was preposterous, but doing so emotionally would be the same as Hank and May had done at the courthouse two years ago. It would be a pledge of their mutual love and devotion. "We don't need some church or piece of paper telling us what's legal or moral. Forget what the rest of the world says is right. We're married."

Rose's matching smile meant Dax's idea wasn't absurd. "I think it's a wonderful idea. I bet Charlie and Jules think the same way."

Dax straightened her posture as the lovely moment they shared shattered with the mention of her once-close friend. "I need to get ready."

She washed up and put on the tux she wore while working in the Beacon Club. Before she slid on the jacket, Rose stepped closer and traced her fingers down the black silk suspenders she'd gifted Dax years ago, stopping at the tips of her breasts.

"I love seeing you in these." Rose made circles with her fingers, making it impossible for Dax to think straight.

"If you don't stop, we'll miss the movie."

Rose patted Dax's chest with both palms. "Then we better get going."

After trotting down the stairs, Dax held the swing door open to the kitchen for Rose. They stepped through, earning whistles from Hank. "Well, aren't you two the prettiest?"

May flew a hand to her chest. "You two are stunning. It's like you're off to your wedding."

"We thought the same thing." Dax walked to the wall hooks with the car keys and grabbed the one for her personal Model T truck. "We gotta get going."

"I poured you a thermos of water and wrapped some biscuits for the trip."

Dax rolled her eyes. The drive was only an hour, yet May packed snacks and drinks for every trip she took to the city. Dax kissed her sister on the cheek. "Thank you, May."

"Which truck are you taking?" Hank asked. "I need to pick up an order at Edith's before she closes."

"Mine. This is a personal trip."

Once seated in the truck, Dax started the engine and coasted down the access road to the front of the Foster House. As she turned onto the main road, she felt the steering wheel pull hard to the right, telling her a tire might have gone flat.

"Crud." Dax wasn't dressed for manual labor, so it would take an hour to fix it and get dressed again. "I think we have a flat. I'll need to change it, so we might be late." Dax steered toward the shoulder.

Rose sighed. "What about Charlie?"

"She won't help me."

"Don't be stubborn. She'll do it for me."

Dax gripped the wheel tighter, deciding to be uncomfortable for a few minutes rather than ruin Rose's birthday. "Fine." She babied the truck the few blocks to Charlie's garage, pulling it in front of an open car bay. "Stay in the car, please."

Charlie appeared moments later with a shop rag in her hands. When she looked up, discerning who was there, she froze. The sadness in her eyes cut Dax to shreds.

"I know you don't want to see me, but I have a flat." Charlie remained silent, so Dax continued, "Rose and I have to be in the city, so I don't have time to change and do it myself." Charlie still said nothing. "I'm willing to pay double if you can finish it quickly."

Charlie's eyes narrowed. "It's always money with you."

"No, Charlie. It's about keeping a roof over our heads and food on the table for my family. You should know. You were once a part of it and could be again."

"The cost is too high."

Yes, the speakeasy business was dangerous, Dax thought, but liquor enforcement had become lax. Thefts had gone down since the legalization of beer and wine. Competitor speakeasies had a gentleman's agreement to respect boundaries and not encroach on another's business. If not for the threat Roy Wilkes posed, it would have been no more dangerous than Charlie's garage or any other shop in town. Charlie knew how civilized the business had become, yet she still didn't have it in her heart to forgive

Dax for her part in the whiskey war against the Wilkes brothers. Dax would stake her life on something else being at play.

"I'm sorry you feel that way." Motion from inside the car bay caught Dax's attention. Brutus lumbered out, snorting and wagging his body. He seemed slower and thicker than Dax remembered but still got wide-eyed when he approached her. Dax kneeled on the pavement and rubbed behind his ears. "Hey, Brutus. It's so good to see you."

"Come here, boy." Charlie patted her thigh. Her sharp command said Brutus was no longer her friend either. He dutifully returned to his owner. "Go inside." He waddled through the opening and disappeared inside the garage.

This was sad, so very sad. All of them should have been closer than this. They should have been friends and chosen family, not enemies.

"I'm sorry I don't have time to have a long overdue talk," Dax said. "Right now, I need to know if you can fix my tire. Otherwise, I need to get to work on it myself."

Charlie took an uneasy breath. "I can do it. It should take about twenty minutes." She turned on her heel without another word, breaking Dax's heart. Again.

Someday, Dax thought, *we'll have that talk.*

CHAPTER SIX

Dax turned the corner onto San Francisco's Market Street. The three red neon-lit letters spelling "Fox" on the theater façade brightened the night sky and were discernable from three blocks away. The parade of luxury cars lined up to drop off their legendary passengers at the Fox Theater was long and intimidating. Her truck paled compared to the Lincoln Roadsters, Imperial Phaetons, Cadillacs, and even one elegant Duesenberg. As Grace Parson's special guest, Dax had her name on the VIP list, warranting her a spot in line and free valet parking. Nevertheless, she could not have Rose Hamilton showing up in something this old and pedestrian.

"I don't want to wait for our truck when the movie is over. Would you mind if I parked by City Hall? It would mean walking a few blocks."

Rose rested a hand on Dax's thigh. Her loving look gave the impression she understood Dax's uneasiness. "I'd walk a thousand miles with you."

Dax navigated the streets, finding a spot to leave her truck. After they got out and Rose put on her coat, Dax felt instantly guilty. Five blocks to the theater in her flat shoes would be a snap, but Rose had worn her pointy stage shoes with tall heels. While Dax would never wear heels to save her life, she'd seen Rose after a long show enough times to know they hurt like heck after a while.

Dax wished she could link arms with Rose and let her lean most of her weight on her, but the street wasn't empty. Someone might see. After four blocks, Rose's stride hitched. Dax dashed a few feet ahead and bent forward at the knees, offering her back. "Hop on. I'll carry you the rest of the way."

"Don't be silly." Rose rested a hand on Dax's shoulder when she straightened. "Just give me a minute to rest the dogs." She shifted her weight from one leg to another, twirling each ankle several times to work out the ache. "If I didn't have stockings on, I'd go barefoot."

"If you didn't have stockings on, we'd be back in the truck, steaming up the windows."

"You are incorrigible." Rose swatted playfully at Dax's arm. "We should get going. Greta wants to have a drink with you before the movie starts." She resumed walking.

"You mean Greta wants to have a drink with *us*." Dax caught up, strolling shoulder to shoulder.

"Oh, please. You told me about Greta's invitation to her summer house." The teasing notes in Rose's voice signaled that the failed meeting with Charlie hadn't soured her birthday.

"That was a long time ago, and she knows you're the love of my life."

"I hope she remembers."

And Dax hoped Grace remembered she was the love of Rose's life. "It won't matter because I have eyes only for you."

Rose gave her a shoulder shove. "As I have for you."

At the next corner, the bright lights of the Fox Theater marquee came into view. The letters on it announced the special premiere of *Queen Christina* and listed the starring actors before the title. "This is magnificent." A sense of wonder charged Rose's voice as if she dreamed of having her name up there one day.

"Have you ever thought of going into the movies?"

"No director would want to work with me," Rose said. "Grace and Greta make it look so easy, but I still stutter around people I'm uncomfortable with."

Dax had all but forgotten about Rose's malady. When Rose sang on stage or was alone with her, May, and Hank, her voice was smooth as silk. She only stuttered while speaking to people she didn't know well or trust. Still, Rose's answer didn't dismiss a hidden desire to act on screen.

"I wish I could kiss you right now," Dax said, "because I think you're perfect."

"And I feel perfect when I'm with you, which is why I've loved you since we were teenagers." Rose could not have said anything sweeter. Dax had made plenty of mistakes, but Rose was the one thing she'd always gotten right.

They crossed Market Street at the corner, blending into a crowd of men in tuxedos and women wearing fancy coats. The line to enter through the main entrance moved quickly. When they reached the front, a man with a clipboard asked, "Name?" without looking up.

"Rose Hamilton and Dax Xander."

He looked up, a glint of recognition in his eyes. "Of course, Miss Hamilton. I heard you sing at the Beacon Club last year. You have an amazing voice."

"Th-thank you."

"I see both of you are special guests of Miss Parsons." He handed Rose a gold embossed card with the name of the Fox Theater and *Queen Christina* imprinted on the front. "This will get you into the VIP area. I believe Miss Parsons arrived ten minutes ago. I'll be happy to show you the way."

Dax didn't like the leering look in the man's eyes or how he placed his hand on Rose's back. Drunk patrons frequently made advances at the clubs, but Dax had Lester behind the piano, Jason at the bar, and two guards in the room every night to keep them in line. She was on her own tonight. She stepped between Rose and the man, forcing his arm down.

"We can find our way, thank you." Dax ushered Rose inside.

Ten steps in, Rose stopped. "That was a little rude."

"He had the look."

"What's the look?" Rose asked.

"We run into it every night at the clubs. He was hoping to take you home tonight."

"Oh, come on. Every night? I haven't had a handsy customer in years."

"Because I've trained everyone. We stop the letches before they get to you."

"I can't believe it happens every night."

Dax clutched Rose by the elbow and searched her eyes. "You really have no idea how desirable you are." She leaned in and whispered, "It's not only the men. I bet you've turned every woman in your audience into a lesbian in their fantasies. No one can resist you."

Rose blushed. "We better find Grace."

Dax scanned the lobby, taking in its grandeur. It was the picture of opulence, seemingly transporting her into a palace or a Parisian church. Each wall was decorated with gold and dark red touches. Roman columns and dramatic arches flanked every door leading to the auditorium. Dax was in awe over the intricate finishing work, thinking each piece must have taken several craftsmen days to complete. A grand staircase lined with a plush red carpet was roped off, guarded by two men. Dax gestured for Rose to head there.

Halfway there, a man called out, "Rose Hamilton."

They stopped and turned toward the voice. The face and red curls looked vaguely familiar, but Dax could not place them. She remained guarded, expecting a theater full of letches tonight.

"Yes?" Rose squinted as if trying to shake loose a stubborn memory. "Phillip Gandy?"

The moment Rose said his name, Dax remembered him. He was the first boy Dax had punched for teasing Rose about her speech.

"You remembered. I'm flattered," he said.

"W-W-What are you doing here? I haven't seen you since high school."

"I'm a crime-beat reporter for the *San Francisco Chronicle*, filling in for the entertainment reporter tonight. I saw your picture in the *Chronicle*, advertising the reopening of a hotel in Half Moon Bay. So when I saw your name on tonight's guest list, I had to come. I'm surprised. You turned out to be quite the singer."

Dax didn't like the tone of his last comment and stepped between him and Rose. "What kind of crack was that? Are you looking for another sock in the gut?"

Phillip eyed Dax with curiosity. "Didn't you go to Alameda High?"

"Yeah, and I put you in your place for making fun of Rose."

"I was a stupid kid then." He took a step backward and focused on Rose. "I'm very sorry for teasing you back then. I'd like to make it up to you by running a featured story on you in the *Chronicle*. It could give your singing career a well-deserved bounce. Please say yes."

"I'm flattered, Phillip, but I'm happy with my career as it is."

He handed her a business card. "Think about it. If you change your mind, please give me a call."

"Grace is expecting us." Dax placed a hand on the small of Rose's back. "We should get going."

"You're right." Rose focused briefly on Phillip. "It was nice seeing you."

Dax ushered Rose toward the roped-off area. "Bounce your career, my ass," she muttered. "More like giving *his* career a bounce."

"He seemed genuinely sorry."

"Being sorry doesn't matter. He doesn't get to throw insults and then interview you fifteen years later for a story."

"I love your protective side," Rose whispered.

"You can thank me properly later." Dax approached a man guarding the roped-off area, pointing at Rose's golden pass. "We're looking for the VIP section."

The man nodded and unhooked the velvet rope, allowing Dax and Rose upstairs. Signage on the wall pointed upward to the mezzanine level. Rose removed her coat at the top as they entered a wide hallway decorated in the same ornate red and gold finishings and draperies as the lobby. A tuxedo-clad young man approached her before she could fold it over a forearm. "May I take your coat, ma'am?"

"Yes, please." Rose exchanged it for a coat-check number. She stuffed it into her clutch bag and visually searched the crowd. Dax did too. She recognized many of the people as guests of the Beacon and Seaside Clubs. Men were standing with men and women with women. Many exchanged caresses Dax would not expect in a public place.

"I see Clive." Rose tugged on Dax's jacket sleeve and nudged her toward the wall opposite the bar.

They skirted the sea of elegantly dressed men and women imbibing legal champagne and likely some illegal liquor. Clive locked eyes with Dax and waved them over. "Glad you made it," he said before kissing them both on the cheek. He returned his stare to the middle of the crowd. Dax traced his gaze, expecting to find Grace. That man rarely let her out of his sight.

"She looks happy," Dax said, spotting her.

"She's in her element," Clive said. "We're all safe here. Every person in this room is like us or accepts us. But once we leave this floor, be careful. Understand?" Dax acknowledged with a firm nod. He gestured a hand toward the center. "Shall we?"

Dax offered Rose her arm and instantly felt at ease when she took it. Grace's face lit brightly with joy when they reached the large group in the center. She spread her arms wide, greeting Rose and pulling her in for a deep embrace. She let go a second shy of the embrace being inappropriate for Dax's taste.

"Happy birthday, my dear Rose." The unmistakable look of love was in Grace's eyes.

"Birthday?" someone in the group said. Others followed and raised their glasses. "Give the woman some champagne." One shoved a glass into Rose's hand. "Happy birthday, Rose Hamilton." The group gulped their drinks, cheered, and swept Rose among them.

Dax knew Rose was safe but was uncomfortable with the others hugging and touching her. Clive whispered when she clenched her fists, "Get used to it. People like Grace and Rose thrive on this."

"They shouldn't touch her like that."

"Set your boundaries with her later. Just don't cause a scene tonight." Clive tugged on her arm until she faced him. "This isn't one of your clubs, so follow my lead. I'll let you know what's not acceptable with this crowd. Okay?"

Dax sucked in her impatience and pride. "Okay."

A woman broke away from the group, holding a champagne glass in each hand. Her dark-brown hair and blue-gray eyes were unmistakable. "We finally get to share a drink since you're not working tonight."

"Thank you, Miss Garbo." Dax accepted the glass. Her policy of never drinking at the clubs during a shift extended to every employee, including her.

"Are you ever going to call me Greta?"

"Not as long as you're a customer of one of my clubs."

"Not seeing you in your tux won't work, so I'll have to settle for formalities."

Dax sipped her drink. "This is really good."

"It's from my private stock. It's a shame you don't offer it at the Beacon or Seaside."

"I'll be happy to order a few bottles, or if you prefer, I can store anything from your private collection in our cooler to have on hand for when you visit."

"You must consider me extra special to offer storage space."

"I'd do the same for any close friend of Grace." Dax sipped again.

"This is never going to happen, is it?" At Dax's hard no, Greta downed her drink in one gulp. "You can't blame a girl for trying." The lights flashed three times. "That's our cue. Time to get to work." Greta pressed a hand on Dax's chest. "Rose is a lucky woman. She never has to worry about you straying."

"No, she doesn't."

Grace, Rose, and a man approached. Dax recognized him as Greta's off-and-on public romantic interest and frequent costar. She wasn't sure if their relationship was a cover or if they shared a genuine attraction.

"John and I need to borrow Greta for the introductions. We'll join you in the loge soon." Grace took Greta by the hand and led her down the long hallway beside John.

Clive asked Dax and Rose to follow him. Halfway down the hallway, he led them down a few steps and pulled back a red velvet curtain, revealing their seats. They were in a VIP box between the orchestra and mezzanine levels. Clive directed them to sit in the second row closest to the curtain, leaving the seat nearest the edge to the audience open.

"Grace will sit there," he said before taking a seat directly behind hers.

Dax sat at the end, leaving the middle seat for Rose to provide her with a better view. Neither had been to a movie premiere, but she wanted to make this night memorable for Rose. This evening was about finally mingling with the crowd she'd admired in their world, not hers at the clubs.

The lights in the auditorium went down, and the stage curtain slowly opened from the center. The four thousand six hundred people in the audience applauded. An announcer spoke over a speaker system. "Ladies and gentlemen, welcome to the Fox Theater for the premiere of one of MGM's most anticipated movies of the year. Greta Garbo, John Gilbert, and Grace Parsons are pleased to bring you *Queen Christina*." He paused for the applause to die down. "May I direct your attention to the north wall balcony?"

A spotlight clicked on, shining on the three stars like a light from heaven. They waved to the crowd before Greta stepped up to a microphone. "On behalf of Grace and John, I thank everyone for coming tonight. We hope you will enjoy Christina's story of strength and compassion as she's forced to choose between love and her royal duty to country. So, for the next one hundred minutes, please sit back and enjoy *Queen Christina*."

The spotlight dimmed, and the movie began. A minute later, the three starring actors stepped into the loge. Greta and John took the front row, and Grace slid past Dax, sitting on Rose's other side.

Despite the excellent acting and action on screen, Dax watched Rose more than the movie, but she didn't miss a thing.

She wasn't there for the film. She was there to witness the awe on Rose's face. And when the lights came up again, she still had her eyes on Rose. The smile on her lips was worth the drive. Worth the disappointment with Charlie. Worth swallowing her pride by encouraging Rose to spend her birthday with her former lover. Dax would not pry her stare away if offered all the world's money.

The applause in the auditorium was plentiful but not as roaring as Dax expected. The long expressions on Grace, Greta, and John suggested they agreed. Rose, however, seemed oblivious to the movie's mild reception.

They exited the private box to the mezzanine hallway. Dax had expected more celebration after the movie from the same people as before, but only half remained. She caught up to Clive and asked quietly, "Is this bad?"

"It's not good."

"From what I could tell, the movie was excellent."

"You were watching Rose most of the time and didn't see a good number of people walk out of the theater during the movie."

"They did? Why?"

"The kiss Greta and Grace shared on screen."

"What? I saw that part. It was merely a hello kiss between two fully clothed women. There was nothing wrong with it."

"Nonetheless, it offended them," Clive said.

Dax looked about the hallway. John was at the bar slamming down a cocktail, Rose was consoling Grace, and Greta stood alone in the middle, with her arms akimbo and head down. Dax went to her and placed an arm around her shoulder. "Don't let the bigots bother you, Miss Garbo. It was a great movie."

"It's my finest work." Greta lowered her head more, weighed down by disappointment. "I'll never get another role where a woman is in command of her destiny and bucks what is expected of her."

"How about we all get out of here and head back to Half Moon Bay? The hotel isn't open yet, but several rooms are finished enough for you, Grace, and Clive to sleep in. Being around people you trust enough to be yourself will make you feel better."

Greta popped up straight, squaring her shoulders. "Perhaps you're right. Being among friends would be good for the soul."

Dax glanced at the bar. Greta's costar was working on his third glass of whatever. "Will Mr. Gilbert be joining us?"

"He's not happy with me at the moment, so I doubt he'll come."

"Then let's get going." After she explained her suggestion to the group, everyone collected their coats and descended the stairs to the main lobby, where several patrons were milling about. Some clamored for autographs. The theater security staff politely held them back, but Greta and Grace graciously signed them.

"I'll get the car," Clive said to them. "Come out in ten minutes."

"Rose and I parked five blocks away, so we'll meet you at the Seaside," Dax said.

She and Rose exited the theater and walked with Clive toward the corner. A group of women were on the sidewalk and stopped talking when Dax approached. Two stepped into her path while inspecting her with disapproving eyes. Dax's hair was short and slicked back, and she wore a tailored black tuxedo highlighting her breasts and curved hips. It was as clear as the neon Fox sign that she was a woman who didn't conform to social dress norms.

"You're one of them," one said.

"An abomination," another said. "Just like that distasteful movie."

Dax stopped, unable to go around them without walking into traffic. She considered pushing through but didn't want to come across as the aggressor. Clive rushed forward, opening his coat flap and displaying the pistol he had hidden in a shoulder holster. He extended an arm and used it like a battering ram to clear a path for Dax and Rose.

Dax threw a protective arm over Rose while they endured the gauntlet of haters and bigots. One woman spat in her face when she passed. For the first time since Riley King was alive, she felt physically threatened for who she loved and how she dressed, but she was more afraid for Rose. Dax would defend herself, but counterpunching wasn't in Rose's nature.

As they cleared the crowd, the last woman elbowed Rose in the upper arm. "You should be ashamed of yourself." Dax's blood boiled. She prepared to fight back when Rose recoiled under her arm, but Clive pulled her and Rose through before she could react.

Clive pushed them farther down the street, but Dax's fury failed to wane. "Let it go, Dax." He then whispered into her ear so only she could hear. "It's your job to be strong for the woman you love."

She tightened her arm around Rose when she trembled beneath it. Dax wished she could have built a cocoon of armor but realized it could not protect them from hatred. They would never be safe traveling into the city, making Grace's plans for the Seaside more necessary than Dax had imagined.

CHAPTER SEVEN

Grace glided her lips down Greta's neck while drifting a hand down her silk evening gown. She stopped at a tempting breast. It had been months since they last shared their bodies like this, each previous encounter out of a need for a distraction, not romantic love. Tonight was nothing different. Love was between them, but she'd opened her heart to only two women, losing one to suicide and the other to Dax. Greta was beautiful, an incredible lover, and a force of nature, but Grace refused to set herself up for more heartache when she needed focus and strength.

Greta lowered a shoulder strap on her dress and bandeau, slid farther down in the back car seat, and placed Grace's hand on the exposed breast. The touch was erotic and fulfilled a physical craving, but this was not the breast Grace longed to have in her palm. Every woman she touched sparked a fantasy of having Rose beneath her body or between her legs, but the possibility of it becoming a reality again was dim.

Ironically, each woman she bedded since letting Rose go was a substitute for her since Rose had started as one for Harriet.

Grace could not consider an entire bottle of barbiturates dissolved in a glass of scotch a coward's way out. She saw it for what it was—a way for Harriet to stop living in the shadows. Grace refused to consider it an option, but Rose's continued affection and the cruel beast she now faced made it more attractive. Intellectually, Grace knew being kind was Rose's nature, but the occasional caress and kiss on the cheek were pure torture.

Her lips and Greta's met with an animal-like hunger, marked by tongues stroking at a feverish pace. Greta slipped a hand under the front tail of Grace's button-down shirt, which had become untucked, and trailed it up her abdomen. The intimate contact made her muscles quiver and her skin tingle. Neither had an ounce of concern about offending Clive as he drove toward Half Moon Bay. He'd been in this position before, and the roles had been reversed several times, with Grace behind the wheel while he got to know a one-night conquest.

Her belly grew hotter with each flick of her tongue. If she hadn't agreed with Clive to limit passion in the car to boundaries of courtesy, she would drop to the floorboard and take Greta into her mouth with a relentless fervor until they both tumbled over the edge. She struggled to keep her promise until a hand squeezed her left breast, sparking a dull pain.

Grace jerked back without warning. "Don't."

The haze of lust slowly dropped from Greta's eyes, but confusion tightened her expression. "Did I hurt you?"

"I think it's the cramped quarters." Grace straightened. "Perhaps we should wait until we reach the Seaside to continue this." She tucked in her shirt.

"Maybe this was a mistake," Greta said, fixing her dress. She turned Grace's head gently by the chin. "You're distant."

"I think I'm taking tonight's movie reception too personally."

"This isn't the confident Grace Parsons who taught me to put everything into a performance and let my work speak for itself. What happened to letting criticism roll off your back because you can't please everyone? This must be about something or someone else."

Grace shifted on her bottom to gaze out her window and focus only on how pathetic she'd become. If she was so transparent that Greta could see her pining, something would have to change. She had a choice—send Clive to check on her businesses to avoid heartache or make her feelings known to Rose and hope her rebuff would stop this madness once and for all. But if the pain she experienced moments ago meant what she thought it did, the decision may have already been made for her.

Clive slowed at the city limits and turned into the newly paved Seaside parking lot. The portico lights at the main entrance were on, thanks to Dax, serving as a beacon in the dark night. The new sign and the redesigned building façade were modern and would draw in hundreds of tourists weekly.

Dax had parked her truck under the drive-thru covering and left ample room for Clive. He pulled in far enough so everyone could get out without the light drizzle touching them. Grace opened the rear passenger door, offered Greta her hand, and kissed her when she stepped out.

"Later?" Grace asked, knowing she'd need more distracting to get through the night.

"I'm counting on it."

While Clive unloaded their bags, Grace and Greta entered through the front door. The lobby was lit but unoccupied. A handwritten note was taped to a column flanking the reception desk. It read, *In club*.

"This is very nice," Greta said, spinning on her heel like a whirly top, taking in the refurbished lobby. The area still needed carpet and decorations but was close to being finished. It wasn't as grand at the Fox Theater or most of the hotels Grace had frequented, but it was a dramatic upgrade. It included brass and dark wood finishings, brighter lighting, and a taller ceiling, achieved at the cost of losing two rooms on the second floor.

"Our lovebirds are downstairs," Grace said, gesturing past the desk. "Care to ride the new elevator?"

Clive entered and left their luggage by the desk before pressing the elevator's call button.

"This is quite the addition to your little oasis," Greta said as the door slid open.

"I wanted the Seaside to have all the conveniences our friends and family are accustomed to," Grace said before entering the car. "Nothing but the best for our people. The biggest addition is the creation of adjoining rooms with pass-through doors for privacy."

"You're doing a great thing here, Grace."

"I hope I don't go bankrupt in the process." The door closed behind them when Clive pressed the button for the basement.

"I didn't realize it was an issue," Greta said. "Is your inheritance not enough?"

"I've been carrying the businesses in town until the hotel reopens. Let's say we better show a profit soon, or it will become an issue."

"Don't worry," Greta said. "I'm happy to back you, and so will our friends. We need a place like this."

"You don't know how relieving it is to hear you say that." The door opened, and Grace stepped out. She took a few steps but stopped, turned to Greta, and clutched her by the upper arms. "If something happens to me, I'll need someone in Hollywood to keep the lines of communication open about this place. Can that be you?"

"Of course. I'd be honored to take up the mantle," Greta said, searching Grace's eyes. Worry in them suggested she suspected something was wrong. Next week's doctor's appointment would tell Grace if her concern was warranted.

They entered the club through the new double doors beneath the lighted sign, "The Seaside Club." The lights were soft, slow music played over the speaker system, and Rose and Dax were dancing in a tight embrace in the middle of the parquet hardwood floor. They were beautiful together, foreheads pressed together, caressing each other's arms. It was apparent to the three newcomers they were in love and devoted to one another. The undeniable fact stung more than Grace cared to admit.

Grace glanced toward the bar at the side of the room and smiled when she spotted Jason pouring champagne into crystal flutes. Clive was instantly drawn to him. Grace and Greta followed. He leaned over the bar and kissed him on the lips. "You're a pleasant surprise," Clive said.

"Dax called the minute she got into town," Jason said.

"I'll have to thank her."

Greta handed Grace a glass and raised hers. "Here's to a world without bigots."

"I'll drink to that." Grace sipped her drink and stepped closer to Greta until their bodies pressed together. The heat between them reignited, but Greta wasn't on her mind. Every man and sapphic woman in the world would give their right arm to be this close to Greta Garbo, but Grace would give every penny she had to trade places with Dax. Still, she kissed Greta with the same fervor as in the car.

The music stopped, and Dax and Rose walked over when Grace broke the kiss.

Rose leaned in, whispering into her ear, "It's good to see you happy like this."

The pit that developed in Grace's stomach proved she was the best actress in the world. She was anything but happy and wouldn't be until she held Rose in her arms again. "How could I not be on a night like this? I'm with friends and beautiful women, and it's your birthday."

"For another three minutes," Dax said. Her expression drew long as she squeezed Rose's hand. "I hope those women in front of the theater didn't ruin your day."

"No, they didn't. I'd call it a perfect day," Rose said. "But there is one thing you could do to make it better."

"Name it," Dax said.

"Remove hard liquor from the clubs until repeal is passed. I don't trust Roy Wilkes. He'll make trouble for fun, so we don't want to give him a reason to arrest any of us."

Dax's shoulders slumped. "I understand why you and May are scared, but I'm working on a solution." She explained the situation to the others and her meeting with Burch's man. "We should hear from him soon."

"We'll need an alternate plan," Clive said. "Burch is a businessman first and will consider his bottom line. I know from experience he's averse to unnecessary risk."

"What do you propose?" Grace asked.

"Mine and Hank's special skills," Clive said.

"I was thinking the same thing," Dax said.

Rose lowered and shook her head. "Haven't we had enough violence? The safest plan is to stop selling illegal liquor until repeal is passed." She placed her hands on her hips to stress her point. "Or Wilkes is thrown out of office."

"I'm afraid it's not possible," Grace said. "There's no telling when either of those scenarios will come to fruition. We'll need the income stream from offering liquor at both clubs to start recouping the remodeling expenditures."

"There has to be another way." Rose flailed her arms, clipping Greta's glass and spilling champagne on her evening gown. Her mouth fell open with shock. "I'm so sorry. I'll get some club soda."

"Got it," Jason said, emerging from behind the bar with a small bottle and towel.

Greta dabbed the spots.

"Can I help?" Rose said, her cheeks flushing with embarrassment.

"No need, dear," Greta said. "I've spilled on my dresses more times than I care to remember, which is why I stick with champagne or gin."

"At least let me take it to the cleaners in the morning. I can have it back to you before lunch."

"It's not necessary," Greta said, "but if you insist, I'll go change."

"I'll show you to the room I have you staying in tonight," Dax said.

"Jason and I will help with the bags and set up the beds," Clive said before heading toward the exit with Jason.

"I'll be right back." Dax kissed Rose before leading Greta out the doors, leaving them open and Grace alone with Rose.

Grace refilled her champagne glass at the bar and another for Rose. "You look like you could use a drink."

Rose snatched the flute from Grace's hand and took a long gulp. "I ruined a Schiaparelli."

"Don't feel bad. I stretched its neckline in a way Elsa didn't intend during the drive here."

Rose scrunched her nose with an impish grin. "Are you two serious?"

"A distraction." Grace sipped her drink but didn't clarify that she needed the distraction from the pain of letting Rose go.

"Ah, then I don't have to worry about you."

"She's not the one who could break my heart." Grace should not have phrased her response in such a way, but seeing Rose happy with Dax had knocked her off balance. Deflection was in order. "I couldn't bear seeing you hurt, which is why I think a preemptive strike on Wilkes is called for."

"Promise me you won't unless necessary. I see why Charlie refuses to mend the fracture between her and Dax. Protecting the people you love is one thing, but sparking violence is another."

The disappointment in her eyes was a reaction Grace could not stand seeing. While Dax and Hank had shielded her from most of the gritty details, Rose wasn't completely blind to the dangers of the illegal liquor trade. She understood all bets were off once Roy Wilkes put on a badge.

"I promise I won't start a fight, but if he comes after any of us, I'll use every available resource." Grace pulled Rose into a tight embrace and whispered, "I won't let him hurt you."

Rose wrapped her arms around Grace's back, pressing their bodies together in a way Grace had wanted for years. But having Rose in her arms only reminded her of how much she'd lost after bowing out of the race for her heart. After years of filling voids with warm bodies, Grace concluded they were no substitute. She pulled back and traced Rose's cheek with a fingertip. "I will always love you, Rose Hamilton."

"I love you too."

Grace knew Rose didn't mean it the same way, but hearing those words broke her resolve to keep her distance. To remain satisfied with a broken heart. She pressed her lips against Rose's in a passion-filled kiss. It was wrong but felt right. It was loving but surfaced pain when Rose pushed away, ripping their lips apart.

"Grace, you know I love Dax."

This was Grace's Waterloo. *Do or die*, she thought. "I won't apologize for loving you. I first pursued you like the others, in order to relive what I'd lost, but you were different. Unfortunately, I didn't realize when I let you go that you had healed me. The void Harriet left was gone, but a new one formed at the realization of losing you." Grace clutched Rose's hand and pressed it against her chest. "I should have fought for you, Rose, because this feels empty without you."

Tears filled Rose's eyes when she stepped back. "I'm sorry I hurt you, but I've loved Dax all my life. My heart belongs to her."

Moisture pooled at the lower rims of Grace's eyes when she squared her shoulders, summoning the strength to take the higher road. Again. "Promise me one thing."

"Anything."

"If things change between you and Dax, I'll be your first call."

"I promise." The sympathy in Rose's eyes wasn't what Grace had hoped for, but its softness opened the door to possibilities.

The sound of someone clearing their throat sounded, turning both their heads toward it. When Dax and Clive walked through the open doors, Grace stepped backward, adding more distance between her and Rose and recognizing her failed attempt to rekindle their affair.

"I have you and Greta on the first floor across the hall from Clive and Jason." Dax slid her arm around Rose's waist and whispered into her ear before redirecting her attention to Grace. "We need to head home. Thank you for hosting us tonight. The premiere was a wonderful experience."

"It was my pleasure," Grace said.

After Dax and Rose retreated through the doors, Clive stepped close to Grace, kissed her on the forehead, and hugged her briefly. "You've had a rough night, my sweet."

She sighed deeply. "You have no idea."

"But I do. I rushed down after dropping off your bag."

Grace gasped as a sense of dread swept through her. "Does Dax know?"

Clive shook his head. "She was there for some of it. I know you're feeling desperate, but you're strong. You'll get past this."

"Promise you'll never leave me." She lowered her head, fighting back the tears.

Clive lifted her quivering chin until their eyes met. "I swore my life to you years ago. I will never leave your side."

Soon, Grace was leaning her back against the headboard and pulling the covers over her breasts, weighing the last few hours' events. The movie in which she'd agreed to take a supporting role to Greta's lead in order to push the envelope of the prudish Hays Code may have just killed her acting career. While the poor reception was worth the risk to show the world that two women kissing was a natural act, not something to revile, it still cut her to the quick. Two hours later, she'd made a fool of herself by telling Rose the cold, hard truth. The thought of ending things the way Harriet had crossed her mind briefly, but she had Clive. She would never be truly alone.

The bathroom door opened, and Greta stepped through in all her glory. Each curve and line were perfect but were no substitute for Rose. However, Grace would rather see Greta's sad face than Rose's. Seeing Rose hurt or disappointed would be unbearable.

Greta slid beneath the covers and joined Grace at the headboard. "Are you seeing a doctor soon?" Greta Garbo was no fool. She'd likely felt the lump in Grace's breast.

"Next week in Los Angeles."

Greta reached for Grace's hand and laced their fingers together. "You can beat this."

CHAPTER EIGHT

One Week Later

Charlie poked her head from the engine well of the car she'd worked on since sunrise and glanced toward her office where Brutus camped out most days to sleep. His bed was empty, giving her pause. She wiped her hands on a clean shop rag and stepped to her office, discovering the floor unoccupied. Her concern picked up steam as she remembered the tendency of dogs to find a cave-like space after sensing the end was coming. She took slow, tentative steps toward her desk, fearing what she might find.

The day she saw him in a cardboard box among his litter mates in the San Mateo parts store eight years ago, she'd fallen in love with him. She couldn't imagine a day without one of his slobbery kisses or a night without him fighting for space on the bed until she kicked him off.

Most of his energy had returned after she'd stopped feeding him chocolate, but the stairs were still challenging. He tried last night and got halfway up before pinning back his ears in pain when his bad leg gave out. Charlie had carried him the rest of the way, and he slept on his bed of blankets in the corner until morning.

Charlie reached the desk corner and eased lower to peek underneath the gap between the drawers. Every muscle relaxed in palpable relief when she discovered the space empty, but her search wasn't over. She still had to find where Brutus had wandered off to. A cursory visual inspection of the garage bays hadn't solved the mystery. The stairs were out of the question, leaving only one option.

Charlie stepped toward the open bay door. Fog and clouds were absent today, allowing the sun to deliver a seasonably warm late morning for the first week of summer. Emerging from her garage, she discovered a heart-melting sight. Brutus was asleep on the driveway on his belly with his back legs splayed flat on the cement, his traditional sunbathing position. He looked like a flying squirrel. He hadn't had the gumption to do this in months.

She kneeled at his side and stroked his back. "Enjoying the sun, boy?" He responded with relaxed, narrowed eyes and gentle panting, bringing tears to her eyes. "You *are* better." Realizing she'd been slowly poisoning her loyal companion had been a sucker punch to the gut after the burns he sustained during the fire Frankie Wilkes started. Running his zoomies at the end of the day might be out of reach, but seeing him enjoy his favorite pastime let her hope for a few more good years with him.

His tail wagged slowly but gained enough speed seconds later to dust the driveway from stem to stern. Charlie followed his stare to the sidewalk, discovering the reason for his excitement. A smile sprouted and grew wider the closer it came. Brutus struggled to get up by pushing off his one good back leg but accepted a well-deserved scratch behind the ears before easing back down.

"Back to sunning yourself," Jules said. "You must be feeling better."

"He's getting his energy back like you said he would." The relief of having her constant companion back was more potent than Charlie had imagined. "Are you heading to the clinic to start your shift?"

"Yep, but I wanted to drop lunch off from the Foster House for later." Jules held up a to-go sack. "May sends her love and tossed in extra biscuits for Brutus."

Charlie gave her companion one more pet before standing. "He loves her biscuits, but is it safe to let him have some? You said to keep him on a bland diet."

"Half of one won't hurt him now. Spoil him in moderation." Jules winked.

"I missed you last night," Charlie whispered. Having had Jules in her bed more nights than not in order to keep an eye on Brutus had spoiled her last week. Keeping up appearances to keep the town busybodies off the scent was a pain in the butt but necessary. "Have you eaten? I'm sure there's enough to share."

"I had a late breakfast with Rose. Maybe I can stop by for a meal break around six."

"Can you stay tonight?"

"I should sleep another night at the boarding house. My neighbors are starting to give me the side eye." Jules checked the delicate watch on her wrist. "I should get going. My shift starts in fifteen minutes."

"Mind if I walk you to the clinic? Brutus could use the excuse to stretch his legs." Three blocks there and back should be the right amount of exercise to help get him back into shape. And the extra time with Jules was the right medicine Charlie needed.

"I'd love that."

Charlie jogged inside, placed the lunch sack on her office desk, grabbed her light jacket and newsboy cap, lowered the bay door, and locked up her shop. The traffic on the main road made it impossible to hold hands without risking being seen, so they walked as closely as social graces allowed in public. Brutus favored a back leg but kept up step for step. He smiled through his panting as extra drool leaked from the corners of his mouth. He clearly enjoyed the outing.

Charlie and Jules chatted about Brutus's progress and planned a beach picnic on their next day off together. "I've been reading about new physical therapy techniques. Walking through the sand would stretch his muscles differently," Jules said. "If he works through the scar tissue on his burns, he could get back to his old self."

If not for the lack of money, Jules would have completed medical school and been a doctor years ago. Instead, she transferred to nursing school but kept up on recent developments and techniques better than Doc Hughes did. Half Moon Bay would have been better off with a caring doctor like her than a tired, old sawbones set in his ways. Charlie could not be prouder of her.

"And maybe get his zoomies back?"

"It's a possibility."

Charlie had thought she'd never see Brutus zoom through the garage again like a mad dog. If he did, if he recovered fully, maybe she could start putting the guilt she carried from the night the garage burned down behind her. Things were finally looking up.

They reached the clinic and continued to the private side door for employees. It was off the beaten path and traffic was nonexistent, giving Charlie the courage to kiss Jules on the cheek dangerously close to her lips. Unable to help herself, she let it linger longer than she should have. She was happy about Brutus. Proud about having the most brilliant woman in town as a girlfriend. If the world were different, she would take Jules in her arms and give her the kiss she deserved. It would pack enough of a toe-curling punch to drive them back to her residence above the garage to make love until the sun went down.

Bravado got the best of Charlie. She sent a hand to Jules's waist and pulled her closer, debating whether to drift over her lips and make this kiss more memorable. The moment she decided to move, Jules pushed her back. "Are you crazy? People might see."

The shrill of a police siren sounded behind her. Before she could get her head turned, a man grabbed Charlie from behind and growled, "Hands up." He snapped her back several feet, sending a look of terror to Jules's face. "Are you okay, miss? Is this man bothering you?"

Jules didn't respond, but the fear in her eyes magnified the moment before the man spun Charlie on her heel. The man was a San Mateo County Sherriff's deputy with a look of superiority written all over him. "What kind of jerk does this to a lady in the middle of the day?" His qualifier made it sound like pawing a woman on the street after dark would be okay. He flipped Charlie's cap off and took a long step back. "No one told me you were a girl. What kind of pervert are you?"

His stare drifted to Jules as if sizing her up as a pervert, too. Jules opened her mouth to say something, but Charlie shook her head vigorously, encouraging her to say nothing. She was in trouble, and if Jules acknowledged anything the deputy might have seen, it could spell disaster for her. As far as he knew, Jules was a victim of Charlie's unwanted advances.

Jules pulled her light jacket tighter around her torso and dipped her head. She remained silent.

"You're a sick one." The officer drew his fist back and landed a punch on Charlie's belly. Thank goodness she hadn't eaten the lunch Jules had dropped off. It would have ended up in a sloppy puddle on the sidewalk if she had.

Brutus barked uncontrollably and was in danger of the officer taking defensive action to shut him up. Charlie feared acknowledging being his owner. If she did and the deputy hauled her away, Jules would have to take control of him. And when Brutus minded Jules, the deputy would know she was friendly with Charlie and welcomed the kiss. She could not take the chance.

"Shut your dog up, lady," Charlie said.

Jules grimaced, likely realizing how much saying those words pained Charlie. "Brutus, down. Come here, boy." He quieted and nuzzled against Jules's leg but was still visibly agitated. She stroked his back to calm him.

The deputy tossed Charlie against the side of the patrol car, slamming her nose into the metal frame between the front and back doors. The pain was instant and debilitating, telling her it was likely broken. He socked her in the kidney before forcing her hands behind her back and shackling them in cuffs. "You're under arrest."

"Arrest?" Charlie spat blood from her mouth. "For what?"

"Lewd and disorderly conduct and for being a freak." He pulled her back, opened the door, and shoved her inside the back seat hard enough to bang her head against the opposite door. He slammed the door shut.

Charlie righted herself in time to see him talking to Jules, but she refused to raise her head or respond. Instead, she continued to pet Brutus. The deputy threw his hands up in frustration, jumped into the driver's seat, and drove down the side street. Charlie craned her head to peer out the back window. Tears streamed down Jules's face, breaking her heart.

"Where are you taking me?"

"City jail until we can take you to county. Now shut up." He took the righthand corner extra fast at the first intersection, sending Charlie into the passenger side door with an excruciating thud. At the second turn, it became clear he was flinging her around intentionally to maximize the pain. He skidded to a stop in front of the jail, sending her colliding with the back seat and confirming her suspicion.

The deputy yanked the car door open, pulled Charlie out by the arm, and fast-walked her inside the tiny city jail. An officer at the front desk looked on with curiosity. "That's the one."

"It would have been nice knowing Charlie was a woman."

The desk officer shrugged. "Well, you got her. What's the charge?" His snicker sounded evil.

"Perversion. I caught her mauling a woman in public."

"What about the other woman?"

"She was a basket case, so I let her go."

"One down. One to go," the desk officer said.

Who else are they going after? Charlie thought.

The deputy holding Charlie grabbed a skeleton key on a metal ring and pulled her past the desk toward the two-cell holding area. He unlocked the one on the left, punched her in the gut again, pushed her inside, and locked the door.

Charlie doubled over and croaked, "Don't I get a lawyer or something?"

"At county." He laughed. "Good luck finding anyone who wants to defend a pervert."

Charlie sat on the bunk inside her eight-foot by eight-foot cell and wiped the blood from her nose with a coat sleeve. How could she have been so stupid to take such a chance with Roy Wilkes as the new sheriff? He'd been in office for one day and already had his deputies roaming Half Moon Bay, looking for any reason to get even with the people he blamed for his brother's death. If she kept her mouth shut, these deputies might not discover she was more involved than anyone thought. Only Hank and Jules knew the truth. They'd never spoken about it. The night of the whiskey war was best kept buried in the past. Otherwise, Charlie would never find a day of peace for the rest of her life.

CHAPTER NINE

Dax and Grace counted on Rose as the main attraction to put as many butts as possible in the seats to justify Grace's massive investment in the marina properties. Accordingly, the pressure to select the right songs for two performances each night, four days a week until Labor Day, was high. If she did her job well, those sixty-two days could pull in enough money to put the Seaside and every business in town in the black until next year.

Rose was convinced putting together a fresh set list of songs would draw in more rich patrons for her summer shows. It was only ten days before the Fourth of July holiday arrived and, with it, the official start of the Half Moon Bay tourist season. She and Lester had spent the last three months compiling a list of possible songs and testing them during weekday performances to gauge the audience reception. All that remained was picking the top twenty-four pieces and arranging them in unique sets.

A creak on the hallway floor sparked a slow-forming grin. Dax had emerged from their bedroom, pulling up her suspenders. The way each strip of cloth accentuated her breasts perfectly sent tingles coursing through Rose's body. They did whenever Dax wore them. Every. Single. Time.

Rose shifted on the couch to view her straight on and waited for Dax to notice her between yawns. Her slouch and the dark circles under her eyes suggested she was still exhausted after closing the club and coming to bed after two this morning. Like Rose, she had a heavy weight on her shoulders with tourist season less than two weeks away. At least she was safe. While tuned into the police frequency on her new radio last night, Rose had heard that the police had broken up a large brawl in a nearby town's speakeasy and taken two people to a hospital. Dax was right when she gave her that radio. It had helped Rose sleep easier, knowing she was safe.

Dax finally opened her eyes fully and focused on Rose. She stopped and matched her smile. "Good morning, beautiful."

Rose stood, walked closer, and draped her arms over Dax's shoulders. "Good morning, sexy. You look tired."

Dax wrapped her arms around Rose's waist. "I am, but I have to meet with Burch's man this afternoon for a special meeting."

"Do you think Captain Burch will help keep Roy Wilkes in check?"

"I don't know. Burch is a businessman, so it's about the bottom line for him, not the people."

Footsteps sounded on the stairs from the Foster House restaurant level. Dax gave Rose a brief kiss and stepped back before Lester appeared at the top, carrying a cup of coffee in one hand and a stack of index cards in the other. "Morning, Dax. Morning, Rosebud."

"Good morning, Lester." Dax straightened her suspenders again. Rose sighed at the delicious sight. "I have a tuner coming on Tuesday to make sure the piano's in top shape for tourist season."

"Thank you, Miss Dax. I noticed three keys were a little loose."

"All right then. I better get to work." Dax gave Rose's hand a gentle squeeze before disappearing down the stairs. Lester knew about her and Dax, but out of courtesy they never showed more affection in front of him beyond holding hands.

Lester focused on Rose. "Ready to nail things down today?"

She greeted him with a friendly hug. "Let's do it. A lot of people in town are depending on us to get this right. I have an idea that might sound strange, but hear me out."

Once Rose explained her plan, Lester laid the index cards on the coffee table. Over the next thirty minutes, they cobbled together interchangeable set lists using six blocks of four songs. Each performance would consist of three blocks of longer pieces to fill forty-five minutes. By shifting blocks around each night, they would not repeat the same combination for the entire week. It was more work for Rose and Lester, but the variation would keep the patrons guessing, enticing them to attend more performances.

They gave each block a code name based on important people in their lives. Lester chose his three daughters—Max for Maxine, Emma, and Linda. Rose chose the three prominent women in her life—Dax, May, and Jules. Finally, they wrote out the combinations for all eight weekly performances, one in each club for four nights a week.

"This is really good," Lester said. "I never considered the block concept."

"Performing the same two sets every night gets old. This will keep things fresh."

Lester smiled. "You certainly have a head for the business side of singing."

"I picked up several pointers from Grace over the years. The most important ones were to not be just a pretty face nor let the men controlling the industry run roughshod over me. She taught me to consider my work a business and be my best advocate. I run the show."

"I knew you were special from the first day we met, Rosebud. You came prepared with a list of songs *you* wanted to perform, not what Frankie Wilkes told you to sing. You didn't need Grace Parsons to teach you the ropes. You had it all figured out the first time you stepped onto the stage."

Rose remembered the day she and Lester met at his piano at the Seaside Club. It was hard to believe it was eight years ago. Come to think of it, Brutus was just a puppy and she was twenty-two and under the thumb of her cousin Ida, working for tips and a room in her house. Accepting the trial singing gig from Frankie Wilkes was Rose's second-best leap of faith since taking her first steps as a toddler. The first was kissing Dax under the poplar trees in Sweeny Park when they were teens. Nothing in life could ever surpass it.

Rose was no longer the shy, insecure person who first took the stage, but Lester had a point. She'd had it within her all along to become as confident in her talent and abilities as she was today. "Maybe I didn't figure it out on the first day, but I have now."

Rapid, loud clomps came from the stairs, drawing Rose's attention. Few people accessed the upstairs residence, so it had to be someone close to her on a serious mission. If it was Dax running up to sneak a kiss, Lester staying longer than expected would disappoint her. However, it was Jules who appeared at the top, her hair a mess and eyes puffy from crying.

Rose stood, her chest tingling with concern. "Jules? What's wrong? Aren't you supposed to be at work?"

"It's Charlie." Jules was out of breath. Panic filled her eyes. "She's been arrested."

"Arrested? For what?" Rose approached, clutching her by the elbows.

Jules glanced at Lester, appearing hesitant to answer. Of everyone in Rose's circle, Jules was the only person never short of words. Her relationship with Charlie was the only topic she was guarded about, especially in public.

Rose redirected her attention. "Lester, would you mind giving us a moment?"

"I think we're done, Rosebud." Lester stood, gathering his index cards. "I'll see you in the dressing room about seven thirty." He turned. "Good luck, Miss Jules. I hope things work out with Miss Charlie."

After Lester disappeared down the stairs, Rose turned to Jules. "Tell me what happened."

"Charlie walked me to work. When we got to the clinic, she kissed me on the cheek. It lasted longer than it should have, and her wandering hands didn't help. You know how handsy she gets."

"Get to the point, Jules."

"A deputy saw us. He thought Charlie was a man who was coming onto me too strong. When he discovered she was a woman, he beat her up and tossed her into the patrol car."

"Where did he take her?"

"City jail." Jules buried her face in her hands. "There was so much blood. I think he broke her nose."

Rose gasped. "This has to be Roy Wilkes's doing."

Jules looked up, fear deepening on her face. "What do we do?"

"We'll get her a lawyer and get her out of there."

"She can't afford a pricy lawyer."

"Don't worry about the money. We'll take care of it. I'll have Grace find the best lawyer in San Francisco to represent her."

"But that could take days."

"Let's go to the club and get Dax and Hank. We can call Grace from there." Rose gently stroked Jules's arms before urging her downstairs.

CHAPTER TEN

The Foster House dining room was quieter than usual when Dax descended the stairs, leaving Rose and Lester upstairs. The sound of flatware scraping against porcelain dishes was barely noticeable. With the restaurant between the breakfast and lunch services, only a few stragglers remained, sipping coffee and reading the morning paper.

Ruth acknowledged her with a playful wink from the beverage station. "Morning, Dax. You're up a little early."

"Club business today." Which was code for meeting with her illegal liquor smuggler. Ruth responded with another wink.

Dax pushed through the swinging door to the kitchen and bumped into Rose's cousin on the way in. Ida caught herself before she could drop the tray of clean glasses for the lunch rush.

"Whoa, Ida. I'm sorry."

"You spent a bunch of money and time putting in a window in the door to avoid traffic jams. One would think you would make good use of it and look before barging into the kitchen."

While Ida's snarky comments weren't directly insulting, they had become tiresome. Dax had promised May to keep the peace, but with Roy Wilkes taking office and tourist season right around the corner, this was not the day to push her buttons. "Look, Ida, you may not like me, but—"

"Dax," May said from the center island. "May I have a word with you?"

Dax sighed. "Sure."

May invited Dax into her office and closed the door behind them. The former bedroom was much roomier since May and Hank moved into their house across the highway. May pointed to the chair. "Sit."

Dax knew better than to argue with May on her turf and did as she was told. "Yes, May."

"I know Ida gets on your nerves, but she's the best waitress we have on staff."

"I don't doubt it," Dax said, "but she needs to show me some respect."

"The same goes for you. Since the day she showed up here asking for a job, you've treated her like she was the enemy."

"Can you blame me after the way she treated Rose for five years?"

"If Rose can treat her civilly, you can too."

"But—"

"No buts, Dax. What do you expect when you kick a dog every day? He'll growl every time you step into the room. It's not as if you're protecting Rose from Ida's poor behavior these days. It's been eight years. People can change. Lord knows you have."

"Me?" Dax pointed to herself. "How did this become about me?"

"Can't you see she's jealous? Rose started off shamed, working for pennies. Now she's the most popular singer in California and rubs elbows with Hollywood stars. And you started out helping Papa with his carpentry work. Now you run the nicest nightclub on the West Coast and oversee a hotel renovation guaranteed to keep this town afloat for years. It's been the opposite road for

Ida and her husband. They had a decent business for decades. Now it's gone. And don't forget Ida carries the pain of being forced to give up her child. Showing kindness costs nothing and might help her see it goes both ways."

Dax lowered her head. Her sister could put things into perspective and make her feel guilty to the bone in a way no one else could. "When you put it like that…"

"When you open your eyes to the truth, holding a grudge against Ida is hard." May lifted Dax's head by her chin. "Try."

"I will. You're a good person, May O'Keefe." Dax stood and kissed May on the cheek. "I gotta head downstairs to the club before meeting with Burch's man today. How about dinner together tonight before I start my shift there?"

"I'd like that." May opened the door, signaling the lecture was over.

Dax walked down the interior stairs to the Beacon Club, going through the storage area and past Rose's dressing room. She pushed open the swinging door to the main floor. The normally dimly lit space was bright, with every light on for inventory and cleaning. The janitor was wiping down the tables, and Hank and Jason counted stock behind the bar.

"Gentlemen, what's the word?"

"Sales picked up from last week," Jason said, "but it's not as brisk as it was this time last year."

"The beer and wine bar down the street is still peeling off locals," Dax said.

"But tourists are still coming for entertainment," Jason said. "And Rose knows how to draw them in."

"Yes, she does." Dax let a smile grow. Rose Hamilton was why people with money flocked to Half Moon Bay all year, especially in droves during the summer. The town had beaches, fishing, marina boat rides, and horse rentals, but Rose was the primary attraction. Everyone west of the Rockies with money to burn came here to have Rose Hamilton sing to them like a lover. Dax tucked away her pride in Rose and focused. "Considering everything, what's your prediction for tourist season?"

"I think we're solid," Jason said. "But with increased beer and wine sales, I'd cut back to two-thirds of the whiskey we ordered last season."

Hank winced, telegraphing a different opinion.

"What is it, Hank?" Dax asked.

"What if Wilkes chokes off our supply? We have a month in reserve to carry us until we can source another supplier. I'd increase your order and store it at the Seaside until we figure out Wilkes's game."

"You make a good point. I'd rather have too much liquor for the summer than not enough," Dax said. The pressure was on her to make enough profit to justify Grace's investment. "I can dip into my personal reserves to cover us for the season."

"Dax!"

She followed the voice, glancing toward the swing door. Rose appeared. She had an arm wrapped around Jules, comforting her. Dax rushed to them. "Rose? What's wrong?"

Rose guided Jules to a table, inviting her to sit. Dax gestured to Jason, asking him to bring a glass of water. Jules's hands shook while she drank it.

"Charlie's been arrested." Rose further explained about the kiss, the deputy, and the beating.

"Roy Wilkes," Dax whispered. Saying his name made her realize a second whiskey war had begun. A chill coursed through her as she clutched Jules's hand. "I'm so sorry. We'll get her out."

"We need to get her a lawyer," Jules sobbed.

"The closest one is in Redwood City. I can drive to town and try to find one."

Rose shook her head. "No lawyer off the street will defend her once they hear the charges. Grace must know one in the area who will."

"Then let's call her." Dax went behind the bar and pulled out the telephone she had installed last year to separate the club's business from the legal Foster House business. She had the operator dial Grace's private line at her house in Hollywood.

"Parsons' residence," the housekeeper answered.

"This is Dax Xander. I need to speak with Mrs. Parsons."

"I'm sorry, Miss Xander, but she and Mr. Parsons are out for the day. May I take a message?"

Dax was vague regarding details but explained the urgency before hanging up. She turned to Jules and Rose. "I don't have to meet with Burch's man for another hour. I'll go to the jail and see about posting bail."

"Do you really want to do that, Dax?" Hank asked. "You'll give Wilkes another reason to come after you."

"Charlie may not reciprocate, but she is my friend. I won't let her sit in a cell a minute longer than necessary." Dax turned to Jules. "You should stay here until this blows over. We'll be safer if we stick together."

"I think you're right," Jules said.

"We're finished with the inventory." Jason stepped forward. "I can take you to the boarding house to pick up some things."

"I'll go with you." Rose squeezed Jules's hand. "When do you have to be back at work?"

"Tomorrow, I think. I begged off sick today." Jules appeared rattled, prompting Dax to bend at the knees to look at her in the eye.

"No matter what it takes, I'll get her out of there."

After popping upstairs to tell May about the morning's events, Hank returned downstairs to prepare the club for opening later. Jason took Rose and Jules to the boarding house while Dax drove to the city jail. Four county deputy patrol cars were parked out front, raising Dax's suspicions. Half Moon Bay had no police force and relied on the county sheriff for assistance. Besides the speakeasy and regular illegal liquor cargo Captain Burch dropped off, the town wasn't a hotbed of criminal activity. Looking the other way had become a way of life for the former sheriff and for Prohibition agents, explaining why a patrol car rarely made it to town more than once a week. Something else was at play.

Dax walked inside. Two deputies were at the desks with their feet propped up on the corners. Another two were nearby, drinking coffee. All eyed her like she was a circus sideshow. Dax broke the awkward silence. "You're holding a friend here. When will she see the judge so I can post bail?"

One deputy stepped closer, folding his arms across his chest while looking down on Dax like she was the scum at the bottom of the marina. "I bet you're one of them."

"One of what?"

"Pervert."

"If it means not being interested in a hairy, smelly thing like you, then you're right."

The other deputies laughed.

"Watch your mouth," he said with fire in his eyes.

"Aren't you the one from the Foster House? Dax, right?" another deputy asked.

"Yeah. What's it to you?"

"Just asking," he said, but Dax didn't buy his question as benign curiosity for one second. He gave the impression that she and everyone associated with Frankie Wilkes's death were targets.

"Then perhaps you can tell me when my friend might be offered bail."

"Likely never. The judge in Redwood City doesn't like her kind. There's no way he's granting her bail. She'll likely stay in jail until the trial."

"Trial? When is that?"

"That's up to the district attorney. But if I know Chet, it won't be for a month or two."

"Can I see her? She'll need someone to watch over her garage."

"Not until we finish booking her."

"When will that be?"

"Check back around dinner time."

"Fine." Dax left the jail feeling worse than when she entered. A bleak picture formed. Roy Wilkes had aligned the entire county justice system against her and her friends, from the police to the district attorney to the judges. She needed help to limit his reach before this went any further.

Dax hopped in her truck and drove south to the lighthouse, where the reconstruction of the fire-damaged building was closer to completion. The ocean-filled breeze nipped at her cheeks when she stepped toward the residence. Mrs. Monroe, the keeper's wife, answered the door and invited Dax to sit at the kitchen table with her.

"Good morning, Miss Xander. It's nice seeing you again. How was Miss Parsons's movie premiere?"

Dax recalled the patrons who had stomped from the theater following the on-screen kiss between Grace and Greta and the tepid applause when the credits rolled. The disappointment among the actors was so palpable she'd feared a gauntlet of pitchforks as they left the theater. The reviews in the *Chronicle* the following day had skewered the movie, twisting the knife of defeat. Salty critics had unfairly judged the film on social mores, not the storyline or quality of the performances, showing more about the critics' biases than the movie's flaws. But none of that needed mentioning.

"It was quite the experience. The theater was like a palace."

Mrs. Monroe harrumphed. "The reviews seemed unkind."

"The critics couldn't get past their own prejudices to be objective."

"How unfortunate," Mrs. Monroe said. "I'll have to rally the community to see it."

Dax narrowed her eyes in confusion. Did she mean people like her and Rose? "The community?"

"Immigrants. Most of us came from countries where those in charge told us what to think and do every day. We came here to be free. We won't let some critics decide for us what is or is not a good movie. Besides, Miss Parsons is the kindest woman on the planet."

"Yes, she is," Dax said. Grace was kind, but she was also in love with Rose. The kiss she stole the night of the premiere had crossed the line, but Rose had handled it with poise. Dax had seen everything but didn't let on until Rose volunteered the information when they got home. They woke the following day more sure of their love, trust, and the absence of secrets between them.

A knock on the door prompted Mrs. Monroe to push herself away from the table. "That must be Captain Burch's man. It's been nice catching up with you, Miss Xander."

"Likewise."

Mrs. Monroe opened the door before disappearing deeper into the house. Dax stood, expecting to see Burch's man, but was taken aback. "Captain Burch, this is a pleasant surprise." He'd trimmed his gray hair and beard and had dropped several pounds since they last met six months ago, but he was still an intimidating six-foot-tall presence with broad shoulders in his captain's uniform.

He shook her hand. "Let's sit, Miss Xander."

"All right." Dax sat, following his lead. She got the impression labeling his surprise visit as pleasant was premature.

"Miss Xander, I wanted to deliver this news in person out of respect for our friendship." Dax shifted uncomfortably in her chair and listened. "Mr. Wilkes is proving to be a slippery one. I cannot circumvent the deep ties he has with Sacramento. Perhaps Mrs. Parsons will have better luck."

"What does this mean for our liquor deliveries?"

"They are suspended until further notice."

"Suspended?" Dax sprang to her feet. This was her worst nightmare. "The Seaside Hotel and Club reopens in ten days. Where am I supposed to get enough liquor to serve guests?"

"I understand your frustration, but I received a phone call from the United States attorney for the area. He threatened to shut down my entire operation if I continued doing business with you. Many people rely on this supply chain. I'm very sorry, but I can't put it in jeopardy. I've reached out to my competitors to see if they are interested, but all have declined. Your only option is the resale market."

"With all the renovations, we can't afford the markup unless I dip into my personal reserves."

"That won't do." Captain Burch shook his head. "How much stock do you have on hand?"

"A month at most."

Burch rubbed his hands together as if concocting a solution. "Mind you, I can't risk things by directly supplying you, but I have several customers in the Los Angeles area. They should be far enough away to ensure any dealings with them won't get back to Mr. Wilkes. I can speak to them about increasing their purchases and selling you their surplus at cost. But I will be upfront about the reason."

"Would anyone agree, knowing the risk?"

"I can think of two."

"I don't know how to thank you, Captain Burch."

"Don't thank me yet. This will take several weeks to set up, and you'll have to transport the load yourself."

"It's better than nothing." Between the Seaside and Beacon Club, Dax figured she would need four trucks weekly during the tourist season and only one after Labor Day. She had access to three—hers and two from the Seaside—and Grace could supply a fourth. Vehicles would not be the problem. Personnel would. She would need four drivers plus one or two people per vehicle as security. Finding and paying for eight to twelve people would add up. She'd have to do the math, but depending on how many people she could scrounge up from the staff, it might be cheaper for her and Grace to scavenge cases of liquor from the local resale market despite the exorbitant prices.

"I'll send word next week with names of those willing to help. Do I have permission to have them contact you?" Burch asked.

"Of course."

Dax left, thinking the day could not get much worse. Her best friend was in jail, her businesses were in jeopardy, and her investor could go bankrupt. Much was unknown at this point, but she knew one thing for sure. When she got home, she would need a stiff drink.

CHAPTER ELEVEN

Grace closed her eyes for the short drive from her mansion to the hospital, pushing away the harsh realities it might impose by revisiting and relishing the memory of the first night she saw Rose Hamilton sing on the Seaside Club stage. Frankie Wilkes had claimed he'd found a rare gem—a canary with a mesmerizing voice, incredible looks, and a stage presence seductive enough to make everyone want to take her home. Once her filming schedule cleared, Grace went to see for herself, and she wasn't disappointed. Frankie was right. The performance was so magical she wanted to take Rose to her room.

Grace fondly remembered Rose's blue gown with a hint of sequins glistening in the stage lights. It had been gathered at the waist, showing off her delectable shape, and its neckline had dipped low enough to distract everyone in the room, especially Grace. The note she'd sent to the stage immediately following Rose's performance, inviting her for a drink and whatever else she might want, proved it.

Their first kiss was as enchanting as Rose's performance, but it was only the appetizer. Grace had never been anyone's first, and despite telling herself Rose was merely a distraction in a long line of them, being part of her sexual awakening was soul-binding. She'd felt to her bones Rose's joy in giving and receiving pleasure.

The experience had opened the door Grace had once sworn never to unlock after losing Harriet, and she was desperate to relive it over and over again. Trying to rekindle their connection last week had been a fool's errand, though. Those moments with Rose in her arms were a sad reminder that deep love was rare. Grace had missed her chance, but she wasn't alone. However, while she loved Clive and Greta for their loyalty and companionship, neither of them was Rose.

The car door on her side opened, spilling the sound of city traffic into the cabin and knocking Grace from her memories. Clive offered his hand. "We're here, my sweet."

She squinted at the sunlight pouring in. The sun in Hollywood was particularly harsh this morning without clouds in the sky to filter its rays. When she reached for Clive's hand, he added an extra pull to his grip to help her from the car. His assistance was welcomed. The diagnostic procedure performed earlier this week at this same hospital was necessary, but it had zapped her energy. She shuddered to think how she would feel after today if things went as she suspected.

Once on her feet, she replied, "Thank you, dear. I suppose we should get this over with."

He closed the door and hooked her arm with his. "Perhaps it will be good news."

"We both know that won't be the case." Grace traced his cheek with a finger. He shaved close today, leaving his skin extra smooth. He knew how much she hated the feel of stubble. "But thank you for keeping my spirits up these last few days."

They walked up the steps to the main entrance of the Cedars of Lebanon Hospital in the heart of East Hollywood. Before stepping inside, Grace paused to inspect the façade. Its curved, smooth surface and horizontal accent lines defined art deco modernism. The facility was only three years old and was home to the best doctors on the West Coast and the most advanced medicines and medical equipment money could buy. Grace's generous donations had facilitated its construction and had earned her VIP treatment when she called Doctor Shapiro for a consultation.

Clive held open each door as they passed, like any man with manners would. However, since leaving the house this morning, his attention had been extra gentle, making her feel like a fragile antique figurine. One that the slightest jostling would shatter into a dozen pieces. She knew he intended the opposite—to make her feel loved—but his attentiveness was underscoring his worry like spotlights on opening night.

When they reached the doctor's office, Clive remained by Grace's side but said nothing while the receptionist checked her in for the appointment. Two other couples were seated in the waiting area, but an assistant ushered Grace and Clive into Doctor Shapiro's private office without delay, continuing the VIP treatment.

"The doctor is with a patient and will be right with you, Mrs. Parsons. Can I get you anything to drink?"

"Some water would be nice." Grace wasn't thirsty, but sipping on something might take the edge off.

The woman filled two glasses from a pitcher on a credenza behind the doctor's desk, placed them on the small end table between the guest chairs, and left after Grace thanked her. The water was chilled to a refreshing temperature and coated Grace's mouth nicely but failed to quiet her nerves. Her hand shook as she brought the glass to her lips for a second time.

Clive steadied her hand and helped return the cup to the table. "Would you like something stronger?"

"No. I want a clear head for this."

The door opened, and the doctor walked in. Clive stood and shook his hand. "It's a pleasure to see you again, Doctor Shapiro."

"Likewise." Shapiro turned toward Grace, bending at the waist to see her face. "Mrs. Parsons, I'm glad you could make it today." He shook her hand, circled his desk, and sat in his chair. "Like I said on the phone yesterday, I have the results from the samples we took on Tuesday."

"I take it they're not good," Grace said.

"The lump *is* cancerous, but the tests show it hasn't spread to your lymph nodes. We've caught it early, which makes it treatable."

Grace had known the truth for weeks—since discovering the lump during a shower—but had refused to address it until after the premiere. A life-altering diagnosis would have tainted the special event, and she'd wanted to enjoy it. As it turned out, considering the movie's unenthusiastic reception, she would have preferred getting all the bad news out of the way in the same week.

Hearing the word Grace feared the most made her realize it didn't matter when she received the diagnosis. It made her numb. Fate had caught up. Her mother had died of breast cancer months before the war started. Developing it herself had been on Grace's mind since.

Something touched her knee.

"Grace, are you okay?" Clive kneeled in front of her. "Would you like some water?"

Grace finally focused on him. "No. I'm fine. Where were we?"

"We were discussing a treatment plan." Clive returned to his chair.

Grace shifted her attention to Doctor Shapiro. "You were saying, Doctor?"

"We've made tremendous advancements in cancer treatment since your mother passed away. And since we've caught it early, we have several options available. The most aggressive is a complete mastectomy, during which we remove the entire breast."

The idea of having a piece of her body chopped off was a nauseating thought. Her livelihood depended on maintaining a pleasing body and face. She could choose costumes to hide her scars and wear a specially constructed brassiere to make her appear natural. However, the question remained whether she would feel whole.

The doctor continued, "However, the growth is small enough to recommend a lumpectomy. With either option, after you heal, you should undergo a course of radiotherapy to kill off residual cancerous cells."

"Radiotherapy?" Grace asked. "Do you mean using X-rays?"

"X-rays in high doses is one form of radiotherapy, but it comes with many unwanted side effects. French scientists are seeing better results using radium in low doses over several weeks. Based on the size of your tumor and its early stage, you're a prime candidate."

"Radium?" Clive said. "Didn't Eben Byers die of radium poisoning last year?"

"I understand your concern, Mr. Parsons. Mr. Byers drank radium-laced water daily for five years and developed multiple cancers. However, in small doses, cancerous cells die when exposed to radiation. I'm recommending a targeted treatment, where we expose the remaining breast tissue to a low dose for an hour a day, five days a week, for three weeks. The amount of radiation I would expose your wife to would be equivalent to the recommended X-ray therapy dose. Exposing her to it over time should reduce the side effects tremendously."

"What are those side effects?" Clive asked.

"Fatigue, swelling, skin redness, tenderness, and hair loss." Shapiro lost Grace at hair loss. No one would pay to see a bald actress on a movie screen. Shapiro seemed to sense her aversion, adding, "All temporary."

"How long would Grace have to decide about the radiation?"

"We'd want the skin and tissue to be completely healed before starting the treatment course, but I wouldn't wait more than a month or two."

"What if I chose to only have you remove the lump and forego the radiation?"

"Even if I get the entire tumor, the cancer's chance of returning is great. You don't have to decide on every treatment element today. However, the sooner we remove the tumor, the better your chances of remission will be."

"How soon could you do the surgery?" Grace asked.

"Today. I reserved an operating room for this afternoon and can reschedule the rest of my appointments for the day if you agree to the surgery."

"That soon." Grace's head swirled at the speed at which things were happening. She'd lived with knowing she likely had had breast cancer for at least a month and she'd packed a bag, just in case. But today, within minutes, the doctor confirmed the diagnosis and was virtually wheeling her down the corridor to chop it out. "I have a grand reopening for my hotel in ten days. Will I be able to participate in the activities?"

"Barring complications, you should be up and around in three days, but no lifting more than a pound for a month."

Grace nodded. The timing would work. With Dax in charge of the opening day events, Grace's role would be limited to handshakes and buttering up the VIPs to spend more money.

"When did you eat last? We should wait at least four hours since your last meal to ensure your stomach is empty."

"She hasn't eaten since last night." Clive volunteered the tidbit before she could get her head to stop spinning.

"Good. I can move things up, and we can start prepping her immediately." Doctor Shapiro circled and leaned his bottom against his desk while taking on an anxious-to-please expression. Grace had seen it from hundreds of clerks and servers but didn't expect it from him. A starstruck doctor might be preoccupied and make mistakes.

"I don't want my celebrity dictating the order of things. I won't cut lines."

"Your celebrity hasn't made a difference, but your generosity has, Mrs. Parsons. Your timely donation last year kept this hospital from closing and allowed us to move into this new facility to continue serving the community. That rightly makes you a priority." He put her slightly at ease, but line cutting still felt wrong.

"I'm open to having the surgery today, but those people in your waiting room were here before I arrived. Please, don't send them home without seeing them."

"All right, Mrs. Parsons. I'll have my staff prep you for surgery while I tend to them."

Clive offered his arm, and he and Grace followed a nurse down a cold, white corridor to a section of the hospital labeled "Surgery." At the double swing doors, the nurse raised a hand in a stopping motion at Clive. "I'm sorry, Mr. Parsons. Hospital rules. No visitors beyond this point."

He took Grace's hands into his. The love in his eyes was born from years of devotion, not romance. He kissed her like he'd done a thousand times since their wedding day, but this instance lingered longer than the rest. As a war veteran, he was no stranger to danger and death, but with Grace's mortality in question, he was clearly rattled.

He squeezed her hands before breaking the kiss. "No matter what the rules say, I'll be by your side when you wake."

Grace stroked her fingertips gently down his cheek. "I look forward to it." She stepped through the doors, resolved that by the end of the day, a portion of her breast would be gone and with it, hopefully, all the cancer.

* * *

Grace's celebrity and money had their advantages, but none as crucial as Clive being allowed into her room while she recovered from the anesthesia. He watched from a corner while two orderlies transferred her from the gurney into the bed. After the men left, he stepped closer while a nurse checked her bandage and the tube running to her arm from a glass container on a nearby stand. Clive had spent some time in an Army field hospital and had seen blood administered through similar containers, but the fluid in Grace's bottle was clear.

"What's in the bottle?"

The nurse continued her work and answered without looking at him. "It's a saline solution to manage her fluids after surgery."

"Is that normal?"

"You'll need to ask the doctor. He should be in soon."

"Thank you."

After the nurse left, Clive dragged a chair to the bed but inspected Grace before sitting. She was still unconscious. Her skin looked paler than before the surgery, which could not have been a good sign. He'd nursed her through several ailments and hangovers, and this rivaled her skin color during her most debilitating bout.

Her hair was mussed, something she would never stand for, so he found a towel on a corner shelf and soaked it with water from a pitcher the staff had brought in while he waited for her return. After wetting Grace's chin-length hair, he fished a brush from her overnight bag and gently straightened it until it resembled the slicked-back look she preferred while in her tuxedo. The studio had a different vision for her hair and often had the stylists puff it up for a more feminine appearance. The look was attractive, but her wet style made her downright alluring, and he'd nearly replicated it.

"Much better, my sweet." He was sure she would be pleased.

Once he returned her brush to its proper place in her bag, he sat bedside in the chair and held her hand, thinking how grateful he was for her having survived the surgery. After fourteen years together, he could not imagine living without her. They weren't romantic or sexual partners, but they were life partners just the same. The life they'd built together was rooted in love, respect, and trust.

Clive recalled the night they first met, a month after his return from the war. Killing so many men had changed him, and he had to do something with his pent-up anger. Channeling it into bedding any woman when drunk enough and every man who gave him the signal wasn't the wisest choice. His downward spiral had him bound for the undertaker or a prison cell for moral turpitude until Grace plucked him from a Los Angeles bar. She gave him a place to live, but more importantly, she gave him purpose. He gladly became her protector after seeing how she made it easier for others like them to live and love by getting them jobs in Hollywood and pointing them to friendly establishments. They had a marriage of convenience, but everything else about their life together was real.

He squeezed her hand. "We'll get you through this."

The door opened, drawing his attention. Doctor Shapiro walked inside, still wearing his white surgical garb. His expression was unreadable, other than he appeared tired.

"How did she do, Doctor?" Clive stepped aside from his chair, giving Shapiro room to examine her.

"Like a champ." The doctor drew back the sheet covering Grace's chest, exposing only the breast he operated on. He inspected the bandage and quickly returned the covers before using his stethoscope to check her breathing. "Her lungs sound clear."

"She looks so pale. Is that normal?"

"She lost a bit more blood than I'd anticipated, but not enough to give her a transfusion, so I put her on saline to build up her fluids." Once Shapiro finished his examination, he focused his attention on Clive. "I got the entire tumor and discovered the tests were right. The cancer hadn't spread."

"That's good, right?"

"Very good. However, I had to remove a significant amount of tissue to ensure I got it all, which is why she lost a bit more blood."

"How much of her breast is gone?"

"About twice the size of a silver dollar. It should heal nicely and not be noticeable with the right brassiere."

The wound was more considerable than Clive and Grace had prepared for, but they would cope. In her business, appearance was everything, from her looks to concealing her sexual predilections. She had to appear desirable to men and acceptable to the studio executives.

"She should wake in another half hour, but I'd like to keep her over the weekend to make sure her incision is healing and she can keep down food."

Clive looked around the private room. It was big enough for two patients but had only Grace's bed, three chairs, and a wash basin. "Grace will expect me to stay by her side. Can you bring in a cot?"

"It's highly unusual." Shapiro rubbed the back of his neck, appearing reluctant. Clive remained silent, leaving the doctor to wrestle with his conscience. Grace was this hospital's top benefactor, making her its most valued patient. "I'll have a second patient bed brought in and double meals delivered."

"Thank you, doctor. My wife will be grateful for the accommodations. I assume you've briefed the staff on our need for privacy."

"Yes, and I've assigned our most trusted people to care for your wife," Shapiro said. "I've ordered morphine for the pain when she wakes up and every six hours to keep her comfortable. I'll check on her before I go home for the evening and twice daily over the weekend. The nurses know to call me if there's the slightest change in her condition."

Once the doctor left, Clive resumed his bedside vigil, waiting for Grace to wake. Her nurse came in twice, taking her blood pressure and pulse and leaving satisfied they were within a normal range. He remained patient, and forty minutes after the doctor left, Grace's hand moved. He clutched it and rose to his feet, leaning closer. Her head moved. Her eyes fluttered open.

"My sweet." He squeezed her hand to let her know he was there.

"My love." Her voice was croaky, and she raised her head. "Did he get it?"

"Yes, my sweet. He got it all."

Grace smiled, letting her head flop back to the pillow, a look of pure relief in her eyes. The immediate danger had passed, so the rest could wait. Radiation treatment was a decision for another day.

CHAPTER TWELVE

Hank began restacking the beverage stock after his and Jason's weekly inventory, admiring the remodeling of the Beacon Club after the country decriminalized the sale and possession of beer and wine three months ago. They'd removed the sliding wall used to hide the bar from agents during a raid, opening up the club floor more. Dax had also built a hidden vault inside the storage room to separate the hard liquor from the legal beverages. The configuration was simple and would be easy to tear down once Prohibition was repealed.

Pushing aside the news about Charlie and what Dax might face at the city jail, he focused on the inventory and the challenges facing the club in the coming weeks. Keeping up with the stock levels had become critical after a competitor popped up down the street following the legalization of beer and wine sales in the country. Sales had varied wildly for the past few months, and the start of tourist season was approaching. Running out of anything would be disastrous for the clubs and the remodeled hotel.

Leaving the storage room open for Jason to double-check his final numbers, Hank moved on to preparing the dining room for opening. While repositioning the chairs that had been stowed upside down on the tables for early morning floor cleaning, he let his mind return to Charlie's predicament and how Dax had dropped everything to help her despite their three-year estrangement. Though Charlie thought otherwise, her friendship was genuine.

During his service in the war, Hank learned dying was much easier than living. As the Army's number one sniper, he had seen firsthand how fragile life was. A person was living one second and dead the next following a perfectly placed bullet. Death was often instant and always final. Conversely, life dragged on for most and was a constant struggle for survival. Nothing was ever permanent. Shelter and food came at a price, as did everything else it took to get by, including love and friendship. In his experience, those last two were rare and fleeting, so when he found them, he enjoyed them while they lasted, fully expecting to lose them. Dax was the polar opposite. When she made a friend, it was for life.

Never in a million years had he envisioned marrying again after a drunk driver killed his first wife, but May had taken him by surprise. So had Dax and Rose. Living with Grace and Clive for a decade had prepared him for the family dynamics he was now part of, and Dax and Rose as life partners seemed as normal to him as his and May's relationship. It was a damn shame the rest of the world didn't see it the same way.

The buzzer at the bar sounded, telling him someone upstairs was trying to reach him on the intercom Dax had installed last year. He hurried toward it, expecting his wife to be on the other end. Pressing the button hidden behind the bar, he said, "Hello?"

"Hello, Mr. O'Keefe." May lowered her voice and slowed her cadence into a seductive tone. "The last rack of glasses for the club is cleaned and ready, but we're busy with an early lunch rush. I thought you might want to come get them and, if you don't think your wife would be upset, maybe sneak a kiss."

"People might start talking about us."

"Let them."

"I like a woman who throws caution to the wind. I'll be right up." Hank closed the intercom and circled the bar, giving in to an insistent smile. His wife's flirting had become more playful since their wedding two years ago, a sign their romance was growing even stronger. After losing his first wife, he had given up on love, but once he found it with May, he promised to never take his second chance for granted and to avoid his youthful mistakes during his first marriage. He never let May go unappreciated, and she had done the same. Neither had wavered in their commitment.

He weaved through the club tables, past the stage and storage area, and bounded up the stairs. At the top, he pushed the door open. May was busy at the stove. Two servers picked up their orders. Four plates remained under the warmers. The tickets hanging from the order wheel on the warmer counter said May was running behind, but Sheila had arrived early for the start of her shift and was unbuttoning her coat.

"Busy is right. What's up today?" Hank asked.

"A pipe broke in the kitchen at Cameron's Café, so we're the only game in town for lunch until it's fixed," May said.

"We're lucky it's not tourist season yet."

"It felt like it already was, so I called in Sheila and another waitress."

"Happy to help." Sheila hung her coat, washed her hands at the sink, and jumped in, preparing the next order in the queue.

"Can I help?" Hank asked.

"We have it covered now." May gestured her chin toward the drying rack. "Your last load of glasses is on top."

Hank approached May and wrapped his arms around her waist from behind.

"Quick, before the missus comes back." May continued their playful game.

He kissed her on the cheek before releasing his hold. "You *are* a naughty one."

The swinging door between the kitchen and the dining room flew open. Loud voices flowed through as Ruth rushed in, looking as worried as the time when a car went out of control and flew into a storefront across the street. "Deputies and Prohis. Lots of them."

"Wilkes." Dread swept through Hank. He had left the hidden liquor vault door open! He needed to close it before the agents could find their illegal stock. His heart thumping fast, he pelted down the stairs as quickly as his legs could take him and retraced his route through the storage area, past the stage and through the dining tables. He heard the door at the top of the inside stairs crash open and the sound of stomping feet.

He had a clear path to the storage area, but a quick glance over his shoulder showed a pistol-waving officer had reached the bottom of the stairs and was closing. He still had three feet to go before getting to the storage room and another eight to reach the hidden button that would pull back the wall to the liquor vault. He was at the doorway and one step inside when something hit him on the back of the head, sending him to the floor between the stacks of beer and wine in pain. He'd been hit enough times to know he'd been pistol-whipped, but the power-crazed officer wasn't done. As Hank tried crawling toward the vault, he kicked him in the back and kidneys multiple times like a homeless street dog.

"Stay down," the officer ordered.

Two hands clutched his ankles and dragged him from the storage room. Someone secured handcuffs around his wrists, yanked him up by his jacket, and slammed him against the bar, sending glasses to the floor in a shattered mess. His head injury left him unbalanced, feeling like he was drunk. Focusing required considerable effort, but Hank recognized the officer as a county deputy sympathetic to Roy Wilkes. The man's smile said he was pleased at having been the one to slap on the handcuffs.

Two men rushed inside the storage room. One came out, carrying a bottle in each hand, filled from the two whiskey barrels stored there. "We got it, boss."

At least Hank and Dax had had the forethought to store their surplus barrels in the basement of Jason's house five miles away in El Granada. Their entire stock of rum, tequila, vodka, and gin was about twelve feet away, however, and the sound of breaking glass said it was being rendered into a shard-filled puddle on the floor.

Hank recognized the sergeant with a round belly and only a wisp of hair above his ears and the nape of his neck when he stepped closer. The sergeant was in charge and eyed him with disdain.

"There's a new sheriff in town, and he's settling old scores."

"Tell me something I don't know." Hank held his chin high, unwilling to give this crooked cop the satisfaction of knowing he was as nervous as a cat.

The sergeant punched him in the gut, putting his three hundred-plus pounds into it. The strike packed a wallop. "This will cost you five thousand dollars and a year in Sheriff Wilkes's jail." He laughed. "If you survive that long."

"Hank! Hank!" May shouted from the top of the back stairs, panic in her voice.

"Stay upstairs," he yelled. "They're taking me to jail." He turned back to the sergeant.

"Leave the ladies upstairs alone. This is between Roy and me."

Another punch to the belly. This one contained enough force to double him over.

"No talking. I decide who gets rousted." The sergeant sneered.

Hank narrowed his eyes at the sergeant. Besides the occasional rowdy customer in the club and Wilkes's men getting sticky fingers at the dock with Burch's deliveries, he hadn't confronted a serious threat to the club or his family since the whiskey war. He had known danger lurked as long as Roy Wilkes was alive, however, so he and Dax had kept tabs on their enemy and those who supported him.

"I know where you live in San Mateo. I know your son attends Stanford. If anything happens to my family, the same act will be visited on yours. Do you understand?"

The sergeant visibly swallowed and gestured for two deputies to take Hank. The men grabbed him by both arms.

Viselike holds threatened to cut off the blood flow there as they dragged him up the stairs and through the door to the back of the Foster House. They threw him into the back of a waiting county patrol car, bouncing his head off the metal frame of the roof on the way in. His dizziness returned, more substantial than before. Righting himself on the bench seat was a struggle.

First, Charlie was arrested for indecency, and hours later, he was being hauled in for violating the Volstead Act. This was no coincidence. Someone must have witnessed what happened the night of the whiskey war when Frankie Wilkes and his men met their deaths at his and Charlie's hands. Hank could have sworn he'd gotten them all, but one must have gotten away.

The two deputies hopped into the front seat and drove down the access road at the side of the Foster House. When they reached the end to turn onto the highway, May was at the corner of the building with Ruth buoying her with an arm around her torso and tears streaming down her cheeks. From the day May had agreed to partner with Grace to open the Beacon Club, she had known the risk of someone turning the law against them. The day she had been terrified of had finally come. Hank's heart broke when she buried her face in her hands. She'd suffered enough.

After taking several turns fast enough to toss Hank around the back like a stuffed doll, the driver stopped at the Half Moon Bay city jail, yanked him from the back seat, and marched him inside. "We got the other one," he said to a deputy occupying the front desk. Hank could not be sure because the night of the whiskey war was dark, but he resembled one of Frankie Wilkes's men who had attacked the Foster House.

"Hot dog. That's him." The young deputy jumped to his feet, slapping the top of his leg. "Mr. Wilkes will be happy."

"Let's go. The sheriff is going to love having you as his guest." A deputy from the car pulled him along after grabbing a skeleton key from a peg on the wall and opening a heavy metal door to the back. He unlocked the cell on the right, pushed Hank inside, and secured the bar door.

"When are you transferring me to county so I can post bail?" Hank asked, supposing it would not be anytime soon.

"When I feel like it." The deputy spun on his heel and exited the holding area, slamming the metal door behind him.

Hank glanced at the cell across the aisle. Charlie was standing at the bars. Her face had been badly beaten and her left eye was nearly swollen shut. "My God, Charlie. Are you okay?"

"Yeah. They gave me quite a beatdown, but I didn't give them the satisfaction of seeing me cry."

"That's my girl."

"What trumped-up charge do they have on you?" She twisted her hands around the bars, clearly channeling her anger.

"They raided the Beacon Club and found the liquor stash."

"Sorry to hear that. What about Jason, May, and Rose? Did the deputies get them too?"

Charlie's failure to ask about Dax didn't go unnoticed. The feud between those two had gone on for far too long. He understood her position. She was naturally a peaceful person who abhorred violence, and he respected her for the lines she'd drawn. At times, Hank wished he was more like her, but he was the polar opposite. He had three hundred seventy-eight confirmed kills during the war, had killed the man who had killed his wife, and knocked off six of Frankie Wilkes's men during the whiskey war. He'd done enough killing for a hundred lifetimes.

"No. I was the only one downstairs at the time. I don't think they'll come after our family."

"Are you sure? I'm worried about Jules."

"Trust me. They don't want another all-out war," Hank said. The cross look the sergeant gave him after Hank mentioned his son was his guarantee.

"What's going to happen to us? One deputy said something about going to county." The strain in Charlie's voice revealed her nervousness. She was strong and could defend herself in most situations, but handcuffed, she was no match against armed deputies. Besides continued beatings, Hank feared the guards might do something even more heinous.

"They have to let us see a lawyer before seeing a judge."

"I can't afford a lawyer," Charlie said.

"Jules already talked to Rose, and we left a message for Grace to help. Once she gets involved, we should be out on bail or have the charges dropped within a day."

Charlie shook her head. "I'll never be able to repay her."

"After what you did for all of us, Grace is your fan for life. Money isn't an issue."

"Well, it is for me. I'll figure my own way out of this."

"No, Charlie. This is not the time to stand on your pride. Wilkes knows no limits. Take Grace's help when it comes. Until then, we stick together."

CHAPTER THIRTEEN

After Rose helped Jules gather enough things for three or four days and picked up Brutus from the garage where Jules had stowed him after Charlie's arrest, Jason drove them back to the Foster House in the Seaside company truck. Rose held her hand in the front seat, but the gesture had little comforting effect. Jules was still visibly shaken. If Rose had seen Dax beaten and arrested, she would have been a wreck, too, unable to think of anything beyond breaking her out of jail and stringing up the vicious deputy by the toenails.

Rose squeezed Jules's hand tighter. "Grace will call soon."

"But when?" Jules's voice cracked with worry. "They'll beat Charlie to a pulp or worse if she's not out soon."

Rose had the same fear, but saying so wouldn't help Jules. "If she doesn't call by tomorrow, we'll find her a lawyer."

"But tomorrow is Saturday. No lawyers will be in until Monday."

The timing of things could not be worse. That probably wasn't a coincidence. Rose got the impression Charlie's arrest had been timed to prolong her stay in jail before she could see a judge. "We'll get her out."

Jason drove down the access road at the Foster House and parked in the back. "What the heck?"

Rose followed his stare, noting the outside entrance to the Beacon Club was open. The club was closed, and no delivery was expected, so the door should have been locked. No one was around, and Rose recognized the vehicles in the parking lot as belonging to locals who frequented the restaurant. Her heart thumped faster at the thought of something being wrong.

Jason flew from the truck and dashed toward the club entrance before Rose could open the passenger door. She climbed down and rushed to the truck bed, retrieving Jules's travel bag and letting Brutus out of the back. Jules exited the front compartment. They entered the club, locked the door behind them, and descended the stairs. Brutus was slower, climbing downward with his two front paws on the same step simultaneously.

The lights in the club were at their full intensity as they had been when Rose left. The place was empty and only half the dining chairs had been returned to their homes on the floor. Things looked undisturbed until Rose focused near the bar, discovering several broken glasses on the floor. Her instinct was right. Something was desperately wrong.

Jason emerged from the stockroom, running a hand through his hair. "Hank is gone, and so is the liquor. Some of it is missing, but most is broken on the floor. I think we've been raided."

"We need to head upstairs." Rose willed herself not to panic while dashing past the stage and her dressing room. Thinking of what awful revelation awaited her, she tried to maintain her fast pace up the stairs, but each step she took felt heavier than the one before. How could they not with Roy Wilkes wreaking havoc? Charlie was his first victim, but who was his second? Her breathing shallowed at the possibility of Wilkes's deputies arresting Dax when she checked on Charlie. Then coming here looking for anyone who was there the night Frankie Wilkes was killed.

As soon as Rose pushed through the door at the top, her fears were confirmed. The smell of frying meats and potatoes and the sound of clanking pans and dishes should have filled the kitchen, but the odors were stale and the room was silent. The space was deserted when it should have been bustling with a cook, busser, and waitresses.

"Where is everyone?" Jules asked, coming up behind her.

Jason appeared, Brutus in his arms. He placed him on the floor.

The question sent a chill up Rose's spine. She continued to the dining room without slowing, Jules and Jason trailing behind. Customers, looking uneasy or sorrowful, were lined up at the cash register to pay their bills; none were at the tables. May was sitting in a chair, crying with a hand over her mouth. Ruth had slung an arm over her shoulder, comforting her.

Rose rushed forward, kneeling in front of her. "May, what's wrong?"

May raised her head and glanced at the people in line. Whatever had happened, she clearly wasn't comfortable speaking in front of them.

"Let's go into the kitchen." Rose turned to Ruth. "Would you mind cashing out the remaining customers and closing up?"

"Of course. The girls and I can handle things."

Rose ushered May into the kitchen, followed by Jules and Jason. Once May was seated at the center butcher block, she handed her a glass of water. "What happened? Where is Hank?"

Brutus settled at Jules's feet.

May's hands shook as she sipped her drink. "Deputies and Prohis raided the club. They arrested him."

Rose gasped. Roy Wilkes had taken his second victim. Or was Hank his third? "What about Dax? Was she here?"

May shook her head. "We haven't seen her since she left. Do you think the deputies have her too?" Her breathing increased to a panicked pace.

Rose matched it. "We have to go to the jail."

"Do you think that's wise?" Jason asked. "They might be gunning for you too."

"It's better than doing nothing while Roy Wilkes plucks us off, one by one," Rose said. "At least we'll know who he has in his sights." She turned to Jules. "You can't show your face there. Otherwise, they'll figure out you're friendly with Charlie." As she turned her attention to May, a plan sprouted in her head. "Let's pack a basket and tell the deputies it's food for the prisoners. It might get us in to see Charlie and Hank."

"Grand idea."

Thirty minutes later, Jason pulled up in front of the city jail with three armed bouncers from the clubs in the truck bed. "I'll wait here, ladies, but we're coming in if you're not out in fifteen minutes."

Guns blazing, Rose thought, fearing the whiskey war was far from over. She climbed from the truck and held the door open for May. When she stepped aside, Rose leaned her head into the cabin. Jason had been a loyal friend since her first day singing at the Seaside Club when Frankie Wilkes owned it. She'd thought the extra attention he'd paid her stemmed from an innocent crush until she learned he was different, like her and Dax. He was a kindred spirit, looking out for her like family. She could not have asked for a better protector in Dax's absence.

"I'll yell if things go downhill," Rose said.

"You can count on me." The solemn look in Jason's eyes said he considered her safety his responsibility.

A guard from the truck bed handed Rose the food basket. "Good luck, Miss Rose. We'll be right here."

Rose locked arms with May. Stepping toward the jail, May had regained her composure and was steadier than expected. Her limp was less noticeable, likely due to the heightened anticipation of finding out what Wilkes's men had done to her husband.

Rose opened the door, stirring up the feeling she and May might have walked into a trap. Four deputies and two Prohibition agents were inside, laughing and chatting at the desks like they were celebrating a victory. All heads turned, and the conversations stopped when Rose stepped inside. The room was silent, confirming that Rose commanded the attention of every man in the room. She was no stranger to seduction, using her appearance and stage presence to convince patrons to spend more money in the clubs. She'd fixed her hair and makeup as she would for a performance and put on one of her more daring stage dresses. Its plunging neckline stopped at the top of her cleavage.

Their hungry expressions suggested this might be easy. One man whistled, eyeing her like he wanted her hands on him, not in handcuffs. Under any other circumstance, she would put him in his place, but antagonizing him would not get her and May in to see Charlie and Hank.

Two deputies rushed forward, pushing and shoving to be the first to greet Rose. The taller and brawnier one won the battle. "May I help you, miss?" His stare was focused on her chest, not her eyes.

"Perhaps. We understand y-y-you're holding two people in custody." She raised the basket. "We have food for them to save you the t-t-trouble of feeding them y-y-yourselves." Rose chided herself for stuttering. It was a sign she was nervous. She took a calming breath and concentrated on slowing the cadence of her speech.

"No visitors, but I'll take the food," the tall one said, reaching for the basket.

Rose drew back, placing the food out of his reach. Her dander was up, which meant her speech was about to flow as smooth as fine whiskey. "Let me set the stage for you. Miss Dawson has been here since this morning, and no one has arranged a meal for her from a local café." Rose gestured toward May. "This woman is Mrs. O'Keefe. You're holding her husband. She has a right to see him. I'm Rose Hamilton, and I'm well-known among the Hollywood crowd. Also, the owner of *The Review* newspaper is a personal friend. I'm sure he'd love to assign a reporter to investigate how you refused to let a wife see her husband and starved a prisoner in your custody."

A deputy with stripes stepped forward, looking worried. "Our beef isn't with the family."

"Then you won't mind letting us make sure the prisoners don't go hungry," Rose said.

"We'll have to inspect it."

"Of course." Rose extended the basket toward the taller deputy for scrutiny but refused to relinquish her hold. "We didn't hide a nail file or pistol in the roast beef."

The man didn't attempt to snatch the container while rummaging through it. "It's sandwiches, napkins, paper cups, and a jar of water."

"You'll need to fill the cups and leave the jar here," the sergeant said. Once Rose poured the drinks, he gestured toward the back of the building. "Five minutes."

The taller deputy stepped aside, clearing a path for Rose and May to pass. Another officer opened a steel door, revealing the holding cell area. Charlie was in a cage to the left, and Hank was in another to the right. *Thank God*, she thought, nearly dropping the water cups she was balancing in her left hand. Dax wasn't there.

May rushed to Hank when he stood from his cot, extending her hands through the bars. "Have they hurt you?" The concern in her voice was strong.

While she and Hank talked in whispered tones, Rose went to Charlie's cell. With a guard standing nearby, she could not speak softly like May did without raising suspicion, so she had to choose her words carefully. "Hello, Miss Dawson."

Charlie approached the bars, her bruised and swollen face coming into view. She looked tired after the beating she'd taken. "Hello, Miss Hamilton."

Rose placed the basket and one cup on the floor before handing Charlie the other water. "Do you need me to send over Doc Hughes, Miss Dawson?" She measured the worry in her question, aiming to come across as in control, not emotional.

"Thank you for your concern, but I'll be fine." Charlie didn't sound convincing, but refusing medical attention suggested nothing was broken.

"Are you hungry? We've brought food." She handed Charlie a sandwich from the basket, following her affirmative nod.

"Thank you. It's very kind of you."

"When I heard of your arrest, I was worried you hadn't a chance to repair the cars in your garage. I couldn't reach Mrs.

Parsons to say her car might not be ready for her next visit, but I'm sure she'll be available soon." Rose paused until Charlie nodded her understanding. Help wasn't coming right away. "Is there anything I can get you?"

"I want to make sure everything at my garage is safe." Charlie was clearly worried about Brutus and Jules.

"I assure you, Miss Dawson. Everything is safe and sound." Rose mouthed Brutus and Jules were safe at the Foster House, and Charlie acknowledged with a nod. "Are they treating you well?"

Charlie glowered at her captor through her swollen eye. "About as well as I expect from these galoots." Her contempt came across loud and clear when she gripped the bars and twisted her palms tightly around them.

Rose resisted the urge to step closer and gently squeeze her hand. "Any word on when you might be released?"

"Hank said they're transferring us to the county jail in the morning. Who knows when I'll get to see a judge."

"I'm sure it will be soon."

"Two minutes," the guard bellowed from the door.

"I should see Hank." Rose scrunched her brow in sympathy. Charlie's defiance briefly wavered, revealing her underlying fear. "I wish you luck, Miss Dawson." Rose turned around, feeling emotion growing in her throat. She cleared it, joined May, and handed Hank one of his wife's lovingly made sandwiches and a cup of water. He looked tired but not pummeled like Charlie had. "May added extra meat to hold you over for the night."

"Thanks," he said. "I doubt they planned on feeding us before taking us to Redwood City." He lowered his voice so only May and Rose could hear. "Tell Dax I'm sorry for leaving the vault open."

"Don't apologize," Rose whispered back. "You likely saved the club from destruction. Otherwise, they would have torn the place apart to find it."

"You're probably right." Hank glanced at the guard. "Any sign of Dax?"

"Haven't seen her."

"Time's up," the guard snarled, rattling the key to the steel door.

May kissed Hank between the bars. "We'll get you the best lawyer money can buy. Look out for Charlie. I'm afraid for her."

"I am too." His despondent eyes said he feared his ability to protect her would be limited.

Rose got a chill, realizing if Charlie was lucky enough to survive this ordeal, she would never be the same. And until she found Dax, she too would be a nervous wreck.

Jason's shoulders lowered in relief when Rose and May emerged from the building. He held the truck passenger door open for them. "Let's get you home, ladies."

As they pulled to the back of the Foster House, Rose spotted Dax's truck parked in its usual place and blew out a massive breath of relief. The moment Jason parked, she threw her door open, helped May down, and darted through the kitchen door. She stopped dead in her tracks, discovering Dax and Jules at the center chopping block with Brutus gnawing a bone on the floor between them. All three looked up.

Dax sprang from her stool and swept Rose into her arms. The tight embrace she gave Rose was a desperately needed reassurance she was unhurt and would do what she did best—protect. Everything Rose held dear was wrapped in that hug. Roy Wilkes had upended their lives, putting everyone she loved at risk, but Dax's strong hold said she would move mountains to make right what had happened today.

Rustling noises at Rose's back told her Jason and May had made it inside. She ended the embrace, her infuriating, fruitless conversation with Dax and Grace a week ago about removing liquor from the club temporarily overpowering the good feeling of having Dax here. She must have scowled because Dax looked at her with questioning eyes.

"What's wrong?"

"Charlie was beaten to a pulp, and Hank was caught red-handed. If you'd pulled the booze from the club and only sold beer and wine like I'd asked, we'd have only one disaster to deal with."

Dax jerked her head back. "You're saying this is my fault?"

"For Hank, yes. I blame you and Grace. Now you two have to fix it."

"Rose." May stepped beside Dax, coming to her defense. "That was uncalled for."

The look of hurt in Dax's eyes was unlike anything Rose had seen before. Tears formed in them. Maybe Rose had gone too far in placing blame, but there was no getting around the fact Dax and Grace had had the opportunity to minimize their exposure to Roy Wilkes's strong-arm tactics, yet they did nothing.

Rose reached up to caress her cheek, but Dax pulled back, something she'd never done before. If she intended to return the hurt, she succeeded.

"Can we sit down and discuss things?" May sat at the chopping block next to Jules. "My leg is killing me."

Rose glanced at both women and instantly felt horrible. May was visibly shaken, and Jules was in tears. She'd been too focused on her anger to consider their feelings until now. "I'm sorry. You're right. We need to come up with a plan."

Dax slid more stools closer for her and Rose while Jason approached but remained standing. "How badly hurt was Charlie?"

Rose cupped Jules's hand. "She was standing and didn't look in pain, but her face was bruised and swollen. I could barely see her left eye."

Jules sobbed. Her stoop was so pronounced she nearly doubled over.

"She looked strong, though, and was amazingly defiant." Rose cupped her hand harder. "She'll get through this."

"What about Hank?" Dax asked.

May visibly swallowed. "He said the deputies roughed him up in the club but hadn't touched him in the jail."

"I hope the trend continues," Dax said. "I'm surprised you got in to see them. They wouldn't let me near Charlie earlier."

"They weren't going to let us until we told them I was Hank's wife," May said. "Hank was vague, but I got the impression he threatened the sergeant if he did anything to hurt us."

"You must mean Tallman. We've been keeping tabs on the deputies closest to Wilkes."

"What do you mean 'tabs'?" May asked.

Dax dipped her head briefly before looking her squarely in the eye. "We did what we thought was necessary to protect you and Rose. We learned where their wives shopped and went to church and where their children lived so we could use the information against them if they ever came after you."

"Their children?" May recoiled.

"Only if they were adults. We would never involve a child."

May shook her head, and Rose joined her. She knew the speakeasy and illegal liquor trades were rough businesses, especially since she nearly became a victim in the war Frankie Wilkes waged against them. However, she never thought Dax would succumb to its seedier aspects. Wanting an eye for an eye in the heat of things was one thing, but preparing for it was downright frightening.

"It makes no difference," Rose said. "It's wrong. Our business is with those who would do us harm, not with their families."

"Hank and I would be the first to agree, but we had to be prepared if they fought dirty like Frankie did by burning down Charlie's garage and setting fire to the Foster House." Dax clenched her fists. Her eyes turned dark. Cold. "He almost killed you and May. I won't let anyone get close enough again to try, and Hank agrees."

"Can we focus on Charlie and Hank?" Jules's tight tone spotlighted her frustration at how far afield the conversation had gone.

"She's right," May said. "Hank said he and Charlie will be transferred to the county jail tomorrow but didn't know when they would see a judge."

"My guess is Monday or Tuesday," Dax said. "We'll have to get them a lawyer by then. I left another message for Grace at her house, but her maid wasn't sure when she and Clive would be back. If we don't hear from her by Monday morning, we should head into Redwood City and hire one ourselves."

The underlying message behind the silent nods around the chopping block was loud and clear. Rose, Dax, May, Jules, and Jason feared the worst for Hank and Charlie.

"What about the club?" Jason asked. "We're supposed to open in an hour."

"Keep it closed. We can plan to reopen on Wednesday."

"And the restaurant?" May asked.

"With Cameron's closed for the plumbing problem, we need to keep the Foster House open for our customers," Dax said. "People can go without a snort for a day or two but not food. I'll ask Sheila to work double shifts until we know what will happen to Hank."

After Jason went home and Brutus was let out to do his business for the last time of the evening, Dax set up a cot in the kitchen for May. The idea of sleeping alone in her and Hank's house was too disturbing.

"Are you sure you'll be okay down here?" Dax asked.

"I slept down here for two years," May said. "I'll be fine."

"Holler if you need anything," Dax said before carrying Brutus upstairs. Rose and Jules trailed behind.

While Dax went to the bathroom, Rose walked Jules to her room. Brutus lumbered inside, jumped on the bed, and kicked up the top blanket, forming a comfortable sleeping area at the foot of the mattress.

"It looks like Brutus has picked his sleeping buddy for the night," Rose said.

"We'll be fine," Jules said. "I'm used to his snoring. You should know I left the Foster House number with Doc Hughes in case he needs to call me tonight."

"What time do you have to start work tomorrow?"

"Eight."

"Keeping busy will help take your mind off things." Rose's heart broke for Jules. She and Charlie had been a couple and life partners for over a decade. They had helped each other through many troubling times, but Jules was hamstrung with Charlie behind bars. Besides finding a good lawyer, she could do nothing to help, not even visit her in jail. It was a gut-wrenching situation.

"Good night, Jules. If you need me, knock on the wall."

"You're a good friend, Rosebud. I couldn't have gotten through the day without you."

They hugged, and Rose closed the door behind her. The day's weight had taken its toll, turning her legs as heavy as lead. She entered her and Dax's bedroom to another disturbing sight. Dax had changed into her sleep clothes but was gathering fresh linens and a pillow from the chest.

"What are you doing?" Rose asked, but she already knew the troubling answer.

"You hurt me tonight. Blaming me for what happened today was cruel. I need some time to cool off." Dax refused to face her, which was likely for the best. Seeing the disappointment in her eyes again would be a knife through Rose's heart. "I'll sleep in the other guest room tonight."

Rose's lips trembled, not because of what Dax was doing but because she was the cause of it. She'd let her anger get the best of her and hurt the woman she loved. Dax had her faults, including a distressing violent streak, but she would never hurt Rose like Rose had done to her.

"Okay," Rose whispered.

Dax passed Rose and stopped at the door with her back to her. Several tense seconds passed before she said, "I may be mad at you right now, but I still love you."

Rose forced back tears. "I never doubt your love for me and hope you do the same. I remember the moment I first realized I loved you. Do you remember the time you punched Phillip Gandy in the belly for teasing me?"

Dax nodded. "He deserved it."

"It was the first time you defended me. I didn't know then what to call how I felt about you, but you were in every dream and fantasy I have had since, even when we were apart. I love you with all my heart, but you planning to go after someone's child frightens me."

Dax lowered her head, walked across the hall, and closed the door behind her.

Rose fell to her bed, staring at the ceiling, facing her colossal misstep and a growing mountain of regret. This would be the first night she and Dax slept apart since the day Frankie Wilkes killed Logan Foster. She had the feeling it would be the loneliest night of her life.

CHAPTER FOURTEEN

Dax woke to a cold, empty space beside her in bed, stirring memories of the lonely years before Rose had come into her life again. Every time she crawled between the sheets after her parents sent her away had reminded her that she would likely be alone for the rest of her life. She never considered taking up with a man like Rose had briefly done with Riley King and had never envisioned the idyllic life she'd enjoyed at the Foster House since Logan's death.

Thanks to Grace, she and Rose weren't scraping by like so many people did these days. They made good money. And with May providing cover by making it known that Rose was an old friend and renter, they were able to share a bed every night like any married couple. Despite what others might think, Dax felt married, as she said the night of the movie premiere, which made Rose's attack last night hurt to the bone.

They were supposed to support and encourage each other, not judge and blame. Though if Dax had been honest with Rose, she would have admitted she felt responsible for the arrests and

Charlie's beating. She had bought the illegal liquor and handed off management of the Beacon Club to Hank. He would not have been there if she hadn't taken on the remodeling project at the Seaside. And Charlie would not have been in Roy Wilkes's crosshairs if she hadn't taken on his brother. So, yes. Dax was to blame, but she wanted—needed—Rose to lift her, not knock her down more. The fact she had chosen the latter was eye-opening and heartbreaking.

Flipping back the covers, Dax crawled out of bed and walked to the window, glimpsing the rapidly approaching dawn. The first slivers of light had sprouted on the eastern horizon. She hoped Rose was still asleep in the other room. If she were, Dax would slip into their bed, wrap her arms around her, and push back the hurt feelings, reminding herself of what was truly important—having love in her life and Rose to share in it.

She eased her door open and tiptoed across the dark hallway in an effort to not wake Brutus in Jules's room, but a floor slat creaked in the center, making her cringe. She heard scratching against the wood from down the hallway a second later. Brutus was up and wanted out. She turned and edged the farthest bedroom door open. Brutus lumbered into the hallway, appearing sleepy.

Dax closed the door behind him. "Hungry and potty, boy?" He wagged his bottom. "Let me put on some clothes and maybe steal a kiss first." Dax padded to their bedroom and slowly opened the door. Disappointment set in; their bed was empty. "Stealing a kiss from Rose will have to wait, my friend."

Dax threw on some work clothes. The guards she posted at the Seaside could go home when the work crew arrived in another two hours, an hour after the Foster House opened, but she could help with the breakfast rush until then. After using the bathroom and brushing her teeth, she went down the stairs, matching Brutus's slow pace to make him feel he was wanted there.

Light from the restaurant spilled into the bottom landing. Once on the main floor, Dax turned down the bathroom corridor and entered the dining room. Brutus followed. The breakfast crew was making the final preparations for opening. "Good morning, ladies."

No one replied with their usual chorus of replies. One young server was filling condiment bottles at the beverage station. Her eyes followed Dax. They had a look of curiosity, but she remained quiet. The tension in the room was thick and needed airing out.

"Ladies, can I have your attention, please?" She continued when they paused their work and focused on her. "Hank is still in jail on liquor charges and will be transferred to Redwood City to see a judge. We're hoping to get him out on Monday."

"Is there anything I can do to help?" Ruth asked.

"You could take a load off my shoulders by doing the incredible job you've always done. May, Hank, and I have come to depend on each of you, and we appreciate your hard work more than you realize, but it comes down to one simple fact. Half Moon Bay relies on this restaurant, so we must keep its doors open."

Ruth approached and stroked circles on Dax's back. "We're all family here, Dax. We'll do whatever you need for as long as you need us."

"Thank you, Ruth. We're keeping the club closed until Wednesday. I'll be here through the weekend but will need help picking up the slack if the situation stretches out much longer. Jason can help Sheila with ordering supplies. Could you help him and ensure the crew is paid?"

"I'm happy to pitch in."

Dax hugged her and thanked everyone for their loyalty before heading toward the kitchen. Brutus was sidetracked by a blob of mustard on the floor, so Dax patted her thigh and said with conviction, "Come, boy. Let's get you some proper food."

Pushing through the swing door, she smiled at the endearing sight of May and Rose in the kitchen and recalled the first morning Rose had put on an apron to help her sister after her brace snapped. They'd had some trouble with Riley King, but things had seemed simple then. The restaurant had been making barely enough money to stay afloat and do a few repairs, but Dax could not have been happier. It was a magical time of a decade's worth of dreams and fantasies coming true. They'd shared a few toe-curling kisses, and she'd felt like she would never be alone again. The lonely feeling of waking without Rose this morning overshadowed the hurt she felt last night. It was an experience she never wanted to repeat.

Brutus entered first and romped toward the back door, negating the possibility of catching Rose by surprise.

"Well, good morning, boy," Rose said, pausing her task of chopping vegetables.

"Hi," Dax said softly on her way past the center block. "I gotta let him out." She left the door cracked open so he could let himself back in. They still needed to discuss why she felt hurt, but Dax could not go another minute without touching Rose. She caressed her arm, withdrawing her hand quickly when a waitress walked in. "I missed you last night," she whispered.

"I missed you, too," Rose whispered back. Her voice was softer than Dax's and had a sad tone, making her sleeping alone more regrettable than it already was.

"I need to feed Brutus."

May turned from her position at the sink and gestured toward the chiller. "I made him a bowl."

"Thanks, May." Dax pulled a bowl from the refrigerator and inspected its contents. The pan-seared chicken, rice, peas, celery, and scrambled eggs looked delicious. Brutus was about to eat healthier than most Foster House diners would today. Seconds after she put food and water bowls on the floor near the chopping block, Brutus pushed the back door open and launched toward them. She'd never seen him eat so fast. "Slow down, boy. You're going to make yourself sick."

When the waitress returned to the dining room, Rose sidled next to Dax, shoulder to shoulder, hip to hip. "I'm not sure what Charlie feeds him, but after a few days of May's cooking, he'll never want to leave."

"Speaking of cooking, where is Sheila? When I talked to her last night, she agreed to come in early today."

"Ruth said she called ten minutes ago," May said. "Of all days, her alarm clock didn't go off. She should be here after opening."

"It's okay, May." Dax slung an arm around her shoulder. "She normally doesn't get up this early. I'm sure she'll be right in."

"But I wanted to drop off breakfast at the jail before Hank and Charlie are moved to Redwood City." She glanced toward the swing door, where two boxed meals sat on the counter beneath the warming lights.

"I've got this, May," Rose said. "You and Dax should go."

May wiped her hands on a towel and kissed Rose on the cheek. "You're the best."

"Stay with Rose, boy." Dax squeezed Rose's hand before grabbing her coat and truck key from their wall hooks. "We won't be long."

Minutes later, Dax pulled up to the city jail. The two patrol cars she'd seen parked in front yesterday were gone, and the windows on either side of the door facing the street were dark, suggesting no one was inside.

"We're too late." The fear in May's voice mirrored what Dax was feeling.

"Stay here. I'll check." Dax exited the truck and peered through a window. The entry room was empty. The metal door to the holding cells was open, but that area was also dark. Dax knocked on the window, but no one appeared from the back. The jail was deserted, begging the question as to why. The sun had yet to peek over the coastal mountains to the east, so the county deputies must have whisked Hank and Charlie away during the night. What was the hurry when the court didn't open until Monday?

Dax returned to the truck, climbing behind the wheel. "No one is inside. We can call the sheriff's office to make sure they got there okay."

"I don't trust them to tell us the truth."

Dax gripped the steering wheel tight, twisting her palms around its metal. "Short of going there with a bunch of men with guns, I don't know what else we can do today."

"Maybe the mayor can help," May said. "He could call in his official capacity to check on two of his citizens. We could also ask for his help finding a lawyer since Grace hasn't returned your calls."

"Good idea. Does he still come in around seven?"

"More like eight these days. Starting on the fourth, he'll arrive earlier to shake hands with the rich tourists."

Dax rolled her eyes. "Politicians."

As she approached the Foster House, Dax saw that every parking spot on the street was filled with cars. She pulled around, discovering the back was full of more vehicles than expected for the offseason. The only space available was the slot reserved for the Foster House truck.

"We better hurry," May said. "Rose must be swamped."

Dax parked, helped May out, and walked inside. She expected to find Rose completely frazzled but found the opposite. Rose had six orders frying on the stove and flipped each in succession like a professional. Ruth prepared the toast and potatoes and accepted the fried meats and eggs from Rose like they'd practiced it for years.

Dax recalled how easily schoolyard bullies upset Rose when they teased her about her speech, and she contrasted it to the woman she'd become. She took the stage four nights a week in front of large crowds to entertain strangers from miles around. She had evolved into a confident, unshakeable woman, which made her verbal attack last night even more perplexing.

May removed her coat and stepped farther inside. "Is Sheila here?"

Ruth looked up. "In the bathroom, taking care of things before she starts."

"Of course." May washed up at the sink and took over for Rose. Rose took over for Ruth. And Ruth returned to the dining room, carrying two orders. Everyone switched roles without skipping a beat.

"I'll see if I can help in the dining room," Dax said. She kissed Rose on the cheek, letting it linger an extra few seconds before whispering, "You're amazing." She left without waiting for a reply.

One foot inside the dining room, Dax dropped her mouth open. Every chair was occupied, and several people were waiting to be seated. The place hadn't been this full since the opening night of the Beacon Club years ago. She approached Ruth at the beverage bar and asked, "What's up with the crowd?"

"Word got out about Hank's arrest. They wanted to show their support."

"This is incredible." Dax pushed back on the lump growing in her throat and focused on the busboy. He was overwhelmed. She dug out an apron from behind the bar and grabbed a dish bucket. When she went to clear a table, the room broke out in applause.

"Hang in there, Dax," one man shouted.

"We got your back," another thundered.

The love and support she felt from the customers warmed her heart. She and May moved to Half Moon Bay four years ago, and from the first day, the town had welcomed them. The bond had grown even stronger since. Based on passing conversations with customers in the club, she had the impression several had figured out her relationship with Rose, yet it didn't impact their appreciation for her.

Dax raised her hand in gratitude, and the applause slowed. "Thank you, everyone. Your support means more than you realize. Please be patient if your orders take a little longer. We haven't had this many customers all at once in years."

"Happy to pitch in, Dax," a woman shouted. "Toss me an apron."

"Thanks, Dorris. I might take you up on your offer if this holds up. Thanks again, everyone." She went to work, picking up dirty dishes and wiping down tables, a task she hadn't performed since taking over management of the club. It felt like old times. Simpler times. When the most she worried about was making payroll for the staff and when she could next sneak a kiss with Rose.

The initial morning rush passed quickly once Sheila joined May in the back. When the mayor came in around eight, Ruth took his order and Dax poked her head into the kitchen. "Hey, May. Mayor Abbott is here."

"Thank goodness." May washed her hands at the sink and walked with Dax to the mayor's table, setting a surprisingly fast pace. He was alone in the booth. "Good morning, Tom. Do you mind if we sit? We have a favor to ask."

"Of course not." He gestured toward the bench across from him. "Please sit." May slid in first, followed by Dax. "I was sorry to hear of your husband's arrest yesterday."

"That's what I'd like to discuss," May said. "I need to hire a lawyer, but the town doesn't have one. Can you recommend anyone near Redwood City?"

"My wife's cousin's husband practices criminal law in Palo Alto. I'm sure he'd be happy to represent Hank." He pulled from his interior coat breast pocket a pen and jotted onto a paper napkin the lawyer's name and his firm's location. "I'll call him later today and tell him to expect you first thing Monday morning."

"If it wouldn't be too much trouble, we'd like to meet with him tomorrow. If there's a chance we can get a bail hearing first thing Monday, I would like him prepared. We're willing to pay extra for his time."

"I'll let him know."

"Thank you, Tom." May folded the napkin and stuffed it into her apron. "Charlie Dawson was also arrested yesterday. Do you think he would represent her too?"

"I suppose so."

"I'll be sure to ask. She and Hank were supposed to be transferred to Redwood City later today, but when Dax and I went to the city jail this morning, it was empty. They were already gone. Considering the bad blood between Roy Wilkes and us, I doubt he would provide us with truthful answers. Could you call the sheriff's office to check on them? Make sure they'd gotten there safely?"

"I'd be happy to, May."

"Would you mind making the call while Sheila makes your breakfast? You could use the Foster House phone. It would take a huge load off my shoulders."

"Of course." Mayor Abbott shimmied from his bench.

Dax did too. She glanced at the register near the front where they kept the restaurant phone. The area was busy with customers. "We should use the residence phone upstairs for privacy." Her sister sighed. A dozen stairs were doable with the newer brace but would require more time than the mayor might consider an imposition. "Do you mind waiting downstairs, May?"

"I'll wait here." Disappointment was in May's voice, but she understood the urgency.

"We'll be right back." Dax led Mayor Abbot upstairs to her living room and office. She circled the desk and invited the mayor to sit in her chair. Picking up the candlestick phone, she lifted the earpiece and clicked the hook three times, raising the operator.

"Good morning. How may I direct your call?"

"Hi, Holly. This is Dax. I have Mayor Abbott with me. He needs to call the county sheriff's office in Redwood City."

"Sure thing, Dax. He must be asking about Hank. I was sorry to hear he got hauled in."

"I appreciate your concern, Holly. How about that call?"

"Absolutely."

Dax handed the phone to the mayor.

He raised the mouthpiece and earpiece closer. "This is Mayor Abbott from Half Moon Bay. I need to speak to the deputy in charge." Moments later, he explained about checking on the well-being of two of his citizens. "I see." He passed along a number where he could be reached all weekend. "Thank you. I'll have them call." He returned the phone to Dax and focused on her. His long expression was worrisome. "Hank and Charlie have yet to be booked into the county jail in Redwood City. The desk sergeant said he would reach out to the deputies assigned to the area and that you and May should check back on Sunday."

"Sunday?" Dax's stomach knotted as she conjured up horrid scenarios of what Wilkes's men might do to Hank and Charlie until then. "They might not live that long. We need help now."

Abbott snatched the phone back. "I'm calling to arrange for a lawyer right now."

CHAPTER FIFTEEN

Last Night

The moment the heavy metal door closed behind May and Rose, Hank rested a little easier. His threat to retaliate against the sergeant's family had clearly sunk in. Otherwise, his captor would not have allowed his family to leave. However, his and Charlie's prospects still looked gloomy. He suspected they were Roy Wilkes's pawns in a high-stakes game of revenge.

Charlie remained at the bars and shifted her focus from the exit to Hank. "It was good seeing May and Rose. Rose couldn't say as much with the guard five feet away, but she gave me the impression Jules and Brutus were safe."

"The last I knew, they planned to stay at the Foster House so no one would be alone."

"That's a relief." Charlie sagged her shoulders. "They'll both be safe there. I wasn't sure where Brutus would end up since dogs aren't allowed in the boarding house."

"You may not think it, but we consider you family, Charlie. Especially Dax. She's never given up hope of becoming friends again."

Charlie's eyes welled with tears. The chink in her armor was a sign she was healing. Coming to terms with what she'd done. "I don't know if I could ever go back there again."

"You did what had to be done, Charlie."

The night of the whiskey war Frankie Wilkes had brought six men with him. Correction, seven, Hank decided after seeing the deputy in the outer room and accounting for the number of bodies that night. They'd successfully eliminated the Foster House guards while losing only two team members, leaving Hank outnumbered and outgunned. His only advantages were his experience and training. He hadn't counted on Wilkes setting fire to the place when he had the seventh attacker in his sights. The flames had blinded him enough to miss Frankie Wilkes emerging from his hiding place. If Charlie hadn't shown up when she did, picked up a dead man's gun, and fired, Wilkes would have killed him. He'd been a sitting duck.

Hank's heart still went out to her. He would never forget the pale, blank look on her blood-spattered face when she dropped the gun at her feet. Her hands shook so hard he'd thought she was having a seizure. But when the fire grew more intense, she snapped out of it and beat back the flames with her jacket. She was a damn hero but had begged him to tell no one what she had done. Hank had thought he was the only one who knew the truth, but the fact he and Charlie were both Wilkes's prisoners said the seventh attacker, who had run away like a frightened dog with his tail between his legs, also knew.

"Dax said the same thing after I killed Riley King. It didn't make it right then, and it doesn't make it right now. Taking a life to save a life is an awful tradeoff, not some act of good over evil."

"I agree. Killing is horrible, even when the law says it's justified. When I returned from the war, I promised myself never to kill again."

Charlie cocked her head to one side. "Then why did you agree to shoot Frankie?"

"Because I also made a promise to Grace. She saved my life, and I'd given my word to repay it whenever she asked."

"How many times did she ask?" Charlie's eyes narrowed, clearly suspecting the worst of the actress, which could not have been farther from the truth. Through her generosity and compassion, Grace Parsons had saved more lives than Hank had taken.

"Once. Getting rid of Frankie was the only way to save the people she loved."

Charlie's nod said her appreciation for Grace was unmarred. "How do you live with the guilt?"

"You don't. You have to forget."

"How do you do that?"

"Being loved and loving them back made me a different person. The bad things from my past don't exist in my present. You have love with Jules, but as long as you reject the others who love you because of what happened, you'll never let go of the past. Dax loves you, Charlie. If you let yourself love her back, you have a chance of moving on."

Charlie's lips trembled. "It sounds easier said than done."

"You'll never know until you try."

Loud voices from the other side of the metal door drew Hank's attention. He focused on what they were saying. Two, no, four deputies were arguing about being outnumbered by armed men from the Beacon Club outside the jail. Two deputies feared for their lives, while one posited they could take on a bunch of locals. Hank recognized the voice of reason as the sergeant's. Considering Hank's threat, he rightly feared for his family's lives.

Minutes later, the metal door clanked and swung open. Two deputies carrying handcuffs stepped inside. "Time to go," one said, stepping up to Hank's cell. His tone was bitter, laced with anger and fear. "Stick your hands between the bars."

Hank complied. The deputy cuffed him while the other did the same to Charlie. They opened their cells and ushered them to the street and into separate patrol cars—minus any punches or accidental head bangs into the car door frame while getting in. They clearly wanted to get out of town quickly. The show of force from the Beacon Club had spooked them enough to rush him and Charlie out of there before men loyal to him and Dax could mount an attack.

Headlights from the two patrol cars speeding inland lit the route on the winding two-lane road cutting through the coastal mountains toward the San Francisco Bay. Until they'd crested the summit and descended to the city, they'd passed only one car traveling west toward the coast. The traffic grew thick as they approached, as did the number and closeness of the buildings.

Hank had forgotten how cramped the city felt after moving from Grace's home, but not that he hated it. The town of Half Moon Bay had been a breath of fresh air after living in Hollywood. Grace's home was beautiful and quiet, with a lush garden, but once he left its protective confines, he'd found the bustle of the Los Angeles basin stifling. The Bay Area gave him the same closed-in feeling.

The patrol cars slowed at the San Mateo County Sheriff's Office building and pulled around back. A sign on the cinder block wall read, "Prisoner Intake." They passed it, continuing to the far end of the building. This was not a good sign. Separating him and Charlie from the other prisoners meant Wilkes had special plans for them.

They parked in an area without lighting and pulled Hank from the back seat. Charlie and the other deputies joined them and walked through an unmarked back entrance. Two deputies peeled off toward another section of the building while the other two escorted Charlie and Hank deeper inside. They weaved through dark corridors of what appeared to be an abandoned part of the facility. Entering an old communal bathroom with dim lighting, they stopped in the shower room. The space was ten feet long by six feet wide with three spigot and faucet handles spaced evenly apart on each long rust-stained wall. Metal bars three feet off the ground ran the length of both walls, and a drain was in the center of the floor.

A deputy secured another pair of handcuffs to the bar on the left wall and connected the other end around the restraints on Hank's wrists so he was chained to the wall with his hands head high while seated on the tile floor. The other deputy did the same to Charlie on the right wall. The one who had shackled Hank moved and stood at the entrance, but the one with Charlie stayed.

Hank smelled his seething anger and flinched when he threw a powerful punch into Charlie's abdomen. "This is what we do to perverts," the guard growled before he launched his fist into her face.

The pounding stoked a rage in Hank rivaling what he'd felt the night he killed six of Wilkes's men at the Foster House. He hated seeing anyone beaten who didn't deserve it, but he particularly detested anyone who would strike a woman. This deputy had no business wearing a badge or walking around on two unbroken legs.

After the fourth punch, his blood boiled. Charlie appeared unconscious. The deputy unzipped his trousers, undid his belt, and stepped between Charlie's legs, leaving no doubt what vile act he intended.

Hank tugged hard at his restraints. A bolt securing the crossbar to the tiled wall loosened. He pulled on it repeatedly until a section popped from a bracket connecting two lengths of the bar together. He slid his handcuff to the end. Now loose, he lunged toward the deputy, who had dropped to his knees, ready to violate Charlie in the worst possible way.

Hank hooked his chains around the man's neck and pulled him back to the grimy floor on top of him to give his partner nothing to shoot at. Maintaining his hold for about forty-five seconds would render him unconscious, but the other guard would jump in long before them. His only hope of ensuring this brute would never hurt Charlie again was to break his neck as soon as he could.

Charlie remained limp with her arms restrained and dangling from the crossbar as the man gagged and grabbed the chains frantically, kicking his feet wildly. The other guard darted over and positioned himself to pull his partner off Hank.

Hank loosened his hold long enough to reposition his hands on the man's head. He was preparing to pop it upward in a twisting motion when Charlie called out, "Hank, no!"

It would take only thirty-three pounds of pressure to snap this man's neck, but that clearly wasn't what Charlie wanted. Her gentle soul could not stand more killing, and Hank could not lay more guilt at her feet, the knowledge that he'd taken a life to protect her. He released his hold.

The moment he gave up, the other officer pulled his partner off and helped him to a sitting position. Hank raised his cuffed hands in surrender, looking to no longer pose a threat, while the brute coughed and gagged on his spit for several seconds before rising to his feet.

The two deputies dragged Hank to the wall and stood him up, shackling him to the showerhead. The brute then unleashed a vicious beating, hammering Hank's belly, kidneys, and face. The coppery taste of blood filled his mouth. His legs wobbled and buckled, but his hands were still hooked over the showerhead, keeping him upright.

"Please don't leave him like that," Charlie called out. "At least lay him on the floor."

The other deputy unlocked the cuffs, dragged Hank across the room, and chained him to Charlie's bar. "You'll get more of the same if you make trouble."

"Keep a sharp eye on this one," a man said from near the entrance. The voice was unfamiliar; someone new must have entered. Hank struggled to lift his head enough to focus on the man's face. He'd seen his face in the papers and once before in person from a distance while scouting his loyalists. The extra-tall frame and broad shoulders were unmistakable. It was Roy Wilkes.

"What do you want from us, Wilkes?" Hank choked out before spitting out some blood.

"Revenge, but not before you tell me where you store the rest of your liquor."

"Your men got it all."

"Come now," Wilkes said. "I've kept tabs on your purchases. I know you've stocked up for the hotel opening. Where is it?"

Hank spat at the brute, rubbing his throat. "This asshole was inside the vault. Ask him."

"We'll get it from you one way or another. We'll have to find the right motivation." Wilkes focused his attention on the brute. "Make sure he doesn't get away."

"Yes, sir," he replied before Wilkes retreated out the door.

The guard double-checked Hank's bindings and the chain. His partner locked the bathroom door on their way out, leaving Hank and Charlie with their injuries.

"Are you okay, Hank?" Charlie's question was laced with worry.

Hank shifted to face her, feeling every bruise and maybe a fractured rib or two. She looked exhausted, making him unsure how much more she could take. "I should ask you the same thing."

"I can take it." Her defiance was inspiring. Few men could have taken the beating the deputies gave her and still be standing. Luckily she hadn't seen what else the deputy had had in store for her.

"I hope so because we need to hold out for as long as we can. They didn't book us into the jail, which means no one knows we're here. We need to give our friends and family time to find us."

CHAPTER SIXTEEN

Back to Saturday

Rose and Sheila churned out breakfast orders while Dax and May met with Mayor Abbott. Rose became curious when they were gone for ten minutes and became worried after twenty when the rush finally died down. What on Earth could they still be talking about?

Rose removed her apron. "If you have things under control, Sheila, I'll check on Dax and May."

"I've got it." Sheila waved her spatula like a conductor's wand and glided from the prep station to the stove. This woman thrived on staying busy as much as May.

Rose hung the apron on the wall hook, entered the dining room, and spotted Dax and May in a corner booth. When she was halfway across the floor, it was clear that May was upset. Whatever news the mayor uncovered, it wasn't good.

Reaching the table, Rose sat next to May in the booth, cupped her hand, and waited for someone to tell her what was happening. Dax detailed the mayor's call to the sheriff's department, including the instructions to call tomorrow.

"Tomorrow?" Rose jerked her head back. "That's crazy."

"The mayor arranged for us to meet with a lawyer in Redwood City tomorrow afternoon after church services," Dax said. "We'll have him call."

Rose squeezed May's hand. "That's good. Hopefully, he can get us some answers."

"I had to promise him an extra twenty dollars to come in on a Sunday." Dax shook her head. Her trust in the legal system rightly didn't stretch far.

May rubbed her temple with her free hand. "This nightmare has given me a headache."

Dax stood from the booth. "Let's get you home so you can rest in bed."

"I think I should."

They returned to the kitchen and gathered May's things. Rose linked arms with her and walked with Dax across the highway to the O'Keefe house at the corner. Dax had replaced the front steps with a wooden ramp and railings before Hank and May moved in to make it easier for May to get in and out of the house.

Once inside, Rose warmed a pot of water for tea while May showered and changed into her sleeping clothes. Dax sat at the kitchen table and rested her head against the upturned palm of a bent arm, watching Rose move around the kitchen. Rose had spent enough time here to know where May kept everything. When the kettle whistled, she poured the water and fixed the tea precisely to May's liking.

Turning, she stopped. Dax had a satisfied expression, making Rose think she might be past feeling hurt from last night. "What are you thinking?" Rose asked softly.

"What it would be like if we had a house of our own."

Rose let a smile form. "I've thought about it too." When she was a teenager, she envisioned her and Dax living in a house that Dax had turned into a carpenter's dream and Rose had made into a beautiful home with elegant fabrics and decorations. Her dream wasn't far from what they had now, but the Foster House wasn't theirs. She still wanted a place of their own.

"One day we will." Dax said it with enough certainty that Rose didn't think her dream was far-fetched. "But I want to buy some land and build us a house."

The thought of building a house that no one else had stepped foot in, one explicitly designed to their liking, pleased Rose more than she thought possible. "I'd like that." She picked up May's teacup. "I'll be right back."

Rose went down the hallway to May and Hank's room, knocked on the door, and walked inside at May's invitation. She looked worn out. "I brought you some tea. I thought it would help you fall asleep."

"Thank you, Rose." May patted the section of the mattress beside her. "Sit with me for a minute."

Rose sat and handed May her drink. "I added a splash of milk and a squeeze of lemon."

May sipped. "It's perfect. Now, tell me what is going on between you and Dax today. You two seemed distant."

"We said some things last night that stuck in each other's craw."

"This is about Hank and Dax threatening to go after their families, right?" May continued at Rose's confirming nod, "You know firsthand Dax has always been a protector."

"Words and fists are one thing." Rose had been the beneficiary of Dax's protective side since they were teenagers. When a bully used words to insult Rose, Dax used her fists to defend her. When Frankie escalated things, Dax was the first to suggest using guns. She had to one-up her enemy every time to win.

"But you think she's gone too far."

"Hasn't she?"

"I thought so at first, but the more I thought about it, the more I realized she had no other choice," May said. "The Wilkes brothers have proven nothing is off-limits. Roy won't let her back down, and now she has to make it look like she can give as good as she got."

"And it scares me."

"Being able and amenable to doing something doesn't mean she will. Dax and Hank are good people. I have to trust they will do the right thing when it comes down to it. If you don't trust Dax, you have nothing."

Rose sighed. "I agree."

"Then fix it before you leave this house." May crawled beneath the covers.

Rose issued May a sharp two-finger salute before tucking her in. "Yes, ma'am."

Retracing her steps, Rose thought more about Dax's record of protecting the women she loved. Of all her traits, it was the one she loved most. However, restraint wasn't her strong suit. Dax would go to any length, which needed to be the starting point of their conversation.

She entered the kitchen, intent on first reminding Dax of two vital facts—her love for her hadn't changed and neither had the attraction. Dax was at the counter fixing a cup of tea. Rose marched behind her, spun her around, placed her hands on either cheek, and pulled her in for a searing kiss. She pressed their bodies together with enough force to send Dax back on her heel until she hit the counter with her bottom.

When she disengaged, Rose studied Dax's eyes. The sadness from last night still lingered. "I love you, Dax. That will never change."

"But you're afraid of me."

Rose pulled back farther. "I could never be afraid of you, but last night, I feared what you're capable of doing."

Sorrow turned to hurt in Dax's eyes. "I could never intentionally hurt someone's child to get back at them."

Rose caressed Dax's cheek. "I know that in my heart."

"I hear a 'but.'"

"But your history tells me you're guided by your emotions, not your head."

"Can you blame me? It's my job to protect you and May."

"I understand your instinct to protect May. You had to protect her from Logan for years, but Hank is her husband. It's his job now. I also understand your need to protect me. You've been doing it since we were kids. You're not afraid to pick a fight with a bully like you did in school and for Heather." Saying that name still stung. During their years apart, Rose had shared her body with Grace, but Dax had given Heather a piece of her heart. It was a piece Rose could never get back, and she could not help but feel a tiny bit jealous.

"I can't stand seeing someone I love hurt." The knife twisted a fraction. Dax still held back a piece of herself for a woman she would likely never see again.

"And that's one of the reasons I love you. It also makes you dangerous. Everyone thinks there are lines they'll never cross until they do."

Dax opened her mouth but closed it quickly and lowered her head.

Rose placed her hand on Dax's chest. "But I know you have a good heart and wouldn't intentionally hurt anyone unless you had no choice but to protect someone you loved."

"The unintentional part scares you."

"Yes, but with my fear in the open, maybe you'll ignore this"—Rose patted Dax's chest near her heart before tapping her index finger against her temple—"and listen to this. And about blaming you for Hank's arrest, I'm sorry. It was uncalled for."

A wry smile grew on Dax's lips. "I guess someone let their emotions get the best of them."

Rose matched her smile. "I guess so."

"We better head back. With the town's full-blown support, we might have to hire extra staff." After washing up, Dax led Rose out May's front door. As they dashed across the highway, they dodged several cars. One honked at them before the driver stuck his head out the window and shouted, "We have your back, Dax."

Dax waved. The goodwill of the town clearly lifted her up. She continued to the sidewalk with Rose, brushing her hand against Rose's before entering the Foster House through the main door. The welcome touch reminded Rose they would be okay.

When they stepped inside, Ida raised her chin at them from behind the register, punctuating it with a harrumph and snide look. "I guess all hands on deck doesn't include you two."

"You know what, Ida?" Dax stepped forward, standing toe to toe with her, looking like she was about to unload both barrels on her, but then she softened her expression and leaned closer. She spoke barely above a whisper. "I know you've had heartache in your life, but we're all family at the Foster House, and no one's past matters here, even the way you treated Rose. We only care about keeping this place going and how you contribute to it. Holding a grudge can be exhausting. It's time to let go of your past and enjoy what you have now." She squeezed Ida's hand briefly. "No matter what you decide, you'll always have a job here. Families look out for each other."

Dax walked farther inside, leaving Ida and Rose speechless. When Ida's eyes filled with tears, Rose knew Dax had gotten through to her. She doubted Ida would accept her and Dax with open arms anytime soon but predicted a slow thawing of her icy demeanor. Just when Rose thought Dax could not get any sexier or she could love her more than she already did, she did this.

Rose scanned the dining room. Her heart thudded faster when she found Dax behind the beverage bar. She'd hung up her jacket and was putting on an apron. Rose walked at a fast clip, stopping at Dax's feet. Her chest heaved. "Meet me upstairs. Now."

Rose spun on her heel, dashed up the private stairs to the residence, and went straight to her and Dax's bedroom, closing the door behind her. After shedding her light jacket, she kicked off her shoes and unzipped her day dress, letting it fall to the floor. When the door crept open, she stepped beside the bed, wearing only her undergarments.

Dax appeared in the doorway. She paused, eyeing Rose up and down, coming close to leering like the customers at the Beacon Club. But Rose welcomed the look. It was what she wanted.

"You're giving credence to Ida's complaint." Dax grinned.

"Shut the door."

Once Dax closed them inside, she strode toward Rose, sliding off her ever-so-sexy suspenders one at a time. "They'll have to be shorthanded downstairs for an hour."

Rose pressed her hand against Dax's chest, pushing her onto the bed. She landed in a reclining position. Rose straddled her, leaning in for a kiss. "More like two hours."

CHAPTER SEVENTEEN

Two days in a hospital bed, albeit a surprisingly comfortable one, were more than Grace could lay still for. The doctor had said through the weekend, but with the poking and prodding she was receiving at all hours of the day and night, she would get better rest in her own bed at home. She would hire a private nurse if necessary, but whatever the doctor said, Grace would leave to spend Sunday morning at home.

Clive folded the last of her clothes and placed them into her overnight bag while she brushed her hair in bed with the aid of a hand mirror. "You look beautiful, my sweet."

"I look pale, and my hairdresser would faint if she saw me in this condition."

Clive closed Grace's bag with all her things inside before sitting at the foot of the bed. He handed her a lipstick case. "Your favorite shade. You always say good lipstick can camouflage a multitude of sins."

"Which is why my lipstick bill has doubled in the last few years."

"I know." He patted her leg before sitting in the guest chair. Only he and Greta, to a certain extent, were privy to her downward spiral until last week's debacle with Rose. The pathetic attempt to rekindle a one-sided love was a fool's errand. The embarrassment would have necessitated a fresh tube of lipstick the next day if Greta hadn't confronted her about the lump after quenching a physical need. Focusing on her health was better than lingering in heartache.

Greta was no different from every woman she'd taken to bed. They all reminded her of Rose but failed to distract her from the misery of having let go of the only woman who had effectively replaced Harriet in her heart. However, Greta had a way of making her wish they both weren't so broken. A life with her would have been pleasing.

The door swung open. Doctor Shapiro stepped through right on time. He'd made Grace his first stop for yesterday's morning rounds and had promised to do so again today. He was a doctor eager to please the hospital's largest benefactor. Though she didn't ask for special treatment, she would appreciate it if it meant she could be home by brunch today.

Clive rose and stood bedside, giving the doctor room to examine her.

"Good morning, Mrs. Parsons. You look much better today." Shapiro reviewed the patient chart hanging from a clipboard at the foot of the bed.

"I feel much better."

"Let's take a look under the bandage." Shapiro gently moved her gown out of the way and lifted the bandage on the breast he'd operated on. "Everything looks like it's healing nicely."

"Good enough to send me home today?" Grace put on her acting face to get the answer she wanted. "With all the chaos and attention I've generated, I'm not getting much sleep. I would recover more quickly at home."

"I've inquired about a home nurse," Clive said. "We can have one to our home to check on her twice daily starting this afternoon."

"Let me take a look at the rest of you first." After pressing on a few areas and asking if she felt pain, he listened to her breathing through a stethoscope and took her blood pressure. "Your vitals are good. How is the pain on the incision?"

"Moderate. Nothing a good shot of whiskey wouldn't cure."

Shapiro laughed. "I'm sure it would, but I'll send you home with a script for a mild opioid. Be sure to not mix the two. One pill every four to six hours should control the pain. Your nurse can contact me directly if you need anything stronger."

"Not that I don't like your company, Doctor, but how quickly can you grant my parole?"

"I'll write home care instructions with a note to see me next week in my office. The nurses should have you in the car within a half hour."

"That is music to my ears, Doctor."

As Grace had hoped, she was in her Hollywood home having brunch an hour and a half later. The maid, who also doubled as their cook, was surprised to hear of Grace's operation and pleased to see her home so soon afterward. She made Grace's favorites and served her and Clive on the back patio, delivering the morning *Los Angeles Times* as usual.

"Shall I get your sweater, Mrs. Parsons?" she asked.

"No, thank you, Lana. The sun feels good."

The warm sun and cool midmorning air provided Grace with the perfect balance after being cooped up in a sterile room for two days. Communing with nature was refreshing, but not entirely serene. She had to wonder if Doctor Shapiro had gotten all the cancer as he had said. If he hadn't, she surmised that her days of enjoying mornings near her lush garden were destined to be fewer than she envisioned.

"Is there anything else I can get you, ma'am?"

"No. This is wonderful. I would have gone on a food strike if I was served one more hospital meal."

"We can't have that. It's good to have you home, ma'am. I left your mail and phone messages in your office. Shall I bring them?"

"Not now. I want to enjoy the peace and quiet a little longer. I'll rejoin the world after I eat."

"Very well, Mrs. Parsons." Lana scurried off to attend to her duties.

Grace nibbled on her eggs, fresh fruit, and toast and drank her juice and coffee while bathing in the warmth of her newfound freedom. She unfolded the newspaper and mentally noted the date before reading the headlines. It was June 25, 1933. *One year*, she thought. She'd seen many women diagnosed with breast cancer and undergo radical treatment, only to die within a year. If Grace could see one more June 25th, she had a good chance of beating this thing.

"You look tired, my sweet." Clive put down his section of the *Times*. "Would you like to settle in the sitting room or your bedroom?"

"Sitting room. I'd rather rest on our couch than another bed, even if it's my own."

"You make perfect sense." He pulled back Grace's chair and steadied her by the arm when she stood. After she took a few steps toward the patio door, her legs felt weak, making her wobble.

"I have you, my sweet." Clive scooped her into his muscular arms and walked her through the house to the sitting room, placing her lengthwise on the white velvet couch. The jostling irritated her wound, spiking the pain at her incision.

He grabbed the blanket from the back of the couch and draped it across her lap and legs. "I'll be right back with a pillow." He kissed her on the forehead before leaving.

Grace could always count on her husband to dote over her. For every cold, stomach flu, and hangover, Clive was by her side, seeing to her needs. Like any married couple, they were devoted to one another, but romance was reserved for their particular predilections. Clive filled his bed with a man less frequently than Grace filled hers with a woman, but they loved each other deeply.

Their lavender marriage wasn't perfect, considering the heartache both had encountered over the years, but Clive was the ideal lavender husband. He loved her and protected her secrets with his life. His loyalty ran so deep that she was sure she could never truly repay his steadfastness.

Clive returned minutes later with the promised pillow, a glass of water, her pain medication, and the stack of mail and messages from her office. After fluffing the pillow and placing it behind her back, he offered her the glass of water. "Do you need a pill yet?"

"Yes, please. Moving around has aggravated things."

Clive opened the pill bottle and handed her one pill. "The nurse will be here around three. You should try to sleep until then."

"I'm sure the pain pill will help. Until then, I should catch up with what I've missed. I've been waiting to hear from the studio about the filming dates for my next movie."

"Rest, my sweet." Clive positioned her mail and messages on the end of the coffee table close to her. "It will be right here waiting for you when you wake."

"Perhaps you're right." Grace closed her eyes, feeling the section of her breast throb from Doctor Shapiro's knife. Oddly, her breast felt whole despite a quarter of it being chopped from her body. The mutilation was hopefully lifesaving, but it would take some getting used to.

Soon, the euphoric effect of the opioid took over, placing Grace into a twilight state. Thoughts of Rose, Clive, Greta, and Half Moon Bay filled her head until sleep thankfully took over.

CHAPTER EIGHTEEN

When Dax opened the Foster House back door, letting in the cool, sunny afternoon summer air, Brutus darted from the busy kitchen toward her truck. She hated telling him, but he would not go on this car ride. Neither would Jules. They could not chance her being associated with Charlie. However, if things went well, by the end of the day, Hank and Charlie would have met with the lawyer and had a bail hearing set.

Dax let Brutus romp across the parking lot to do his business and return to the truck before giving him the bad news. She bent at the knees and scratched him behind the ears as he panted. "You gotta stay with Jules, boy." He wriggled, staring at the truck door. When Jules stepped beside Dax with her arms folded at her chest, Dax asked, "Can you check on the guards at the Seaside and bring them lunch? May has boxes for them in the fridge."

"Happy to," Jules said. "Can you call when you know anything?"

"Of course. I hope Charlie will accept my help."

"Tell her I'll never speak to her again if she doesn't."

"I will." Dax was sure Charlie would not listen to her, but she might listen to May or Rose. However, if the last few years were an indicator, she would not accept help from them or even from Grace. Grace would have to work behind the scenes to secure Charlie's release.

When Rose and May arrived, Dax circled the truck and opened the passenger door for them. Dax entered the driver's side and rolled down the window to speak to Jules again. "If we're not back by dinner time, May left a bowl for Brutus in the fridge."

Jules gripped the windowsill of Dax's door. "If you get in to see her, tell her I love her."

"I will." Dax wasn't sure how much longer Jules could hide in the wings without going out of her mind. She looked exhausted and on the verge of trying something crazy like breaking Charlie out of jail by herself. "In the meantime, Charlie needs you to care for her little guy."

"You've lifted him." Jules snickered. "He's not so little."

Dax rolled up the window. Before driving off, she glanced west toward the ocean. The horizon was filled with dark clouds, a sign that the heavy storm the town's fishermen predicted this morning during breakfast was on its way.

The drive over the coastal mountain highway was long with its many twists. Since the accident that injured her leg, May didn't like traveling at high speed, so Dax took each turn extra slowly. May stared out the side window, lost in thought. She sat in the same stoic silence as Jules had since Charlie's arrest.

Rose sat in the middle with her hand resting on Dax's leg. The touch was reassuring but did nothing to break the tension in the cabin. Soon Rose started to hum. Dax instantly recognized the song Lester had written to honor her and Rose's story, speaking to a secret love. It was her favorite song Rose sang at the club. It could have been the anthem for every couple like her and Rose, and Clive and Jason.

At the next turn, Rose started to sing. Her soothing voice was the perfect break from the soul-crushing silence. It was a bright reminder of what made the Beacon and Seaside Clubs special. Other small coastal towns had restaurants and hotels to bring in tourists, but none competed with Half Moon Bay. Rose attracted the famous and wealthy for hundreds of miles to experience a hypnotic voice none of the big cities offered.

Once they were on a straightaway, Dax glanced past Rose, discovering May mouthing the words to the song with tears welling in her eyes. When Rose finished, May said, "The song is beautiful. I knew Lester had written it for you two, but I never truly understood the pain you experience every day by having to live apart until now."

"What changed?" Rose asked softly.

"I thought about what my life would be like if Hank had to stay in jail. Heartbroken came to mind. I couldn't live like Jules and Charlie, having to spend most nights apart and packing in so much during the few nights they shared. It's cruel."

Dax kissed Rose's hand before she had to change gears again. "Rose and I are lucky because of you. No one in town questioned us living in the Foster House because you were there. Even after you and Hank moved out, your daily presence in the kitchen keeps the busybodies at bay."

"Half the town knows about you two," May said. "Most aren't upset by it, and those who are keep their mouth shut because you keep Half Moon Bay afloat."

"I'd rather them accept us than be afraid of losing their cash cows," Dax said.

"It's sad to say, but acceptance is a long way off," May said.

Dax followed Mayor Abbott's directions the rest of the way to the lawyer's office, soaking in the depressing fact that she and Rose would be safe only with people like themselves or supporters like May. She parked in front of the five-story-tall building where Joseph Grant's law office was. A sinking feeling set in when she realized the office might not be on the first floor. And since it was Sunday, the elevator operator might not be working. May's brace allowed her to get along better, but going up beyond one floor was still problematic.

May opened the passenger door before Dax could swing around and climbed from the cab gingerly while holding onto the side of the truck.

"You should have waited, May. I would have helped you out."

"I guess I'm a little anxious."

Rose slipped out and closed the passenger door. "We all are."

Once they were inside, Dax read the wall directory. "Damn." She sighed. Grant was on the second floor, and the lobby elevator was closed for the weekend. She turned to May. "I'll go up and ask him to come down."

"No," May said. "If I go slow, I can make it up one floor."

They had arrived fifteen minutes before their scheduled appointment, so time wasn't the issue. May's stubborn streak was. One floor was two flights of eight or ten stairs each. She could likely make it but would be tuckered out by the time she reached the top.

"Stubborn," Dax mumbled. "This is ridiculous. Let me have him come down."

"You don't get it, Dax. It took extra money to convince him to see us today. I must show him how determined I am to get Hank and Charlie released. If a crippled woman climbing up two flights of stairs doesn't impress him, I'll know what type of man I'm dealing with. Someone who'll respond only to money, not emotion."

"Dang, May," Rose said. "You're tricky."

"Lean on me." Dax offered her sister her right arm.

May climbed each step slowly, leading with her good leg and dragging the one with the brace to the same level. It took three or four times longer than Dax or Rose would have climbed, but she made it to the second floor, breathing hard and sweating buckets. She would never admit it, but Dax was sure she was in pain.

She handed May a handkerchief to wipe the sweat from her brow and cheeks. "Do you need a drink of water?"

"I'll be fine. We better get going." May limped down the corridor, stopping at the door marked Law Offices of Joseph Grant, Esquire.

Dax tested the knob. It was unlocked. She opened it, revealing a reception area, but Grant's secretary wasn't at her desk. "Mr. Grant?" she called out while ushering May to the closest chair. Rose sat beside her. "Rest for a minute. I'll look for him."

As Dax moved toward a secondary door, it opened, and a man in an expensive tailored suit appeared. "Mrs. O'Keefe?"

"I'm her sister, Dax." She guided him to the outer room and introduced May and Rose. He gave Rose an extra look of recognition and interest.

"Oh my." He looked at May with concern. "If I'd known about your malady, I would have made other arrangements. Can I get you some water?"

"That's very kind."

Grant went to his office, returning seconds later with a tall glass of water. "This will help, Mrs. O'Keefe. How about we talk right here?" He pulled up a chair and sat across from May.

"Thank you." May took three sips and explained Hank's arrest and his being taken away in the middle of the night. "We haven't seen him since Friday afternoon in the city jail, and they won't say where he is. Will you help us?"

"Of course, Mrs. O'Keefe. I can start by arranging to see your husband today. The sheriff must grant his lawyer access. If he refuses, I can bring a habeas corpus petition to the judge tomorrow and force him to produce Mr. O'Keefe in court."

May threw a hand to her chest. "Such a relief. There's also the matter of Charlene Dawson, who was arrested on different charges earlier the same day and taken away with my husband. We're concerned about her and would like you to represent her as well."

"What were the charges?"

"Lewd and disorderly conduct, but it was a trumped-up charge."

"Does Miss Dawson have a history with the arresting officers?"

"She does with the new sheriff, as does my husband." May explained in vague terms about the night Frankie Wilkes attacked the Foster House, saying he had wanted to buy them out, but she had refused. "Now, Sheriff Wilkes blames us for his brother's death."

"Ahh." Grant nodded. "This explains why he made a Volstead Act arrest. No law enforcement agency in the state has made one since last year. They've left that ridiculous business to the FBI."

"Can you help Miss Dawson? I'd consider it a personal favor. Of course, we'd cover your attorney fees."

"For you, Mrs. O'Keefe, I'd be happy to help. Let me call the sheriff's office and get things rolling." Grant stood, went to his secretary's desk, and lifted the phone handset. "Yes, sheriff's office, please…This is Joseph Grant, attorney for Mr. Henry O'Keefe and Miss Charlene Dawson. They were arrested in Half Moon Bay on Friday, held in the city jail, and brought to your facility sometime yesterday. I'd like to meet with my clients today and arrange a bail hearing as soon as possible…I see. I'll petition the court first thing tomorrow morning. You can't keep me from my clients forever."

A cloud of dread darkened the room as realization spread. Roy Wilkes had no intention of letting them see Hank and Charlie. They were already dead or soon would be.

When Grant hung up the phone, Dax asked, "What's our next step?"

"You go home. I'll draft a petition and deliver it to the court when it opens for business tomorrow. Judge Fletcher is an old friend. I'm sure I can get on his calendar by the afternoon."

"Then what?" Dax asked.

"The sheriff will have twenty-four hours to present Mr. O'Keefe and Miss Dawson in court."

"You're saying I won't know if my husband is alive or dead until Tuesday."

Grant turned to May. "Yes. I'm afraid our system works slowly. You're lucky these aren't the Wild West days when it took a month for the circuit judge to make his way around." He said it as if not knowing her husband's fate for three days, not thirty, was supposed to comfort May.

Dax went to her sister's side as tears tracked down her cheeks. "Let's go, May. Mr. Grant can do what he can from his end. In the meantime, I'll do what I can from mine."

"And what is that, Miss Dax?" Grant asked, his eyes narrowing.

"That's none of your concern." Dax removed an envelope from her interior breast coat pocket and handed it to Grant. "Two hundred dollars should be enough to get you started. You'll find our contact information inside. Please keep us informed."

Rose helped May up and followed Dax out the door to descend the stairs slowly. Down was much easier, and May breathed normally in the truck within minutes. Before Dax put the gears into reverse, May asked, "What do you have in mind?"

"I'm not sure, but Roy Wilkes only responds to force. Otherwise, we'll need to pick off the people doing his dirty work."

"You're talking about using what you know about their families." The disappointment in Rose's voice was gut-wrenching.

"Yes."

Dax pulled onto the street to start their return trip. The dark clouds over the ocean when they left Half Moon Bay were now over the coastal mountains and were moving toward the bay. Dax felt the wind push the truck at the foothills, requiring a quick steering adjustment. The rain started to fall, lightly at first. Within seconds, though, it was coming down in sheets. She turned on the wipers and headlights when visibility dropped to zero. The predicted storm had turned the early evening as dark as night. The western hemlock, oak, and cedar trees along the route were swaying nearly to their breaking point, and their branches whipped wildly in the ferocious wind.

No other cars were in sight, which wasn't a good sign. Dax considered turning back, but driving through the storm seemed better than being stuck in Roy Wilkes's stronghold with dozens of his armed loyalists. When Rose and May clutched hands and held onto each other as if expecting a horrific end, Dax rethought the wisdom of being on this road. However, they'd passed the halfway point at the last turn and were closer to home than the Bay Area. Continuing was her best option.

Dax's heart thumped the fastest it ever had when she reached the summit. For the next quarter mile they would be exposed to the devastating wind and relentless rain. She gripped the steering wheel tighter and tighter until her knuckles turned white. A giant gust sent a large branch hurtling toward their windshield.

"Hold on!"

CHAPTER NINETEEN

Without a window in the shower room, Charlie could not discern the time of day, but she figured she and Hank must have been captive for at least a day based on how hungry she was. The deputies had returned three times since Roy Wilkes showed up, trying to beat the location of the Beacon Club's liquor stock out of Hank in order to bankrupt the Seaside and Grace Parsons. He held out but grew weaker with each pounding, and Charlie could do nothing but watch. She could not feel more helpless. At least the swelling in her eye had gone down, and they hadn't gone thirsty. The deputies had chained them to the shower faucets, not the horizontal bar Hank had ripped from the wall. They didn't work, but they leaked. Between visits from the thugs, Charlie and Hank caught the drips in their palms and sipped enough to stave off severe dehydration.

She considered working on getting loose again but didn't want the noise to disturb Hank. Thankfully he was asleep. If the deputies held to their pattern, he should have four or five hours before the next round. Instead, she drank more water and relieved herself in her pants. It was uncomfortable and embarrassing, but she had no other choice.

The rafters rattled and creaked, reminiscent of the noises the roof over her garage would make when a powerful storm rolled through Half Moon Bay. Minutes later, the sharp, reverberating sound of rain pelting a tin roof started, increasing in speed and intensity within seconds. They were all signs a violent storm was roaring outside. The tiles along the shower walls created the perfect echo chamber, reminding Charlie of when she'd climbed into a tin barrel when the neighborhood kids used it for target practice with rocks. Her ears had rung for a week afterward.

She glanced at Hank and whispered, "Damn." He was stirring.

Groggy, he asked, "How long was I out?" His face was becoming unrecognizable with the swelling and bruises.

"Maybe an hour. If you can stand, you should drink some water. You'll need your strength."

"You're right." Hank groaned, pulling himself to his knees. He slipped, his full weight yanking on the faucet his handcuffs were attached to and shifting its position on the wall. He landed with a thud and a loud moan. After getting his bearings, he moved to his knees and inspected the faucet. "I'll be damned. It's finally loose." He tugged it downward again but failed to move it more. He stood and pulled back, achieving the same result. "I need a better angle."

"Wait. I have an idea," Charlie said. "I'm skinny, so I've learned to leverage what I have to lift heavy things in the garage. If you put your feet against the wall and lean back hard like a plank, you can put your full weight into it."

"You're a genius, Charlie." Hank positioned his feet, launched himself backward, and pulled as hard as possible. The faucet popped loose. He tumbled to the floor with another thud, his handcuffs still intact. The tap followed, creating several sharp clanks. The sound was loud enough to wake the dead and alert the deputies if they were nearby.

Hank didn't move.

"Are you okay?"

"Yeah. I'm trying to figure out which body part hurts the most."

"What did you decide?"

"All of them."

"At least you're loose now."

Hank gingerly moved to all fours, shaking his head forcefully for several seconds. "It should be a good tradeoff, but it doesn't feel like it. Give me a second, then I'll try to get you loose."

"With our combined weight, it should be easier."

"Easier? Yes. Less painful? No." Hank rose to his feet slowly and moved to Charlie. "Do the same thing but with me holding you this time?"

"It should work. I'll try not to hurt you."

"I'd appreciate that."

Charlie positioned herself as Hank had. He wrapped his arms around her chest from behind. "If we get out of here, how about we don't tell May about this part?"

"Or Jules."

"Deal." Hank squeezed tight. "On three."

They counted aloud together. Reaching three, Charlie leaned back, and Hank pulled with a torquing motion, sending the tap flying and him and Charlie to the floor. They landed side by side on their right shoulders. The impact rattled her teeth and jostled her to the bone. Hank's pain must have been magnified by his cracked ribs.

"Are you okay?" Charlie asked.

"You keep asking that, and each time I feel worse. Let's make a pact. Never ask if I'm okay again."

"Deal. What's the plan now?" Charlie asked, moving to her feet. She offered a hand to Hank.

"Get the hell out of here." He accepted her help and stood with considerable effort.

Clanking noise came from the outer area with the toilets and sinks. The deputies were coming in. It had only been an hour since the previous interrogation, so their early return meant something had changed. Charlie had a bad feeling the reason didn't bode well for her and Hank. Catching the deputies by surprise was now their only chance.

She glanced across the tile floor. Her faucet head was against the other wall. "Shoot. The fixtures." She darted toward hers and clutched it into her hands.

Hank did the same with his. He mimicked Charlie by standing by their respective taps, holding their hands as if they were still shackled, and using their bodies to shield their lack of restraints from the arriving officers. "Follow my lead. Use it like a brass knuckle."

Every time Charlie faced the likelihood of having to do violence, the speakeasy business was involved. And the speakeasy meant Dax. Despite what Hank had told her about forgiveness and love, Charlie wasn't sure if she could get past associating Dax with the bad things she'd been forced to do.

The two deputies who had conducted Hank's last two beatings appeared at the shower entrance. The larger one looked determined to do more harm, while the smaller one stood guard again at the entryway.

During the last two visits, the larger one had walked inside empty-handed to administer punishment with his fists. However, he carried keys this time and held them like he planned to unlock their handcuffs. "Time's up," he said.

Hank furrowed his bruised, swollen brow as if he knew what the deputy meant. However, Charlie didn't understand. If their plan was to kill them, why not do it then and there? Why did he have to unlock them first? "What are you going to do with us?" she asked.

"They're going to put us in with the other prisoners and have them kill us," Hank said. "This way, their hands are clean. Right, fellas?"

"You're a smart one," the big one said. "The wife of yours should take a lesson from you."

"What about my wife?" Hank's chest heaved with mounting rage.

"She's sticking her nose where it doesn't belong. Now it means the boss can't afford to keep you two around any longer. You have her to thank for what's about to happen next."

When the deputy stepped closer, Hank gave Charlie a nod. This was it. They either escaped now or died in this jail. They would have only one chance with the element of surprise. She gripped the faucet tighter, prepared to swing it at the big guy with all her might.

The guard angled toward Hank, gesturing for him to turn and step aside so he could unlock the chain securing him to the faucet. Hank twisted his torso to show compliance, but when the deputy moved within striking distance, he cocked his right arm back and, gripping the fixture, launched his hand. The punch landed on the man's face, stunning him and knocking him a step backward. That was Charlie's cue. She pelted him from the opposite direction, landing her strike on the back of his head. He fell to his knees and crashed to the tile floor.

The other deputy rushed forward, but Hank clocked him with a two-fisted uppercut under the jaw, hitting him in the throat. He tumbled to the floor, gagging and clutching his throat.

Hank returned his attention to the bigger threat when the man moved. He straddled him on the ground and pummeled him with the faucet, ripping his face to shreds. Charlie recoiled. It didn't matter how evil this man was. Killing him when he no longer posed a threat was wrong.

"Hank, stop." He continued to strike the unconscious officer like he was possessed. She'd long suspected the war had messed with his head, but he'd hidden it well since moving to Half Moon Bay. The beatings he'd taken from the deputies must have broken whatever he'd thought was fixed.

Charlie darted to his side and grabbed his punching hand in mid-throw. "Not like this, Hank." She softened her tone when he stopped struggling, and met his stare. He had bloodthirsty eyes. "Not like this."

His breathing was labored, making her think he wasn't done. But when his crazed look evaporated, she knew the old Hank was back in control. He gestured his chin near Charlie's feet. "Get the key."

Charlie retrieved them and unlocked Hank before herself.

"Put the cuffs on them." Hank searched both deputies, snatching up their guns and extra ammunition from their waist holsters and cash from their wallets, but seemed disappointed after going through their pockets a second time.

"What are you looking for?" she asked while handcuffing both guards.

"A car key. I'd rather drive out of here than be on foot, especially with a storm passing through." Hank dragged the deputy he'd brutalized to the wall and recuffed his hands so they were looped over the horizontal bar. He pulled over the smaller officer, who was now sucking in air but was still in agony. Hank looped his hands through the bigger officer's arms to chain them together.

"Why not just chain him to the bar too?" Charlie asked.

"I saw the technique used during the war to secure prisoners. The enemy would chain the dead to a prisoner. The big guy won't be strong enough to break free. Being chained together will limit the little guy's leverage."

"Genius."

"We need to get out of here." Hank ripped the sleeves from a deputy's shirt and wrapped one around each deputy's mouth, tightening them as gags. He whacked the smaller deputy in the head with a gun, knocking him out with his partner.

After leaving the shower area, Hank slowly opened the bathroom door before waving Charlie forward. They moved into the dark, vacant corridor and retraced the route by which the deputies had brought them there. Hank stopped at a hallway intersection and looked left and right. He seemed unsure of which direction to go.

Charlie had an excellent memory for the order of things. It helped her as a mechanic while reassembling engines, brakes, and gearboxes. She tapped Hank on the shoulder. "Left. Then right, and we should be outside."

"Got it." Hank turned left, stepping lightly on the balls of his feet. He held his arms close to his torso, nursing his injured ribs.

Wind and rain noise increased in intensity.

Charlie followed. Voices came from the far end of the lit corridor. Their next turn was thirty feet away, but the voices grew louder. Someone was coming. Fifteen feet. Louder. Five feet. One voice became clear. It was Roy Wilkes. Hank made the turn. Willowy shadows on the floor at the hallway intersection meant Wilkes and another man were about to turn and see Charlie unless she hurried. She stretched her legs longer and moved faster, struggling to remain quiet.

Charlie turned the corner down another dark corridor. After two steps, she realized Roy might see her when he passed the opening. She saw Hank lying flat on the floor several feet away. She dropped and remained still while the wind rattled the rafters and rain pelted the tin roof. If they were lucky, Wilkes would look the other way when he walked by.

His voice got crystal clear, telling Charlie he was at the intersection. Her pulse raced at the prospect of getting caught. When his voice began sounding muted, her tense muscles relaxed.

Hank scurried silently to his feet. Charlie did, too, and followed him to the exit. He pulled the door open, letting in a gushing wind and a hard, steady spray of rain. Charlie went through it first. The wind nearly knocked her sideways, forcing her to counterbalance by shifting her weight. The rain instantly soaked her short hair and made it difficult to see in the dark, but she made out they were in a fenced compound.

Hank closed the door softly and caught up to Charlie. "We have to hurry. Wilkes will find out we're gone in a minute."

"Which way?" she asked.

"This way. We need to stay off the main roads the best we can." He darted across the parking lot to the perimeter wall, still holding an arm close to his side to guard his tender ribs.

Charlie followed, staying in the shadows. The wall was too tall to scale, leaving the street-side entrance as their only avenue of escape. Lights around the newer part of the building and parking area threatened to give away their position, forcing them to use vehicles as cover. Hank tested several car doors but found none unlocked. They were out of options and had to flee via the main street, using only the rain as camouflage.

Unlike when they arrived, the guard shack at the front gate wasn't occupied. No one in their right mind would man a post in that flimsy thing with these high winds. Hank and Charlie crouched, sneaking to the shack. He tested the door, and it was unlocked. While Charlie waited outside, he went inside and pressed a button. A second later, the gate clanked and rolled open.

Charlie slipped out as the jail siren sounded, and Hank hobbled steps behind her and slowed to nearly a crawl.

"Run, Charlie. Run. Save yourself."

"I won't leave you behind." She slung his left arm around her shoulder and buoyed him with her right around the small of his back. "We're in this together."

They limped down the street, moving as fast as Hank's injuries allowed. Typically, this road would bustle with local traffic, but the storm had it deserted. While the siren wailed at their backs, they turned at the first corner to get off the same street as the jail.

"Where to?" Charlie started to huff. She was strong from working in the garage, but Hank was six feet tall and outweighed her by at least fifty pounds.

"There's a train yard several blocks from here. The down-and-out class will hide us."

Charlie could not do a few miles, but she could make it a few blocks, even soaked to the bone. She felt a burst of energy and moved faster. While Hank gave directions, she steered them to stay in the shadows. Minutes later, the edges of the Redwood City train yard came into view.

"Go past the fence," Hank directed. "We'll find the working stiffs there."

Charlie picked up speed and turned once they reached the end of the fence line. The area was littered with a half dozen abandoned train cars and piles of old equipment and parts. She made a straight line to the first car. The door was closed, but she and Hank teamed up to open it, revealing at least two dozen men wearing scraggly beards and tattered clothes.

Hank doubled over in pain.

"Can you help us?" Charlie begged. "We're being chased."

One brawny man stepped forward. He appeared to be a leader among this ragtag group of homeless men. "We don't know you."

Hank pushed up his left sleeve, exposing a tattoo composed of a double "A" using curved letters on his forearm. It was a hard-earned badge of honor for those of the 82nd Division who fought in France. So many were injured and many didn't make it home. And of those lucky enough to make it home without a scratch, many, like Hank, hid scars no one could see. "Help an All-American brother?"

The man inspected Hank with a look of respect and waved four men over. "Help them up."

Two jumped down and provided a lift while another two pulled up Hank and Charlie. The leader closed the door behind them. An oil lantern was lit, casting the train car in an amber glow and shadows on the men's faces. The consensus look was skepticism.

"Thanks, Mac," Hank said. "The town clowns are after us."

"It looks like they got in a few good licks," the leader said.

"You don't know the half of it."

"Who's the Jane?" the leader asked.

Charlie got a bad feeling from several of the men eyeing her. She stepped closer to Hank and grabbed his hand. She was the only woman among two dozen men who likely hadn't had the company of one in months or years. Hank was the only thing between her and the pack of leering men, but he was injured.

"She's a friend, and I owe her my life." Hank surveyed the group of men and added, "Understand?" He implied they would have to go through him to get to her.

"You both will be safe here," the leader said, rolling up a sleeve and displaying a matching tattoo. "You have my word."

CHAPTER TWENTY

The branch that was flying toward their windshield was as thick as Dax's leg and as long as the truck. If she steered right, she risked crashing headfirst into a large tree. If she went left, she would cross the middle line into the eastbound lane and risk running head-on into traffic. The steady wind and rain made it difficult to see oncoming cars, even with their headlights on. Her instinct told her most people were smart enough to stay off the road during this squall, so her choice was simple.

Rose dug her fingers into Dax's right thigh through the fabric of her pants.

Dax veered sharply into the other lane. The truck wobbled. It was on the verge of flipping over, but Rose leaned right and pushed May against the passenger door, settling the vehicle upright. The branch skimmed the truck's passenger side on its way by, making a scraping sound. Dax relaxed her grip on the wheel, drifted the car back into their lane, and released a loud breath of relief.

"Phew." She continued down the coastal side of the mountain, protected by the dense trees along the road. Rose still had her fingers dug into her a mile later, and it stung. "Can you let go of my leg?" Dax said. "I think you're drawing blood."

Rose looked down and withdrew her hand. "I'm sorry. I hate the feeling of being tipped over, which is why I rode the rollercoaster at Neptune Beach only once."

"Duly noted. No rollercoasters for Rose." Dax glanced at May. She and Rose were still gripping the other's hand. Her heavy breathing suggested she was shaken, yet she said nothing. Complaining wasn't her way. "We'll be home soon," Dax said. "It looks like we're past the worst of it."

Rose patted their clasped hands before releasing her hold. "Dax is right. The worst has passed."

Over the next few miles, Dax dodged several downed branches on the road and passed a local farmer's barn that resembled a pile of matchsticks.

"My goodness," May said. "I hope the Foster House survived."

"Don't worry, May. The building is solid. It survived February's whopper with only a few leaks. Nothing is knocking it down." Dax's thoughts drifted to the Seaside Hotel. She'd built it to be as strong as the Foster House, leaving remodeling of the administrative offices for last. She'd experienced several schedule overruns, but every public part of the hotel was complete, save the final touches. The work on expanding the offices had begun, but the exterior walls weren't done, making them vulnerable to high wind. She would have to check on it when they got into town.

Once they reached the bottom of the hill and entered Half Moon Bay, the rain stopped and the wind slowed to a light breeze. Leaves, trash, and small branches were scattered in the street. Rose gasped when their headlights shone on Edith's Department store. The large plate-glass window facing the street was shattered. Edith was sweeping broken glass from the sidewalk, and her husband was struggling to nail up plywood.

"I should help." Dax parked near the storefront, making sure to miss broken glass in the gutter. "May, can you get my work gloves in the compartment?"

Everyone climbed out. Dax approached the husband. "Need a hand, Henry?"

"Please. I'm glad you're here," he said. "We tried calling the hardware store to get the right wood, but Holly said most of the phones closer to the marina are out of service, and the phone company can't send anyone out until tomorrow. I had to make do with scraps, but I'm not sure what I'm doing."

"You got a decent start. We can knock this out in a half hour." Dax put on her gloves. "We'll need a few more good pieces. Let's see what you have."

Everyone went inside. Glass shards littered the floor, and puddles of water stretched to the register.

"Oh my," May said. "What happened, Edith?"

"A couple of trashcans flew right through the window. The racket was something awful. And the rain. Goodness. It poured in."

"I'll get a floor squeegee, mop, and bucket. If we work together, we can have this place cleaned up in no time," Rose said before disappearing down a store aisle. Dax smiled. Helping was quintessential Rose Hamilton. She rubbed elbows with Hollywood stars yet was the first to volunteer to mop up after a storm for no other reason than her friend needed the help.

"How did the Foster House fare through the storm?" Edith asked.

"We don't know yet," Dax said. "We were driving back from Palo Alto and stopped to help."

"That's so like you three, helping others before helping yourselves." Edith shook her head, turning to May. "If there's anything we can do to help with Hank, please let us know."

"Thank you, Edith," May said. "Your support means a lot."

Half an hour later, Edith and Henry thanked Dax, Rose, and May, sending them on their way with bottles of ice-cold soda pop. Dax turned onto the coastal highway at the marina. Except for the trash, sand, and kelp debris, the buildings on the street looked intact. The Foster House was closed, though it should have been open for business. That was worrisome, but then again every shop on the street was dark.

"This is a good sign," Rose said. "Things looked much worse in February."

Dax wasn't so sure about her analysis and pulled around back. The parking lot was empty except for the Seaside truck and two other cars. The two lights in the parking lot were still on, though, so maybe Rose was right, and they'd escaped damage. They entered the kitchen and discovered Ida inside mopping up.

"Where is everyone?" Dax asked. "Was anyone hurt during the storm?"

"Ruth made the call to shut down the restaurant before the storm hit and sent the staff home. She called everyone to make sure they made it home safely."

Dax could always count on Ruth to take charge. She'd worked in restaurants her entire adult life and was a natural leader. But Ida was a different story. She was equally experienced, but Ida was out for Ida. Nothing more. Her presence was perplexing. "But you stayed?"

"You said it." Ida raised her chin. "We're family. Someone had to help Ruth clean up and stay on top of leaks. I'll get the bathrooms." She grabbed her mop and bucket and entered the dining room, leaving everyone speechless, especially Dax. She would never have believed Ida could change without seeing this for herself.

"Well, I'll be darned." May scratched her head. "What got into her?"

"Dax," Rose said with love in her eyes. "You should have seen her last night. She killed Ida with kindness."

"Will miracles never cease?" May kissed Dax on the cheek before taking her coat off and hanging it in her office.

The basement door leading to the Beacon Club opened, and Jason walked into the kitchen. His furrowed brow meant he was concerned. "You're back. I was starting to worry something happened to you."

"We stopped at Edith's and helped clean up the storm damage. Their big window broke, and the rain flooded the front of the store. How about here? Any damage?"

"You had a few roof leaks upstairs, and some water came into the club through the exterior door."

"I've been meaning to fix the lower trim."

"Well, the trim is gone now."

"Where's Jules?"

"In the dining room with Ruth. She handled the leaks in your residence earlier."

"I'll update her on Charlie," May said. Bad news would come better from someone in the same circumstance. She continued into the dining room.

"Have you checked the Seaside?" Dax asked.

"Not yet. We just got a handle on things here."

"We should go. I'm concerned about the section near the manager's office. The back wall isn't finished."

"I'm going with you." Rose leaned closer to Dax and whispered, "You deserve something special tonight after taming Ida."

Dax grinned before glancing at Rose's heels. "You might want to change those."

"Give me three minutes."

While Rose went upstairs and May was getting the lowdown from Ruth, Dax retrieved flashlights, more work gloves, and her newsboy cap in case the rain started up again.

"Any word on Hank and Charlie?" Jason asked.

"Nothing good. The sheriff's office said they hadn't arrived at the jail yet, so the lawyer will petition the court tomorrow. Wilkes will have until Tuesday to cough them up."

"Tuesday makes five days since they were arrested." Jason shook his head. "Do you want me to gather the bouncers? We can shoot our way in."

"We might have to. Did Grace or Clive call when we were gone?"

"No. The phones went out during the storm."

"Of course." Dax rolled her eyes. Few things were going right today. At least they'd made it home in one piece, and Ida showed signs of changing for the better. "If Tuesday is a bust and we still haven't heard from Grace, we'll need to take things into our own hands." Storming into a sheriff's office with dozens of armed deputies on hand would be suicide. Dax might have no choice but to leverage the information she and Hank had gathered on several of the officers.

Rose pushed through the swinging door from the dining room, donning her coat. Dax did a double take, focusing on her girlfriend's clothes. Work pants, flat shoes, and a button-down shirt were unexpected and sexy as hell. She was always alluring in Dax's clothes. "I'm ready."

"Yes, you are." Dax added a seductive tone to her response, thinking she and Rose might break into the VIP suite the construction crew finished earlier in the week. She handed her a flashlight. "In case the power is out."

The three entered the dining room to quite a sight. May, Ruth, Jules, and Ida were drinking coffee and laughing at the round table in the center of the room. A few moments of enjoyment with lady friends were precisely what Jules and her sister needed today. Reality would hit them soon enough in the morning.

"We're heading to the Seaside to look for storm damage," Dax told her sister.

"Be careful," May said. "The ladies will have supper ready in an hour."

"If we're not back by then, I'd appreciate it if you could keep a plate for us in the warmer."

The three exited the Foster House through the main door. The street was deserted. This might be their only opportunity to hold hands publicly, so Dax felt for Rose's hand and laced their fingers together. It felt as natural as breathing. It was also infuriating. Every male-female couple in the country could do this without attracting looks or risking arrest. But Rose and Dax had to exist in the shadows, living their truth behind closed doors or when no one was around.

They stepped over trash and bits of kelp for two blocks. Other than being littered with debris, the front of the hotel appeared unaffected by the storm. Dax used her key to unlock the main door and turned on the lobby lights. To her relief, the space was untouched.

"Let's split up and check the rooms on the third floor first and work our way down," Dax said. "Rose, you're with me. I don't want you getting hurt."

"I was hoping you'd say that."

"Sounds good," Jason said. "But no testing the beds until we're done." He winked. "I don't want to be here all night."

A thorough check of the guest rooms uncovered only minor water damage in two rooms. In both those cases, the windows were ajar. Dax made notes, including a list of materials she would need to make the repairs. They went to the basement level next, saving the suspected problem area for last.

Every time Dax walked into this club, she remembered the first time she saw Rose sing. It was mesmerizing and had solidified she was the only woman for her.

Rose climbed on the stage Dax had built for her years ago. She caressed the microphone like a lover and stared into the dining area. Dax approached the side of the stage and remained silent, watching Rose sway to some incredible memory. Her smile dropped, replaced by a frown.

"Are you ready to sing on this stage again?" Dax asked.

"This is where I started. I was so nervous that first night. I was afraid I would stutter, but once I opened my mouth and closed my eyes, the experience was magical."

Dax climbed the steps, stood behind Rose, and wrapped her arms around her waist. "You became the Rose Hamilton everyone loves right here."

"I know." Her voice cracked.

"What's wrong?"

"Sometimes I love the stage too much. It kept me from moving in with you and May right away because I couldn't chance losing my job. That side of me is nothing like the girl you first met. I'm afraid of losing those parts of me you fell in love with."

Dax tightened her hold and rested her chin on Rose's shoulder. "I see that girl every day. She's in bed with me every morning and helping around the Foster House every afternoon. The Rose Hamilton on the stage every night is the same girl underneath the makeup and sexy dress. I see her in how your eyes search for me during every performance and in your smile when you find me. You love singing, and you love me. We're in a place where you can have both without having to choose between them. If you ask me, we're the luckiest people in the world."

Rose melted into her embrace. "Yeah, we are."

Jason emerged from the basement kitchen. "Everything looks good down here. The only area left is the offices under construction."

"We better get going." Dax kissed Rose on the cheek and dropped her hold.

They used the stairwell Dax's crew had remodeled with ornate finishings to lead customers to the club, not hide it from Prohibition agents. Entering the administrative area through the double doors, she was met with bone-chilling cold air. Given there was only a single layer of plywood covering the walls, she had expected a lower temperature here than in the rest of the hotel, but this was too cold. The lights were also off, suggesting the power was out in this part of the hotel. She tried a second wall switch, but it didn't work either.

"Jason, can you go to the utility room and check the fuses?"

"I'll be right back." He disappeared through the double doors.

Dax and Rose continued with their flashlights. The area under construction consisted of several offices. She'd knocked down a wall between three tiny offices to create a larger shared space for the assistant managers. The new area was more functional. She'd also expanded Frankie's old office, including the outer room for the manager's secretary, to give it the roominess the hotel manager deserved. Those sections were the suspected problem areas.

A quick check of the shared office revealed no damage, but a cold draft hit Dax when she opened the door to the manager's suite. The secretary's area was untouched, or so she thought. When Dax stepped inside, her foot landed in a puddle of water. "Wonderful. This will take days to dry."

"There's still time before the grand reopening," Rose rubbed her back between the shoulder blades.

"Maybe." Stepping further in, Dax shined her light torch in the office toward the exterior wall. Several sheets of plywood along a twenty-foot-long section had broken off and flown into the wall that had not been part of the intended construction. Now the entire wall would have to be redone. "Great. There's no way I can get this office ready to occupy before the opening next week."

"I'm sure you'll figure something out," Rose said.

Dax sloshed through a half inch of water and handed her flashlight to Rose when they reached the damaged wall. She put on her work gloves and pulled back sections of sheetrock to determine if the damage extended to the other side of the wall. The depth of the cavity surprised her. It was a newer wall, likely put in when Frankie Wilkes bought the hotel, but the hollow was twice the traditional depth.

Reaching the corner, Dax jumped when something moved inside. "Scared the crap out of me."

"What is it?"

"I'm not sure. Can you hand me my flashlight?" Dax shined her light in the cavity and jumped. "Geez. It's a body." It was a dark, ratty skeleton in some type of naval clothes.

"A body?" Rose's reply ended in an uptick.

"Sorry, Dax, but the fuse won't hold," Jason said, entering the office.

"Jason, come here." Dax waved him over. "I found a body in the wall."

"A body?" He stepped forward, shining his light into the wall cavity. "Wow." He looked closer. "I recognize those clothes. It's Captain Ford. He went missing when Frankie took over the Seaside."

"Who was Captain Ford?"

"He was the whiskey runner who supplied most of the West Coast before Burch took over. I remember when he went missing. Roy Wilkes had been buying from Ford for years, so Frankie asked him to broker a deal. I was in Frankie's office at the start of the meeting to confirm what Ford used to charge. Ford wanted double what he'd charged the previous owner, and Frankie went nuts. When things got heated, he and Roy asked me to leave. Captain Ford never returned to his ship, and no one has seen him since. It was a big deal around here. Federal agents came to town looking for him and asked most of the staff questions."

"I remember that day," Rose said. "They came into Ida's for lunch. I had no idea they were looking at Frankie for murder."

"And Roy," Jason said.

"Let's get him out of there." Dax made a platform from bricks and sections of plywood to lay the skeleton on to keep it dry. She then ripped out more sheetrock until Ford was accessible. Grabbing him, she grimaced at the gruesome thought of Frankie and Roy hiding his body here not long after killing him.

She and Jason laid Ford on the platform. Dax wasn't ordinarily squeamish, but going through his pockets was creepy. She found nothing there that might tell her who had killed him, but something caught her eye when she glanced at his boots.

"Rose, can you shine the light here?" Dax surveyed the area more. Ford's flesh had rotted away, and his clothes had been ravaged from years of insects feasting on the body. She focused on the top of his left boot and pulled from it a small notebook. She moved closer to Rose and the light.

"What's in it?" Rose asked.

"It looks like an appointment book and a ledger of his sales."

"Should we call the police about the body?" Jason asked.

"And talk to who? Roy Wilkes? We wait until we can reach Grace. She has contacts in Sacramento." Dax wasn't sure what good Ford's book might serve, but she stowed it into her pocket, hoping it might be the key to getting rid of Roy Wilkes.

"What do we do with the body?" Jason asked. "The crew and staff will be here in the morning."

Dax could not risk people asking questions and the information getting out before she could figure out how to leverage it against Roy Wilkes. "We have to move it to the Foster House."

"Oh no, you don't." Rose's voice was firm. She fisted her hands and placed them on her hips, forming her fighting stance. She'd drawn her line in the sand. "I am not going to sleep in the same house with a corpse."

Dax considered saying she'd slept in the hotel several times next to Grace with Ford's body buried in the wall, but she held her tongue. "We can store it in the boat we have tarped on blocks near the dock."

"Much better choice." Rose relaxed her arms and softened her expression.

Minutes later, armed with a bedsheet from housekeeping, Dax and Jason rolled the remains onto it. Each took an end, and they walked out the back along the marina in the dark, with Rose shining a flashlight along their path. Arriving at the Foster House dock, they discovered the boat had been knocked down during the storm and was resting against the building. After returning the boat to the blocks and stuffing Ford into it, they entered the restaurant through the kitchen. May and Jules were at the center chopping block with Brutus sleeping on the floor.

"Where are Ruth and Ida?" Dax asked.

"I sent them home," May said.

"Good. We need to tell you what we found."

CHAPTER TWENTY-ONE

The rain made Dax's grip unsteady, causing Rose's hand to slip slowly downward. If she let go, the woman she loved more than life itself would fall to certain death at the bottom of Devil's Slide. She would rather die with her than live, knowing she could not save her dear, sweet Rose.

The rain was relentless, thwarting every attempt to shore up her grasp. Then, Rose's fingers slipped away, and she disappeared into the dark abyss. Dax was paralyzed, unable to reach out or take in a single breath. Everything good in her life, everything that made her want to live, was gone.

She forced her toes to work, then her legs to scoot closer to the cliff's edge. She knew joining Rose was seconds away when her breasts cleared the precipice. She pushed harder and harder to make the reunion come more quickly, but she made no progress. Something held her back, keeping her from her destiny.

She glanced over her shoulder, discovering Frankie Wilkes holding her feet. He released a sinister laugh. "You haven't suffered enough yet, and neither have your friends. I want you to know what it's like to lose everything."

"But I have lost everything," Dax cried out, *feeling a pain so deep only death could heal. "Please let me die."*

"You'll die when—"

Her Big Ben alarm went off with a loud clang, waking Dax from her nightmare. Rose startled next to her and slammed her hand on the clock, silencing the annoying bell.

"I'll go with you." Rose moved to climb out of bed, but Dax pulled her back, wrapping her arms around her tightly. Her dream was over, but not the horrible feeling of loss.

"I never want to lose you."

Rose squirmed and turned until she faced Dax. "What brought this on?"

"I had the dream again."

Rose narrowed her eyes in concern. "It's been years. Why now?"

"With everything going on, I feel like I'm losing everyone I love and can't do anything about it. Losing you is my worst nightmare."

"Roy isn't coming after me."

"Not yet." Deep down, Dax knew he would not stop with Charlie and Hank. They were merely the opening salvo since they were the ones who had fought off Frankie and his men.

"I have faith we'll stop him." Rose scooted closer. "Now kiss me. I want to start every day with a kiss from you."

"I'd like that." Dax brought their lips together in a languid kiss and drifted her hands to Rose's bottom, pulling her in closer until the pressure woke her center. Rose moaned, a sure sign she wanted more as well. Surrendering to her was as natural as breathing, but they had a more pressing matter—getting Roy Wilkes removed as sheriff.

Dax pulled back reluctantly. "As much as I want to continue this…"

"We need to get going," Rose finished her sentence.

They dressed quickly and went to the kitchen for coffee. Dax was surprised to see May in this early on a day when the restaurant was closed. She was in the pantry with her notepad, and Brutus was gnawing on a soup bone near the chopping block. He looked up but bounced back to working on the bone.

"Good morning, May," Dax said. "What brings you in this early?"

"I couldn't sleep, so I thought I'd start the inventory."

"Did you see Jules leaving for work?"

May nodded. "I sent her off with some toast and eggs."

"How was she?"

"Holding up as best she can." May looked as if she was barely holding on, too. "Are you two heading to the newspaper office?"

"Yeah. We figure Mr. Cruz is up, working on today's edition."

"Maybe he can fill in some blanks about Captain Ford." May gestured toward the chiller. "There are a few biscuits from dinner last night. They might convince him to help."

"Your biscuits are more valuable currency in Half Moon Bay than the almighty dollar." Dax wrapped the leftovers in a to-go bag while Rose poured coffee into three paper cups. "We'll be back as soon as we can and help with the inventory."

When Dax and Rose went to the truck, Dax first checked the boat on blocks at the edge of the parking lot. She lifted the tarp's edge, confirming Ford's bones were where she'd hidden them. Unsure what to do with them, she knew Roy Wilkes would get rid of them if given a chance.

Minutes later, she parked in front of the *Half Moon Bay Review* office and its wall of windows facing the street. The lights were on, and three people, including the owner, were inside, hard at work. Rose grabbed the biscuits and a cup of coffee while Dax held the office door open for her.

Mr. Cruz looked toward the door. "Good morning, Rose. Morning, Dax. I'm sure you're here about Hank and Charlie."

"Yes. W-W-We'd like to talk to you about something important." Rose held out the goodies they brought. "May sent some biscuits and coffee to make you more a-a-agreeable to helping us."

"I'll never turn down May's biscuits, but you don't need to bribe me." His long expression made him look sad. "Whatever you need, I'm happy to help."

"Is there somewhere private we can talk, Mr. Cruz?" Dax asked.

"My office." He gestured toward an open interior door and walked Dax and Rose inside.

Once alone, Dax asked, "What can you tell us about Captain Ford, a Canadian ship's captain who went missing in 1925, around the time Frankie Wilkes took over the Seaside? I understand federal agents came to town, looking into his disappearance."

Cruz rubbed his chin. "Ford. It rings a bell." He went to the row of file cabinets against the wall and thumbed through the drawer marked with the year 1925. "If I recall, it was in June before the official start of tourist season...Yes, here we go... June 30th..." He pulled a folder from the cabinet and laid it on his desk. He opened it, revealing a folded newspaper and several handwritten notes. "I keep my investigative notes with a copy of the edition in case I have to go back. The man was Captain Francis Ford. The FBI was looking into his disappearance. When I talked to them, they said he had a meeting with a customer in Half Moon Bay but never returned to his ship." Cruz flipped to another page of his notes. "The FBI lost interest and never came back after two Prohibition agents came to town."

"Those Prohis were on Frankie Wilkes's payroll," Rose said. "They were regulars at the club."

"Why are you asking about a missing person from eight years ago?" Cruz asked.

"Because I found his remains buried in the wall of Frankie's old office at the Seaside Hotel," Dax said. "I have a witness who says Captain Ford met with Frankie and Roy at the hotel."

"Interesting. According to my notes, Frankie denied meeting with Ford. I didn't think anything of his story since Ford was in the illegal liquor trade, but you think Frankie and his brother had something to do with his murder?"

Dax showed him Ford's notebook, flipping to a specific page. "I found this in the wall. It says Ford had a meeting with the Wilkes brothers in Half Moon Bay on June 22nd." Dax turned to another page in the book. "The witness helped me decode the ledger. Ford planned to squeeze Frankie for double what he'd charged the previous owner. The ledger proves it. We think Ford refused to budge, and the Wilkes brothers killed him and stuffed him into the wall."

"Is your witness willing to provide a statement?"

"Yes, but anonymously." Dax could not risk putting Jason at more risk. "You know Roy Wilkes arrested Hank and Charlie. We need to get him removed from office to get the charges dropped."

Cruz tilted his head in confusion. "The charges are too serious to be dropped without an investigation."

How could possessing liquor and kissing a woman on the cheek be serious? "So you won't help us?"

"I want to help, but getting rid of Wilkes won't sweep away the killing of two deputies."

"What are you talking about?" Dax was confused.

Cruz retrieved a newspaper from his inbox and unfolded it. It was today's. The headline threw Dax for a loop: "Locals Wanted for Killing Deputies."

"What the heck?"

"I thought you knew."

Dax read along with Rose, but the words on the page didn't match what the lawyer was told. The article said Hank and Charlie were transported directly from Half Moon Bay to the county jail for processing, where they overpowered and killed two deputies during their escape at the height of the storm.

"This can't be true." Heat built in Dax's cheeks as a setup became clear. "Hank and Charlie were taken from town sometime before Saturday morning. We went to the Bay Area yesterday before the storm, and the deputies told our lawyer they weren't there. So which is it? Everything the sheriff said was a lie."

Cruz picked up his notepad and made some notes. "I'll put this information in tomorrow's edition."

"That's great, but we need to get him removed. Can you run an editorial? Maybe we can get the county board's attention and make everyone see Wilkes is lying." Dax got angrier, thinking where the heck was Grace? She picked the worst time to be unavailable. Her influence could have stopped this before it got out of hand.

"I can, but my circulation is limited. What you want is an editorial in the *Chronicle*. Most state government officials read it every day. Unfortunately, my contact no longer works there."

"What about Phillip Gandy? He's a crime reporter there." Rose turned to Cruz, explaining, "We went to high school with Phillip and saw him at Grace Parson's premiere last week."

"It's worth a try," Dax said.

"We should go today," Rose said.

"I think you should stay. Once we tell May and Jules what has happened, they'll be upset. I don't want them to be alone today." News of Hank and Charlie being hunted by every cop from Half Moon Bay to Sacramento was their worst possible nightmare.

Rose nodded her concurrence.

"Before you go." Cruz grabbed his camera. "Let me take photos of the remains and pages from the notebook. I can develop them within an hour. They might help convince the *Chronicle* editor to run the piece on Wilkes."

"Thank you, Mr. Cruz. I don't know how I'll repay you," Dax said.

"More of those biscuits will be payment enough."

CHAPTER TWENTY-TWO

Grace fluttered her eyes open and moved her legs and was confused instantly. White morning light filtered through the sheer drapes of her bedroom windows, and her legs rustled beneath the bedding covers, but she could not remember coming upstairs. She recalled Clive waking her briefly for the nurse's visit in the afternoon and becoming drowsy shortly after. He must have carried her up sometime later.

When she shifted to sit against the headboard, the dull pain in her breast magnified. A quick glance confirmed a water glass and her pain pills were within reach on the nightstand, but she resisted the instinct to take one. Grace had seen too many friends fall prey to opioid dependency, including her dear, sweet Harriet. She refused to go down that path. Instead, she pushed past the pain, went to the bathroom, and gave herself a sponge bath to start the day.

Getting dressed was more difficult than she anticipated, so she opted for a pair of night pants, a loose button-down shirt, and house slippers. The effort was tiring, but she needed to return to a routine and start doing things herself. She held onto the railing while descending the sweeping staircase, taking each step slowly and cautiously.

When Grace reached the second to the last step, Lana turned the corner and nearly bumped into her with the breakfast tray. "I'm so sorry, Mrs. Parsons. Should you be out of bed?"

"Bed is making me tired. It's time to break the cycle. Where is Mr. Parsons?"

"He's been working in the garage since sunrise, ma'am," Lana said. "Shall I set you up in the dining room for breakfast?"

"I'd like to sit on the patio again. The fresh air should do me some good. Could you bring it out in ten minutes? I'd like to say good morning to my husband."

"Of course, Mrs. Parsons. I'll grab your sweater. It's still a bit chilly."

Grace thanked her and went to the rear of the house to the attached garage. Her legs felt stronger when she opened the door, confirming her plan to ignore the doctor's orders to stay in bed for another day was a much better idea.

Clive had the hood up on their Packard Roadster and was tinkering inside the engine compartment. He was fastidious about his cars and guns, ensuring they were always in top-running condition. When Grace had asked why he was so attentive to them, he'd said, "They are my tools to protect you. I take my responsibility seriously." His response made her love him more.

"You're up early," Grace said, stepping inside and drawing his attention.

"You're up." His expression was bright with surprise and satisfaction. He wiped his hands with a fresh rag and walked toward her. "Did you sleep well?"

"I must have since I don't remember you taking me to bed."

"You were knocked out after the nurse gave you a shot for the pain, so I carried you up when it became apparent you weren't going to wake for dinner. How is your pain today?"

"The same, but I'm going to forgo a pill until I can't stand it."

"If I didn't have these greasy hands, I'd take you by both arms before saying this isn't the same situation. Harriet was troubled before hurting her back, which made her vulnerable to addiction. You won't fall prey. I'll see to it. Don't be afraid to make your recovery more comfortable. You need your strength."

Grace caressed his cheek. "Why are you so good to me?"

"Because other than physical needs, we complete one another." His answer was so simple yet spot on. Grace once thought pretending her lavender marriage was real was her greatest performance, but she was wrong. She was stronger and more confident with Clive by her side and liked to think he was too. They had common interests and motivations and had nursed each other through sickness and heartache. They shared a platonic love more profound than most romantic relationships, even those concocted by Austin or Bronte, and that had made the isolation of a sapphic life bearable.

She smiled. "Yes, we do. Are you hungry?"

"I want to finish tuning up the Roadster."

"I'll ask Lana to have a plate waiting for you on the patio." She kissed him on the cheek, retraced her steps inside, and opened the slider. Her sweater was hung over the back of the chair, and breakfast was on the table, sitting beneath a metal warming dome. The morning newspaper and her messages and mail were on a separate tray. The sun hit the table just right, taking enough chill off the morning to make Grace comfortable in her shirt.

Digging into Lana's beautiful presentation of eggs, fruit, and potatoes mixed with peppers and onion, she glanced at the other tray. It was time to reenter the world by reading the stack of waiting mail and messages.

A quick scan of their return addresses told her the mail could wait. She then picked up the stack of phone messages. The top one was from the studio, saying filming for her next movie would begin in two weeks. The schedule would give her time to attend the Seaside reopening and stay for a week to interact with a host of important guests.

Turning to the next page, Grace read Friday's message from Dax, saying she had an urgent matter and to call immediately. The next note said the same. The third made Grace gasp. Dax said Roy Wilkes's deputies had beaten and arrested Hank and Charlie on separate charges and taken them to the county jail. They needed her help in getting a lawyer and the charges dropped. The final message said they were meeting with a lawyer on Sunday to represent Hank and Charlie for their Monday bail hearings.

"For heaven's sake." Grace pushed herself up, felt the ache in her breast roar again, and quickly returned to her chair.

The patio door opened, and Lana stepped out, carrying a second food tray. "Mr. Parsons will join you after he washes up, ma'am."

"Thank you. Could you string the house phone out here? I need to make an urgent call."

"Does it have to do with Mr. O'Keefe? The article about him this morning was shocking."

"What article?" Grace snatched the newspaper from the tray.

"Page one below the fold."

Grace flipped the paper over. The headline took her breath away. "Two Deputies Killed in Daring Jail Break." The article named Henry O'Keefe and Charlene Dawson of Half Moon Bay as the two escaped prisoners, detailing their arrests. Grace could hardly believe what came next. The story said they had overpowered two deputies while being processed into the county jail and shot and killed them before escaping while a storm ravaged the Bay Area Sunday evening.

"Thank you, Lana." Clive stepped outside after having put on a clean shirt. He focused on Grace. His expression changed in a second from neutral to worried. "What's wrong?"

Grace handed him the paper. "Hank and Charlie are in trouble."

"I'll get the phone, Mrs. Parsons." Lana returned a moment later and laid the telephone on the table before leaving.

Grace asked the operator to connect her to the Foster House.

"I'm sorry, miss, but the local operator reported many phone lines are down following the storm. Service should be restored by the end of the day."

Grace turned to Clive and explained about the phone service. "Dax left several messages pleading for my help. I feel horrible for not checking in earlier. If I had, Hank and Charlie wouldn't be on the run."

"We don't know that. I'll drive to Half Moon Bay today, find out what happened, and call you later this afternoon."

"I'm going with you."

"Do you think it wise? The doctor said you should rest today."

"I'll be too worried to rest at home. I can sleep in the car, knowing we'll get to the bottom of things when I wake. If I have any issues, Jules can see to me."

Clive narrowed his eyes. "Fine. I'll have Lana pack our overnight bags. We'll leave within the hour."

CHAPTER TWENTY-THREE

Charlie woke with a start. Someone had placed a hand over her mouth. It was rough and smelled of grime. She shot her eyes open, discovering a man hovering over her. The crazed look in his eyes left little doubt about what he wanted. She squirmed, but he laid himself on top of her. At twice her weight, he easily pinned her down. His crotch was hard, confirming Charlie's fear. He was about to rape her.

The wisdom of sleeping by the door for an easy escape in the event of something like this happening seemed sound last night, but she hadn't planned on being taken by surprise. Hank was several feet away, sound asleep from his injuries. Her only hope was to make enough noise to wake the others while this man dry-humped her like a dog in heat. She thrashed her head, trying to move his hand enough to scream, but it stubbornly would not budge. Even her grunts were muffled. She heard a zipper a second before he forced her hand to his crotch.

Charlie felt sick.

Then.

The weight on her lifted. Two men ripped the attacker off her, flung him to the train car floor, and pummeled him with punches to the face and kicks to the groin, belly, and kidneys. The others woke but remained seated, watching the punishment being administered.

"That's enough," the leader called out. The men stopped but held him down.

Hank limped to Charlie. His slumped posture and pale complexion said he was still in pain. "Are you okay? Did he hurt you?"

Charlie's lips trembled, diverting her gaze to the floor. The thought of what he did made her sick. "He made me touch him."

Hank narrowed his eyes and formed fists, looking at her attacker like he was fresh meat.

The leader nodded at Hank. "He's all yours. We don't take kindly to anyone who would force himself on a woman."

Hank marched to the man, his pain momentarily disappearing. He lifted the man's head and upper torso by the collar before turning machinelike and striking him relentlessly in the face until he was a bloody mess.

Charlie wanted Hank to stop but could not bring herself to call out. She wanted the man hurt for what he'd done, but the bloodier he became, the more her stomach turned. Torn by the unfolding scene, she felt tears track down her cheeks.

Hank stopped short of killing the man and stood over him. His chest was heaving like last night when he nearly killed the deputy. "You're lucky I don't castrate you."

The leader slid the train car door open, letting in the morning sun and cool air. Two men tossed Charlie's dazed attacker onto the ground. The leader remained at the opening, standing tall. "If you show your face around here again, you'll get more of the same." He watched the man limp off before kneeling in front of Charlie. "Are you all right, miss?"

"Yeah, I'm fine." She moved to stand, and he rose and extended his hand to help her up. She accepted.

"We don't stand for violence or stealing from one another. I hope you don't think we're all like him. Just because we don't have steady jobs or a home doesn't mean we don't have manners."

"Thank you for stepping in. I'm in your debt."

"If anything, we're in yours." The leader tipped his newsboy cap. "You're welcome to stay, but he knows the law is after you. You best be going before he earns a dime for the tip."

"I suppose you're right." Charlie turned to Hank, placing a hand on the small of his back. He looked as if the pain had returned doubly after the beating he had administered. "Do you think you can walk?"

"We don't have a choice."

"What about the train?" the leader asked. "We could sneak you onto a car or scrounge up ten cents for each of you to cover the fare for a streetcar."

Hank shook his head. "That's no good. The sheriff would have deputies at the stations looking for us."

The leader rubbed the back of his neck. "There's a truck driver who makes a run to San Francisco every Monday morning to drop off and pick up auto parts for the garage he works for. He gives us rides into town sometimes so we can look for work. If we leave now, we might catch him before he takes off."

"How far is it?" Charlie asked.

"Two blocks."

"I can make it," Hank said. He stepped to the opening, sat on his bottom, and swung his legs over the edge.

"Hold on," the leader said. "We'll help you down and get you to the garage."

The leader and another man slung Hank's arms over their shoulders and walked him to the garage. The hour was still early, before the traditional start of the business day, so vehicle and pedestrian traffic was light. "We're in luck," the leader said. "The truck is still here."

Charlie was familiar with some repair garages in Redwood City but not this one. With so many people cutting back on spending, older cars were staying on the road longer—and needing repairs. As a result, at least a dozen new garages had popped up in the last few years, and it was hard to keep up.

The men steered Hank inside through the back door. Charlie surveyed the garage. The tools and equipment were dated and stored chaotically. Everything in her garage was new, thanks to Grace rebuilding and stocking her place after Frankie Wilkes burned it down. She prided herself on keeping it clean and organized.

A man dressed in shop coveralls was loading used tires into the back of the station pickup truck. The leader approached him. "Morning, Stanley. We have a favor to ask. Is there any chance you can take these two with you on your morning run?"

Stanley eyed Hank up and down. "What happened to him?"

"I got rolled," Hank said.

"We'd appreciate a lift," Charlie said. "I'm afraid we don't have any money to pay you for the trouble. But I could pay you by leveling your tire changer. It looks out of balance."

"How did you know?" Stanley asked. "It's been a bear for months."

"I have one like it in my garage. Unless you tighten the bolts every month, the frame gets off-kilter. It should only take a few minutes." Charlie grabbed the appropriate monkey wrench and a shop rag from the back bench. Within ten minutes of tightening and cleaning the grime buildup from the blades and other parts, she had the machine running and looking like new.

"Wow." Stanley scratched his head. "If you need a job, we could always use a hand around here."

"I appreciate the offer, but I have a shop of my own and need to get back to it."

"Well, if you change your mind, the offer stands. In the meantime, I'd be happy to take you two to the city."

"That's very kind," Charlie said.

After thanking the men from the train yard, Charlie and Hank climbed into the truck cab. Stanley got behind the wheel and popped a wad of chewing tobacco into his lower lip for the twenty-five-mile drive to San Francisco. He and Charlie chatted about various aspects of the garage business, mutually complaining about the recent scarcity of some parts to repair the older vehicles.

An hour later, Stanley pulled into the same tire dump yard Charlie used occasionally. After helping him unload the tires, she checked on Hank in the front seat. He looked weak. She feared he might have internal injuries. "I'll get you some water and try to round up something to eat."

"Thanks, Charlie." Hank squeezed her hand. "You're a good friend."

She asked Stanley about food and water, and he replied, "Let me buy you breakfast. It's the least I can do."

Charlie accepted his kind offer. After they ate at a nearby diner across from Golden Gate Park, she glanced at Hank sitting across from her in the booth. The bruises on his face had turned a dark shade of purple, and the swelling around his eyes had started to go down. The food and water seemed to bring back his energy.

She focused on Stanley. "Thank you kindly for breakfast, but we should be going. Once I clear up my legal issues, you're invited to Half Moon Bay, and lunch is on me."

"I don't know what trouble you're in, but…" Stanley's blush suggested he had a crush on Charlie. He stuffed five one-dollar bills into her hand. "It's not much, but I hope it helps."

"It will. Thank you."

Stanley handed Hank his cap and gestured at his bruised face. "You might want to hide your mug. It draws a lot of attention."

"Much obliged. Like my friend said, we'd like to repay your kindness. I hope you'll take us up on it."

The morning edition of the *San Francisco Chronicle* left at a table caught Hank's eye. He grabbed it and walked outside with Charlie and Stanley. After saying goodbye on the street and parting ways, Hank opened the newspaper and shook his head. "I knew it."

"Knew what?"

"Wilkes is framing us for the murder of those two deputies last night." Hank handed her the newspaper. The headline on the left read, "Results on State Repeal Vote Expected Tomorrow." Charlie's gaze drifted to the next story. "Two Deputies Killed in Daring Prison Break."

She read the first few paragraphs of the story. "But they were alive when we left."

"Well, they're dead now. Roy is the law and has every cop in the state looking for us."

"What do we do now?" Charlie asked.

"We need to get off the streets, but first, we need to call the Foster House to let everyone know we're safe."

Charlie returned to the café and had the cashier make change for one of the dollar bills Stanley had gifted them. Minutes later, she and Hank located a pay phone inside a corner drugstore. Charlie remained outside the booth, but Hank kept the door open so she could hear. Meanwhile, Hank deposited the nickel and asked the operator to connect him to the Foster House.

"No answer," he said. "I'll try to get the operator in Half Moon Bay." When he put the coin in again, a policeman entered the booth next to them.

Charlie's heart raced at the prospect of the officer recognizing them, so she tugged on Hank's arm. "We need to go."

Hank retrieved their money, clutched Charlie by the arm stealthily, and walked away casually like nothing was wrong. Once on the street, he said, "We need to find a place to hide."

Charlie looked around and saw a street sign saying Golden Gate Park was one block away. She remembered coming to this area years ago with Dax to pick up May's piano. When she talked to May last month, she mentioned she and Dax had driven past Logan's old house. The bank still could not find a buyer, and it was sitting vacant. If Charlie remembered correctly, the house faced the park.

"I know a place. We can go to Logan's old house. Isn't it vacant?"

"It is. I should have thought of going there, but I'm not thinking straight with these ribs." Hank lowered Stanley's hat to cover his face before following the signs to the park with Charlie. When they turned onto the street where Logan's old house was, he suggested, "We should go around back where no one can see us breaking in."

"Wait." Charlie grabbed his arm, bringing him to a stop. "I was here once with Dax. May kept a key hidden on the front porch. Maybe it's still there."

They walked up the weed-laden concrete pathway, passing the foreclosure sign saying the property was bank-owned. Several plants had died, and the yard was littered with trash. Everything was overgrown and in dire need of pruning. Hank stopped, doubled back to the sign, and pulled it from its stakes.

Charlie gave him a curious look. "What's that for?"

"If someone sees us, they'll think the house was finally sold and won't call the police."

They continued to the porch. It was dirty, filled with leaves, cobwebs, and peeling paint. The windows and door appeared intact, so the house might not have been vandalized on the inside. The porch chairs and table were still there but were knocked over, and several legs were broken. A potted plant where May had hidden the key was broken on the wood slats. The damage appeared to be storm related, not from hooligans.

Charlie sifted through the debris and potting soil until she felt something metal. "Found it." She swept the dirt away, wiped the key on her pant leg, and handed it to Hank.

He tried the lock, and it worked. When the door eased open, a noise came from inside. Something or someone shuffled their feet on the floor. A crash.

Hank pulled a gun from his waistband. "Stand back." He burst through the door, disappeared inside, and more scuffling ensued.

Charlie wasn't as concerned for Hank as she was for whoever was inside. Hank was a superior marksman, and his military training made him the ultimate threat. If she went in to help, he might mistake her for an intruder, so she waited patiently at the door.

"Charlie, come in."

She entered, closing the door behind her. Void of furniture, the interior was musty, dusty, and full of cobwebs. Hank appeared from around a corner. "What was it?"

"A pack of feral cats. I scared them out an open back window."
He went from window to window, drawing the curtains closed.
"The power is out, but the water still works. We'll need food
soon, but we could stay here for a while."

"A while." Charlie leaned against a wall and slid to the floor
on her bottom, succumbing to the house's stark, abandoned
feeling. It was a metaphor for what her life had become. Only
three days ago, she had a home, a business, an incredible
girlfriend, and the most loyal dog in the world. Today, it was all
gone without any hope of getting back what she'd lost. She and
Hank were running from a man drunk on power and hellbent
on revenge. An ominous feeling overtook her. Her days were
numbered.

CHAPTER TWENTY-FOUR

The thirty-mile drive to San Francisco afforded Dax too much time to relive telling Jules and May about what had happened overnight and seeing the profound worry and heartbreak on their faces. Their loved ones were taken three days ago, and each day had brought news worse than the one before. None of them, including Dax and Rose, believed the outlandish story coming from the sheriff, which made Dax's trip much more critical.

Reaching the city limits and heavy traffic, Dax downshifted to slow her speed. The car behind her truck since leaving Half Moon Bay slowed, too, mirroring her turns as she made her way toward Mission Street. She wasn't sure the driver was following her—several other vehicles behind her had followed the same route—but it seemed suspicious. There wasn't much she could do about it, but as a precaution she parked two blocks from the Chronicle Building. Armed with the freshly printed photographs of Captain Ford's remains, his notebook, and the original news story from 1925, she walked the rest of the way.

When she turned onto Mission Street, the distinctive five-story clock tower at the corner of the three-story building, surrounded by ornate Gothic Revival detailing, came into view. The building had gone up almost a decade ago to replace the old headquarters. It was the most anticipated relocation in the city. The largest, most influential newspaper west of Saint Louis had moved from the West Coast's first skyscraper to a sprawling building covering an entire city block. When it opened, the *Chronicle* was hailed as "the most modern newspaper on Earth." The paper was precisely what Dax needed to bring down Roy Wilkes.

The interior was as remarkable as the outside, with lobby walls lined in variegated marble and floors made of mosaic marble tiles. Dax checked the building directory on the entry wall and found Phillip Gandy's location on the third floor in the reporter section. She climbed the stairs, admiring the detail on the iron and oak railing and marble wainscoting. She would have to consider adding similar details to the Seaside Hotel lobby someday.

The third floor was less ornate than the lobby but equally spacious. Reporters' desks were lined up in four straight rows of ten, each with a typewriter and stacks of paper on top. Most of the desks were occupied, and several people were milling about. Dax scanned each face until she spotted Phillip, typing at an impressive speed, and his red curls. She chuckled. The reporting business wasn't as glamorous as she'd thought. She'd envisioned men dressed in wrinkled suits and armed with notepads, pounding the streets for a story, not sitting at a typewriter, correcting their spelling errors.

Dax approached. "Excuse me, Phillip."

He looked up. "Dax? This is a surprise. What brings you here?"

"A hot story, but not here. Is there someplace we can talk?"

Phillip looked around the room. Privacy was out of the question with the number of people there. "Come with me." He grabbed his hat and led Dax down the stairs and out a side door to Mission Street. Once away from the building, he said, "Too many eyes and ears in there. Everyone tries to scoop the other. It's exhausting. So, what's this hot story of yours?"

"What would you say if I could link a newly elected county sheriff to an eight-year-old murder?"

"I'd say you have my interest."

"How soon could you run the story?"

"It depends on my editor. I'd have to investigate, corroborate the claim, and give the sheriff an opportunity to refute the allegation. It could take a few days or weeks."

Dax nervously rubbed her neck. "Weeks won't work. I need the story out there sooner so the county officials can remove him from office or we can put him in jail."

"What's the rush?"

"He arrested two of my friends on weak, trumped-up charges, beat them to a pulp, and framed them for murdering two of his deputies."

Phillip nodded. "Today's front page. You're talking about Henry O'Keefe and Charlene Dawson from Half Moon Bay, so the sheriff you suspect of murder must be Roy Wilkes. Who are they to you?"

"You're pretty smart, Phillip. Hank and I work together, and Charlie is a personal friend. Both are good people. There's no way they would have killed those deputies unless it was self-defense."

"The original charge against Dawson said she was arrested for lewd and disorderly conduct with another woman." Phillip eyed Dax up and down. "Were you the other woman?"

"No, I wasn't. I was working with Hank when she was arrested."

"At the Beacon Club? The story said O'Keefe runs the town's nicest speakeasy."

"Can this be off the record?"

"I don't do off the record, but I can promise if you tell me the whole truth, I won't publish anything incriminating unless there's no other way to confirm the story. If you lie to me, I'll make sure you get what's coming."

Dax raked her hands down her face, weighing her options. He would not lift a finger to help if she wasn't honest with him. And if she told him everything, he might print enough to land her in jail. Her choice was obvious. "It's the other way around. He works for me. I manage the club and the hotel renovations and another club in town. We sell beer, wine, and illegal liquor. Rose sings at the club, so I don't want this blowing back on her."

"Dang, Dax. I knew you were the type to never put up with any guff in high school, but this is incredible. How are Charlie and Sheriff Wilkes involved?"

"She runs the town's repair garage, and we're friends, or at least we used to be until some things went haywire. The sheriff's brother owned most of the businesses along the marina in Half Moon Bay, including the Seaside Hotel. Until I showed up, he ran the only speakeasy in town. The competition between the clubs escalated. Frankie burned down Charlie's garage and tried to burn down my sister's restaurant, but Hank killed him in self-defense. Now Roy Wilkes is out for his pound of flesh."

"This is an amazing story, but what about this eight-year-old murder?"

"After Frankie was killed, ownership of his Half Moon Bay properties was up in the air while his brother and his silent partner fought it out in the courts. The new owner decided to remodel the hotel this year, and she put me in charge."

"Who is *she*?"

Dax was hesitant to get Grace involved, but ownership of the hotel was a matter of public record. "You would figure it out soon enough. It's Grace Parsons."

Phillip nodded with understanding. "Ah, now I know why you and Rose were her special guests at last week's movie premiere."

"Yes. After the storm passed through yesterday, I checked on the construction. A wall I hadn't planned on redoing was damaged. That's when I found a skeleton buried in the wall." Dax showed him the photographs, including the original *Half Moon Bay Review* story.

Phillip read the article. "So you're saying the body is the missing Captain Ford."

"Yes." Dax handed him the picture of a page from Ford's notebook. "I found this on the body. It says he was supposed to meet with Roy and Frankie Wilkes in Half Moon Bay on June 22nd. I have a witness who was at the meeting but was told to leave when things got heated. Ford never made it back to his ship."

"This probably isn't enough to convict Sheriff Wilkes," Phillip said.

Dax was frustrated at the obvious but had to do something. "But it could be enough to show he's a dirty cop who framed Hank and Charlie and maybe get him removed from office."

"I agree. Can I keep these?"

"I'll hold on to them for the time being." Dax had no reason to suspect he would bury the evidence or hand it over to Wilkes, but she had a gut feeling those pictures shouldn't leave her hands.

"I'll run this past my editor. If he gives me the go-ahead, I'll need to see the remains and the original notebook, interview your witness, and dig into the missing person's case."

"How long will that take?"

"A day or two." He pulled out his notepad, reinforcing her vision of how a reporter should work. "I'm supposed to meet with my editor after lunch. I can let you know later today whether he wants me to work on the story. How can I reach you?"

Dax wrote down her address and phone number at the Foster House. "But if it's all the same, I'd like to come back today. I can drive you to Half Moon Bay."

He didn't look convinced about the urgency. "I understand you're anxious to get things started, but this isn't how I work."

"I'm more than anxious. This is personal. Hank is my brother-in-law. He and Charlie are on the run for something they didn't do, and it's tearing my sister apart." And Jules, she wanted to say. "They won't be safe until we expose Wilkes."

Phillip's heavy sigh suggested she'd gotten through to him. "All right, Dax. I have a good feeling my editor will approve this in a heartbeat. And since I don't have a car, I could use a lift to Half Moon Bay. Meet me back here around two."

She pulled him in for a tight yet brief hug. "Thank you, Phillip. You won't regret this."

After parting ways with Phillip, Dax glanced at the tower clock. She had three hours to waste before she could meet up with him again. Grabbing a sandwich and a soda at a local lunch counter ate up an hour, after which she drove the city aimlessly until she found herself in front of the old Portman house.

"Heather…" Dax whispered her name and traced her lips as memories of stolen kisses and a bruised face flooded back. She still loved the beautiful redhead, the abused wife of a carpentry customer, though not in the way she loved Rose, and often wondered how her life turned out. Wondered if she'd found someone more kind and deserving of her and how big her children had gotten.

The memory of their last day together returned and steered her toward Logan's old house, where she and May had put up with him for nine years. She parked in front. The weeds, dead plants, and overgrown shrubs were a sad sight. The jewel of the neighborhood was now a monstrous eyesore.

She stepped up the walkway and gasped. For years, May had swept the wraparound porch every morning and wiped down the furniture, clearing it of dew and dirt. She would have fainted at its current condition with cobwebs, trash, leaves, and years of built-up grime. Dax shook her head, stepping onto the porch. The furniture was upturned, and the legs were broken. She tried shoring up a chair, but it was a lost cause.

She leaned over the railing, gazing toward the street she had watched every Saturday, waiting for Heather to walk by on her way to the park with her children. The faint smile she would give Dax when she strolled past was an acknowledgment of their special bond until the last day they set eyes on one another. Her smile was gone, buried beneath bruises and swelling from a beating no wife should have to endure.

Dax remembered flying from this very spot and darting across the yard to give Benjamin Portman as good as he'd given. Her gaze followed the route she'd taken that day. Surprisingly, the For Sale sign was missing, suggesting the bank must have finally found a buyer. The house hadn't interested May since Logan's death, but she might like knowing it would soon be occupied and hopefully loved again.

A sound inside the house, resembling the floorboard beneath the sitting room window, caught Dax's attention. She remembered it creaked whenever she approached the window to open it and turned in its direction. The window curtain fluttered, suggesting someone or something was inside. She went to the window to peek inside, but the drape was closed. She tried the doorknob, but the door swung open like a whirlwind. Someone in the shadows pulled her inside and placed a hand over her mouth.

Dax struggled. Her heart thumped hard at the prospect she was about to be robbed, beaten, or worse when he closed the door. Then she focused on the man's face when he lowered his hand. It was bruised and swollen like Heather's had been that horrible day.

"Hank? What happened to you?"

"Wilkes's deputies."

"What are you doing here? Is Charlie with you?"

"I'm here." Charlie appeared from the sitting room. She looked tired, and her face had bruises but not as fresh or as bad as Hank's.

Dax wanted to wrap her arms around Charlie and pull her in for a long, overdue embrace, but her stiff body language suggested the gesture would not be welcome. Instead, she said, "I'm glad you're safe," gripped her by the upper arms and locked eyes with her. When Charlie's lips trembled, Dax let go, knowing she'd gotten across the real message that she missed her friend.

"How did you two get here?" Dax asked.

Hank peeked through the window curtain. "We hid overnight in a homeless encampment at a train yard and hitched a ride with a garage mechanic. What are you doing here?"

"After we read the story about you two killing the deputies, I went to the Chronicle Building to enlist help in getting you two free. Then…I guess…I came to reminisce." She preferred not to talk about Heather and the part of her life she'd thought was behind her.

"Well, we didn't do it," Hank said. "When we escaped, the deputies were alive, so we handcuffed them to the wall."

"I didn't believe that you did it like the sheriff claimed. Not for one second. I thought it had to be self-defense, but now it looks like Wilkes killed them after you escaped to punish them and blame you."

"My thoughts exactly," Hank said. "I'm happy you're here, but you can't stay. It's too dangerous. Go home and tell May and Jules we're safe." The sound of a car pulling up to the front of the house forced Hank back to the window. "Someone is here."

Dax peeked through the curtain on the other side of the window. "It looks like the car that was behind me after I left Half Moon Bay."

"Wilkes's men must have followed you." Hank stepped back quickly and winced. "We have to get out of here."

"You're hurt. You won't get far on foot," Dax said. "We need to get to my truck."

"Then we'll have to shoot our way out." Hank removed a pistol from his waistband and handed it to Dax. He pulled another one from his jacket pocket.

"I assume these are the deputies' guns?" Dax paused at Hank's affirming nod. "Getting caught with them will help prove Wilkes's lie that you killed them."

"Well, I'm not giving up our only form of defense."

Charlie lowered her head, clearly unhappy with the option of using guns. "All we've done so far is defend ourselves. Even if we got away, leaving a trail of more dead deputies would bring every man with a badge down on us. There has to be another way."

"What about the time we ditched the Prohis?" Dax asked.

"We'll need a diversion," Charlie said.

"What do you have in mind?" Dax smiled. Except for the time Charlie had fixed her flat tire, this was the most she'd spoken to Dax in years.

"Garbage cans are out back. We could create a ruckus with them. When those guys go to check it out, we break for your truck. We can flatten one of their tires before we take off. It should slow them down."

"That might work." Hank peeked out the window again. "They're waiting. I'd bet my last dollar more deputies are on the way, so we gotta move now."

"All right, who does what?" Dax asked.

"I'll knock over the cans in the back," Charlie said. "It should set off the pack of feral cats back there. As soon as the deputies go around back, you help Hank into the truck. He's hurt something awful. You'll need to stick their tire with something."

"I have a screwdriver in the glove box."

"That will do the trick. I'll come back through the house and meet you at the truck."

Hank offered Charlie his gun. "Take it just in case."

"No." Her stern expression left no room for negotiation.

"You're so stubborn, Charlie," Dax said. "Take the damn gun."

"I won't fire it. You better get ready." Charlie disappeared into the kitchen.

Moments later, metal clanking and screaming cats from the back of the house created a racket loud enough to raise the dead. Dax peeked through the window, watching the sedan parked several yards behind her truck. The car doors opened, and two men wearing suits flew out, waving firearms. They ran down the gravel access alley on the side of the house.

That was Dax's cue. She wrapped one arm around Hank's back and held the gun in her other hand. Hank threw an arm around her shoulder while holding a gun in his free hand. She opened the door and rushed outside, guiding Hank down the walkway. He limped and, at times, was dead weight, suggesting he was hurt more badly than she first thought.

Once on the sidewalk, she could see the car more clearly and confirmed it was the one behind her during her drive from Half Moon Bay. She steered Hank to the truck's passenger side and opened the door. He lifted his leg to the running board and tried pulling himself into the cab by holding onto the doorframe, but he slipped.

"I'm too weak," he said. "Go, flatten their tire."

"Not until I get you inside." Dax crouched and pushed him up with her body, putting her legs into it.

Once Hank tumbled into the cab and righted himself, Dax opened the glove box, retrieved a screwdriver, and headed toward the car. Before she was able to disable a tire, however, the front door opened, and Charlie appeared, running. A shot rang out. She ducked and shouted, "Let's go!"

Dax returned to the truck, jumped inside, and closed the door simultaneously with Charlie closing the other. Another gunshot sounded as the men stormed from the house, pointing their pistols at the truck. She started the engine, engaged the gears, and stomped on the gas pedal, screeching the tires. More shots followed, two striking the truck's back end.

Dax turned the corner and got the truck up to twice the speed limit on the residential street. Checking the side mirror, she saw the car from the front of the house also make the turn. Their vehicle was more suited for speed and could easily catch up, but Dax had one advantage. She knew these streets like the back of her hand. She needed to avoid the main roads and the heavier traffic to keep moving.

Dax navigated turn after turn, but the sedan continued gaining ground. And each time they rounded a corner, Hank moaned at the pressure of being forced into her or Charlie. Dax could go around in circles, but the men would eventually catch up. She needed to change the conditions. So far, she'd avoided heavier traffic to not endanger other vehicles, but perhaps a wreck in traffic could cut off the car chasing them.

She was in the Tenderloin and could hit traffic by turning onto Market Street and heading into the Financial District. "Hold on. This could get dicey."

Charlie and Hank hooked arms while Charlie braced her right arm high on the passenger door window frame.

Dax made the turn. Traffic was lighter than expected. She'd forgotten the lunch rush was over, and the going-home crowd would not come out for another two hours. She weaved between cars, but their pursuers kept up. Even running stop lights didn't slow the people chasing them. They were determined to catch Hank and Charlie, dead or alive.

The ferry dock was straight ahead. She had a choice. The Embarcadero ran parallel to the wharves along San Francisco's eastern shoreline. Turning north would take her into the hills. Her truck would be overtaken before cresting the first hill. Going south would keep her on flat ground, but the roads were trickier near Mission Bay. She looked straight ahead and saw a third option was possible. A glance in her side mirror confirmed the pursuer had to slow and swerve to miss a car in the last intersection. This was her only chance of getting away.

Shoremen were casting off ropes for the car ferry at the end of the dock. Dax downshifted, increased her speed, and crashed through the cyclone fence at the entrance of the car ramp. The ferry boat blew its horn, the signal it was about to pull away.

"This is crazy." Charlie's voice was brittle with fear.

"Hold on!" Dax gassed it seconds before the boat pulled away. The truck bounced once, twice on the deck before she slammed on the brakes. They stopped, one foot short of hitting the last car in line.

Everyone's chest heaved inside the truck cab. Dax rechecked her mirror. Wilkes's men had followed her and sped down the car ramp. They launched off the end and missed the ferry, falling nose-first into the San Francisco Bay.

Dax wiped sweat coating her forehead. "Phew! That was close."

CHAPTER TWENTY-FIVE

A gentle nudge woke Grace from her deep sleep. The familiar deep voice said, "We're here, my sweet." Grace fluttered her eyes open. Light filtered through the car windows, warming the inside of their Packard. "We're here," Clive repeated.

"I'm up." Grace lifted her head from the pillow she'd stuffed between her and the door for the drive up the coast. When she shifted to sit straight, pain reminded her of the healing incision on her breast. It throbbed again, but she resisted taking the prescribed narcotics. If she gave in, she feared Harriet's fate of addiction and depression would catch up with her. And in Grace Parson's world, fate was a cruel bitch. It would beat her down until she had no way out but the one Harriet had taken.

While Clive circled the car, she fluffed her hair, pulled her compact mirror from the glove box, and deemed herself presentable after wiping the sleep from her eyes. She got her bearings, noting he'd parked behind the Foster House in Dax's reserved space a few steps from the back entrance. The area appeared uncharacteristically weather-beaten, with kelp and other ocean debris in the parking lot and against the building.

"Nothing like door-to-door service."

Clive opened the passenger door, tossed the pillow in the back seat, and offered his hand. "Nothing but the best for you."

Stepping from the car, Grace felt her legs wobble.

Clive caught her arm. "I have you. Do you need to wait for this to pass?"

"No. We need to know what has happened to Hank and Charlie. Though I would love your arm."

"It would be my pleasure." He escorted her to the door after offering his arm and held it open for her.

Grace walked through slowly, feeling steadier on her feet. Farther inside, she discovered the kitchen oddly vacant. At two o'clock in the afternoon, she had expected the opposite. Even when the Foster House was closed, like today, the kitchen typically bustled with activity from baking or stocking supplies. She continued to the swinging door into the dining room, solving the mystery of where everyone was.

Rose and May were seated at the center table playing cards while Charlie's faithful bulldog lay on a blanket nearby. All three heads turned in her direction when she stepped inside. May's eyes turned sad, shimmering with tears. Brutus popped up from his bed, wagging his tail. But Rose's reaction was Grace's favorite—a slight smile with admiration in her eyes and a look of satisfaction.

"I knew you'd come," Rose said as she pushed back her chair. She met Grace halfway and gave her a tight hug. The pressure made Grace's incision sting, but she hid the pain from the others.

Grace then hugged May loosely to avoid aggravating her injury. "I'm so sorry I've been out of touch, but it couldn't be helped." She sat when Clive pulled out a chair for her. He sat next to her. "We read the disturbing newspaper account of what Hank and Charlie have been going through, but we're here for the real story."

"It's been a nightmare." May detailed both the arrests, the harsh treatment Hank and Charlie had received from their captors, and the lawyer they hired to represent them in court.

"Before leaving home today, I contacted my San Francisco lawyer. He said he'd start looking into things this afternoon. I'll have him contact Mr. Grant. I noticed Dax's truck isn't here. Is she at the hotel?"

"She's in San Francisco." Rose told Grace about the minor storm damage and their findings in Frankie Wilkes's old office at the Seaside Hotel, including the notebook. She also detailed the story of the missing Captain Ford.

"Yes, I remember the story," Grace said. "I'd recently become Frankie's silent partner and had taken an interest in his disappearance."

"Jason was there that day. He said Frankie and Roy met with Ford in Frankie's office, and it had gotten heated. A few days later, the FBI came to town asking questions but backed off after speaking with the local Prohibition agents."

"So, the two agents we had on our payroll to look the other way were part of the coverup?"

"It would seem so. Since we couldn't reach you, we were desperate to do something. Dax is meeting with an acquaintance who is a reporter with the *Chronicle*. We hoped to have him expose Roy's involvement and get him removed from office or prosecuted for murder."

Grace slumped in her chair. *What have they done?* By exposing the Wilkeses, they risked exposing every illegal, dirty thing they'd done to run their businesses. Every federal agent on the West Coast would dissect their books and dealings to make a name for themselves. "We have to stop her."

"But why?" Rose looked confused. Of course, she would. She worked in a speakeasy and occasionally partook in consuming illegal liquor, but she was naturally a good person. She believed the seediness of the business was born out of self-defense, not self-preservation.

"I'm a celebrity. Once this gets out and my association becomes known, it will be sensationalized for months. I can't afford to have my life and business examined by every law enforcement agency and newspaper in the country."

"I never thought of it that way. What can we do? Dax is already there."

"We need to call the reporter she went to see and put the brakes on the story."

"I have his business card, but our phones aren't working yet. We'll have to go to Edith's. While we're in town, I'll also speak to the owner of the *Review* and ask him to refrain from putting it in the paper."

"We should leave now. I need to make several calls, including one to the governor."

Minutes later, Clive drove Grace, Rose, and May into town and parked in front of Edith's Department Store. The front window was boarded up. "What happened here?" Grace asked.

"A garbage can flew through it during the storm. Dax helped Henry board it up yesterday."

"That sounds like our Dax."

Once inside, Rose explained to Edith the urgency of using the phone.

"Of course," Edith said. "You can use our office." She walked them to the back of the store and left them alone after saying, "Take as long as you need."

Rose lifted the phone receiver and asked Grace, "Who do we call first?"

"The reporter."

Rose had the operator dial the number on Phillip Gandy's business card and held the phone so she and Grace could hear since the topic involved her. The call connected to the Chronicle Building operator, and after they were placed on hold for several minutes, Phillip answered, "This is Phil Gandy."

"Phillip, this is Rose Hamilton."

"Rose. You must be calling about Dax. I've been waiting for her to come back."

"Yes, I am, but what do you mean about waiting for her?"

"She told me about her brother-in-law and friend."

"And the sheriff and Ford." Rose finished his sentence to demonstrate she knew precisely what Dax had told him.

"That's right. She was supposed to return after I met with my editor. When should I expect her?"

"I don't know, but I need to talk to you about what she told you."

"What about it?" Phillip sounded suspicious.

"Something has changed since she talked to you. If you publish the story right now, more people I care about will be in danger."

"You mean in more danger than O'Keefe and Dawson?"

"It's a different danger, and I can't risk them getting hurt."

"What about Dax's brother-in-law and friend? Aren't you afraid for them?" Phillip asked.

"Desperately, but we have someone else who can help in ways you can't."

"You're talking about Grace Parsons, the owner of the hotel where Dax found Ford's body?"

Grace cringed. Her name was already part of this mess. Controlling the damage was critical.

"Yes, Phillip," Rose said. "She and her husband have been friends of ours for years. She has influence unrivaled in this state and is willing to step in."

"What do you want from me, Rose?"

"To sit on the story."

"You've got to be kidding. This story has Pulitzer Prize written all over it."

"If our childhood friendship meant anything, please don't publish the story. How can I convince you?"

"I'll need something else," he said.

"Like what?"

"An exclusive. Word has it Grace Parsons and Greta Garbo are having an affair."

Grace seethed with anger. Phillip Gandy was not a man they could trust, which meant her world would blow up unless Rose convinced him to reverse course.

The crease at the bridge of Rose's nose became more pronounced with worry. "I won't justify an accusation with a response, but I will let your employer know you got suspended from school for sneaking into the girls' bathroom wearing a girl's gym uniform."

"I was a kid, looking for a peep."

"Dax and I will tell them all the girls knew you were a cross-dresser, looking to blend in with us, and we saw you trying to pick up men at our club."

"You wouldn't."

"In a heartbeat. If you think the *Chronicle* wouldn't care about employing a cross-dresser who regularly seeks the company of men, then, by all means, publish the article."

"Fine." His response dripped with contempt.

"If Dax gave you those photographs, I expect you to burn them. And if word of this ever sees the light of day, so will your cross-dressing history."

"Dax has the photos, and I didn't even meet with my editor today. He canceled, so no one else knows."

"Keep it that way." Rose hung up the phone with a determined look typical of Hollywood studio executives. And if Grace had the right to say so, she would tell Rose the last few minutes were sexy as hell.

"Remind me to never get on your bad side," Grace said. "Thank you for keeping a lid on things. Now it's my turn." Following a call to update her "fix-it" lawyer in San Francisco, she was comfortable he would take over for Mr. Grant and, if her next call didn't yield the expected results, he would do whatever was necessary to secure Hank's and Charlie's freedom.

Grace had the operator call a tightly held number to Governor Rolph's personal secretary in Sacramento. Few people knew it existed, and fewer had unfettered access to her employer—one of the most powerful governors in the country. Rolph was a favored guest at Grace's Hollywood estate, placing her atop the list. She was confident he would do everything in his power to help. Unfortunately, his blatant refusal to enforce Prohibition laws had put him at odds with the federal government. Hence the urgency to control every facet of this debacle before the FBI or Prohibition agents stuck their noses into it.

"Hello."

"Sara, this is Grace Parsons. I have an urgent matter and need to speak to the governor immediately."

"I'm afraid I won't be able to reach him until tomorrow morning. He's taking the train back from the governors' convention in Denver."

"Then I'll have to meet him in Sacramento. When will his train arrive?"

"He's going directly to Oakland and will ferry to San Francisco for his son's birthday."

"What time is he due home?"

"His train is due between eight and nine, so he should arrive home between nine and ten."

"I'll be there waiting for him. It's of the utmost urgency."

"I'll alert his staff."

"Thank you, Sara." Grace finished the call and relayed the details to the others in the office. "So now we head back to the Foster House. Hopefully, we'll hear something from Dax before I meet with the governor. We'll need the evidence she's collected to convince him."

After a quick stop at the local newspaper and dropping by the clinic to update Jules on the recent developments, everyone adjourned to the upstairs residence to wait until Jules finished her shift.

"Are you sure, May?" Grace asked. Climbing the stairs seemed daunting. Since coming home from the hospital yesterday, she'd only descended stairs herself.

"I climbed two flights of stairs yesterday and was quite proud of myself. I'd like to continue challenging myself to get stronger."

How could Grace argue with May? She'd been crippled for twelve years yet was determined to start rebuilding her strength. "Lead the way, then."

Clive offered his arm. "May I help?"

"Please," May said with a smile. She and Clive followed Brutus and climbed the private stairs slowly while Rose and Grace waited at the bottom. When May was close to the top, Rose offered her arm to Grace. "Shall we?"

"Please." Grace linked arms with Rose. She leaned on her halfway up when her legs turned to lead and her breathing grew labored.

Rose slowed. "Are you all right, Grace?"

"The trip must have tired me more than I'd thought. I'll be fine." She summoned the last of her energy reserves and reached the top, more lightheaded than before but focused on taking one step at a time.

"Are you sure?" Rose narrowed her eyes in concern. "You look pale."

"I should have eaten before we left."

"Let's get you on the couch." Rose provided more support, making the rest of the trek less demanding.

May was already on the couch, and Grace joined her. "Thank you, Rose."

"I'll be right back with something to eat and drink." Rose turned her attention to the others. "Can I grab something for anyone else?"

The others asked for whatever she was fixing, and Rose disappeared downstairs. Minutes later, she returned with a pitcher of water and sandwiches. The late lunch conversation centered on Hank, Charlie, and Dax. Everyone wondered where they were and if they were all right. Rose appeared to grow more worried as the conversation marched on.

Jules soon appeared at the top of the stairs, looking tired. "Any other news?"

"Nothing since we last talked." Grace shifted on the couch and winced when the pain in her breast returned with a vengeance. It had hurt all through their visit to Edith's and their meal. Now, she was on the verge of surrendering to a pain pill.

"We saved you a sandwich," Rose said.

"Perfect. I'm starved." Jules laid her handbag on the desk and joined the others after grabbing her early dinner. The tense conversation repeated, with everyone agreeing they were finally hopeful about Hank's and Charlie's prospects with Grace now involved.

The pain had yet to relent. As hard as she fought, it was time to give in, but she didn't want the others to see her taking opioids. Grace struggled to push herself from the couch.

Clive rushed over and helped her up. "Are you tired?"

"I need to use the restroom and get something from my bag."

He whispered so only she could hear, "The pills are in your handbag on the nightstand in the guest room."

She smiled her appreciation. "I'll be right back." After using the toilet and filling a glass of water, Grace went to their room and fished out her pill bottle. She studied it momentarily, wondering if this was how addiction started for Harriet. Giving into the pain was much easier than bearing through it.

A knock on the door drew her attention. She returned the bottle to her purse and said, "Come in."

Jules stepped inside and closed the door. "I wanted to make sure you were feeling okay. I could tell you were in severe pain."

"It's nothing."

"Recovering from breast surgery isn't nothing."

Grace drew her head back. Clive would have never mentioned her condition to anyone, especially not the women in the next room. "How did you know?"

"I recognized the bulge beneath your blouse. It's bandaging. Considering how you're favoring your left side and the size of your bustline, I'd say you had a lumpectomy instead of a radical mastectomy. How far along was your cancer?"

There was no sense in denying it. Rose was right when she once said nothing got past Jules. "We caught it early, and the surgeon was confident he'd gotten the entire tumor."

"How many days post-op?"

"Three."

"Then you're still feeling a high level of post-operative pain. When was your last dose of pain medication?"

"Yesterday."

Jules shook her head in disapproval. "You're putting your body through unnecessary stress at a time when you need to conserve your energy to heal. May I check your incision?"

Grace nodded, unbuttoned her blouse, and gingerly exposed her left breast.

Jules carefully lifted the bandage and inspected the incision and stitches. "I don't see any sign of infection, which is good, but

I'm concerned about the amount of discharge on your dressing. I should change it. Did you bring extra?"

"In my overnight bag."

Jules dug out the supplies and applied a fresh dressing on the wound. "Good as new. Now, how about that medication?"

"Handbag."

Jules gave her a single pill and a glass of water. "Never take these on an empty stomach. The euphoria will intensify." Maybe the intoxicating effect was Harriet's downfall. Following her accident, she ate like a bird and often took her medication without eating. "You need to rest." Jules pulled back the covers on the bed.

"You won't tell the others, will you?"

"Of course not. It's a private matter."

"You would make an impressive doctor, Miss Sanchez. If you ever want to return to medical school, I'd be happy to help," Grace said.

A glint of possibilities slowly appeared in Jules's eyes. "I might take you up on that."

CHAPTER TWENTY-SIX

Money speaks, Dax thought. She had seen the axiom in practice every week at the Beacon Club. Any patron who threw around enough money went home or to their hotel room with any man or woman they'd set their sights on...except for Rose. Moments earlier, the ferry captain and two deckhands stormed onto the car deck, demanding an explanation as to why some crazy person had crashed through the gate and nearly taken out the aft end of his boat and the cars of his paying customers. She figured money and a good story could resolve this problem.

Dax exited her truck to keep the captain from seeing Hank and Charlie and asking more questions. They ducked low in the cab. "I'm very sorry, Captain, but I feared for my life after witnessing a horrible shooting minutes earlier"—she failed to mention they were shooting at her, Charlie, and Hank—"and the men chased me. I didn't know what to do. Thank goodness your ferry was preparing to pull away. Otherwise, they might have killed me."

The fire in his eyes had abated some with Dax's twisting of the facts. "I'll still have to call the police."

Dax put on her saddest, most terrified face. "But I'm afraid they're connected to the police. I need to get as far away as possible. I'll gladly pay for the gate. Otherwise, I didn't damage your boat." She reached into her pocket and pulled out the money she'd brought to bribe Phillip Gandy if necessary. "Would a hundred dollars compensate you for your troubles and allow me to go on my way?"

His raised eyebrows suggested she'd found his price. "I suppose no harm was done except to the gate." He extended his hand palm up. "But I never want you to use this ferry again."

Dax made the sign of the cross on her chest and turned over the money. "I promise."

He pocketed the money and turned to his deckhands. "See her safely off when we dock."

"Yes, Captain," one said, giving Dax the side-eye.

Once the ferry stopped and Dax cleared the dock ramp, Hank and Charlie sat upright. The truck sputtered, and the front wheels felt wobbly.

"The engine won't last much longer," Charlie said. "We'll need to pull over so I can look at her."

Scanning the area, Dax realized she'd taken the Alameda Ferry. She knew every road on this island like the back of her hand. Unfortunately, everyone she knew from thirteen years ago was dead or had moved away. Except for one person.

"I have an idea." Dax took side streets, staying off the highly trafficked Central Avenue. The circuitous route took her past Sweeny Park, bringing up a smile-inducing memory of her first kiss deep inside its poplar tree grove. She'd put an entire classroom of bullies in their place, including the teacher, for teasing Rose about her stutter and had come here in search of her after she'd run off in embarrassment. Then came the rain and the urgency to take shelter beneath her school uniform coat. Dax remembered her heart beating so hard when she pressed their lips together for a first kiss. It was a miracle it didn't burst through her chest.

She continued through the residential streets and pulled her truck onto an asphalt driveway on the side of a house and around back until it was hidden from the road. The trees and shrubs along the property line were in dire need of pruning, and weeds had taken over the small patch of grass in the backyard. The house needed a fresh coat of paint, but the intricate woodwork was still the best on the block.

"What is this place?" Hank asked.

"My past." Dax and the others exited the truck.

The back door opened, and a man holding a claw hammer stood in the doorway. The years hadn't been kind to him. He'd put on about twenty pounds. Age had taken most of his hair and the muscle tone in his arms and shoulders. Deep lines on his cheeks and forehead spoke to a life of worry and regret.

"This is private property. What do you want?" He lifted the hammer chest high.

"Hi, Papa."

He squinted to look at her better and put on the glasses hanging from a chain around his neck. "Darlene?"

"Yes, Papa. Can my friends and I come inside?"

Her father glanced over her shoulder. She followed his stare. Hank was using Charlie as support with an arm over her shoulder. "I don't want any trouble here."

"Please, Papa. If I ever meant anything to you, please let us in. We have nowhere else to go."

He stood silent for several tense beats before lowering the hammer and moving to the side. "Kitchen."

"My friend needs to lie down. Can I take him to the sitting room?" Dax would have never asked if her mother was alive. The room was reserved for special guests and off-limits to family and certainly to someone dressed in filthy clothes like Hank's.

He let out a loud sigh. "Fine."

Dax went through the door first, and Charlie and Hank followed. "Go through the kitchen and turn left," Dax said. "Put him on the couch."

Before Charlie and Hank disappeared deeper into the house, Hank met her father's stare. "Thank you, Mr. Xander. I know where your girls get their kindness."

"Do I know you?" Her father squinted.

"You met him once, Papa. Now let him lie down," Dax said.

Once they were alone and her father closed the kitchen door, he asked, "Who are these people, and what kind of trouble are you in?"

"The man you almost turned away is your son-in-law."

"You married?" He jerked his head back.

"No. May remarried after that worthless, no-good Logan was killed. Hank is the best thing to happen to her."

"May told me about Logan being killed. The paper said he was shot during a robbery several years back."

"Don't believe everything the papers say, especially in a county where the cops are dirty."

"Now I recognize May's husband. He brought her to your mother's funeral last year. Was she married to him then?"

"Yes."

Her father stiffened—his unhappy stance. "Why didn't she say anything?"

"You'll have to ask May." Her sister didn't have a mean bone in her body, so May must have had a good reason to hold back something so important.

Charlie reappeared. "I'm sorry to interrupt, Mr. Xander, but could I trouble you for a glass of water for my friend? He's really weak."

He gestured to a cabinet near the sink. "Glasses are up there. Help yourself. If you're hungry, I have some leftovers from the café down the street."

"Thank you, but we had our first meals in days a few hours ago. Overeating might make us sick."

Once Charlie returned to the sitting room, her father said, "I don't understand. Are you three down and out? Did you steal that truck?"

The accusation stung coming from her father. Of course, he would assume she could not make her way in the world. That if she was willing to violate the laws of God by kissing a girl, she would break any law. "No, we're not down and out, and we don't steal. I bought the truck two years ago. You can check the registration if you think I'm lying."

"Then you have some explaining to do. Why haven't your friends eaten in days? Why does my son-in-law look like he's gone nine rounds with Jack Dempsey? And who are you running from?"

"It's a long story."

"Long or short, I want to hear it." He crossed his arms in front of his chest like he used to when Dax was a little girl and had done something she wasn't supposed to. She knew he would not budge until he'd gotten an answer.

"A dirty sheriff arrested them on trumped-up charges. After they beat Hank to an inch of his life, he and Charlie escaped. Now the dirty sheriff is setting them up for killing two deputies."

"Did they?"

"No. They said the deputies were alive when they escaped, and I believe them. Hank and Charlie are good people."

"Why would this sheriff go after them in the first place?"

"His brother had a feud with us. He killed Logan and came after the rest of us. We had to defend ourselves. Now the new sheriff wants revenge for his brother's death and intends to finish the job his brother started."

"By the rest of us, do you also mean May? Was she in danger?"

"Yes, but Hank saved us, and after the dust settled, he married her a year later."

He ran a hand down his face, absorbing the brush with death his favorite daughter had gone through. "I'm glad your mother isn't alive to hear this. She would have gone off the deep end with worry."

"Oh, please. Mama wrote off May the day she defended me about the accident."

"Despite her harsh ways, she loved her girls."

"Well, she had a horrible way of showing it." When his eyes narrowed with anger, Dax dug deep to rein in her emotions. She had thirteen years' worth of pent-up feelings about her parents casting her out at sixteen for doing something as natural as breathing. "I don't want to argue with you, Papa. Can I use your phone to let May know we're safe? I'll pay you for the charges."

He nodded.

"Is the phone still in the hallway?"

"We moved it to the sitting room years ago when we started using it for actual sitting."

Dax silently chuckled and was surprised upon entering the sitting room. The settee and never-used fancy pillows were gone. Even the one she'd used to decorate her bed for her ill-fated first intimate encounter with Rose. Dax thought her mother never would have gotten rid of her grandmother's prized possession.

The room had been converted from a showpiece into a livable space, not unlike the main room in the Foster House residence. Hank was stretched across a comfortable couch with his eyes closed, and Charlie was seated in a cushy armchair.

"How is he?" Dax asked.

"Tired." Charlie glanced at Hank. "Jules would know what to do to help him."

"I think the best thing we can do for him is to let him rest and give him plenty of water to drink."

"You're probably right."

"I'm calling the Foster House to let them know you're okay. Would you like to talk to Jules if she's there?"

Charlie nodded, keeping their exchange to a minimum.

The phone was an upgrade to the candlestick one they had when Dax lived here. It was odd seeing how time marched on in this place. She'd had a static image of it in her head for thirteen years, but this wasn't it. Remnants of her childhood no longer existed except in memories.

Dax lifted the phone receiver and asked to be connected to the Half Moon Bay operator.

"How may I direct your call?"

"Holly, this is Dax. Are the phones still out at the Foster House?"

"Hi, Dax. The crew is here now. They expect to have service back up around six."

"Can you get a message to May and Rose?"

"Sure thing. Rose and Grace Parsons placed some calls from Edith's an hour ago. I'll call Henry, and he can run down to the

Foster House."

"Grace is in town?" *Finally*, Dax thought. Maybe now she could get a handle on things, and Hank and Charlie could turn themselves in without fearing a deputy would shoot them on sight.

"Yep."

Dax passed along her father's telephone number. "Have Henry tell Rose I'm in Alameda and tell May and Jules that Hank and Charlie are with me."

"Half the state is looking for them," Holly said. "Are they okay?"

"They're safe for now. I trust you won't tell anyone else about this."

"Of course not. Everyone in Half Moon Bay is rooting for their safe return. Your secret is safe with me."

CHAPTER TWENTY-SEVEN

Rose glanced down the hallway when she heard a door open and squinted to make sure she'd seen things correctly. Jules had said she was going to her bedroom to change out of her nurse's uniform. However, she'd just stepped from Grace's room and turned toward her door. The curious sight had her thinking about last month at the Beacon Club. Jules had stopped by to watch Rose perform and joined Grace at her table. They laughed that night, drank champagne, and whispered into each other's ears. Rose thought nothing of it then, but perhaps it was a sign of something germinating. Her sympathies went instantly to Charlie if it were the case.

Rose could not let her friend make the biggest mistake of her life. She turned toward May and Clive. "I'll be right back." Moments later, she knocked on Jules's door at the end of the hallway. "Jules, it's Rose. May I come in?"

"Yeah, come in," Jules said through the door. Rose opened it, discovering her wearing only her underthings while hanging up her uniform in the closet. She took out a day dress and slipped it over her head. "What do you want?"

Rose suddenly doubted the wisdom of her assumption. Charlie and Jules had been a couple for years. They loved one another, and until now, Rose never thought either would cheat on the other. However, there was no disputing what she had seen at the Beacon Club and here tonight. "I'm going to come right out and ask. Are you and Grace having an affair?"

Jules's face contorted into an odd shape she'd never seen before. It was a cross between shock and eating a lemon whole. "Why on Earth would you ask such a thing?"

Rose explained, but her suspicion sounded absurd the moment she said it. "What else am I supposed to think?"

"Anything but that." The hurt look on Jules's face said Rose was way off base.

"I'm sorry, Jules, but I couldn't stand by and watch you throw away an incredible relationship."

Jules shook her head. "I can't believe you would think so little of me to think I would treat Charlie like that."

Rose plopped her bottom on the mattress. "I know. I feel like a heel for even suggesting it." A heel didn't come close to describing how bad she felt. She felt lower than the scum from the bottom of the bay dredged up during yesterday's storm. "Forgive me?"

Jules offered one of her signature impish smiles, joining Rose on the bed. "It goes without saying."

"If it's not a fling, then what is it? Is Grace okay? I was worried about her earlier today. She was pale and nearly didn't make it upstairs."

"You'll have to ask her later. She's sleeping now." Jules was unusually cryptic, which meant something was wrong. A knock on the door drew her attention. "What is my room today? Grand Central?"

Rose laughed. "Come in."

Clive peeked his head inside. "Sorry to interrupt, ladies, but Henry from the department store stopped by. He said he received a message from Dax."

Rose sprung to her feet. She didn't want to admit it to the others, but she got concerned when Dax didn't meet up with

Phillip Gandy in the afternoon for their second meeting. "What did she say?"

"The message was short. She left a phone number where to reach her and said she was in Alameda with Hank and Charlie."

Jules bounced to her feet. "Are they okay?"

"I'm afraid that's all I know," Clive said. "I checked. Phone service was restored earlier than expected. I thought you two would want to be there when we call Dax's number."

"Yes, of course," Rose said. "Have you woken Grace?"

"Yes, she's coming."

The three rushed to the living room, where Grace and May were huddled on the couch, clutching hands. Jules sat next to May, assuming the same long, worried expression mixed with a dash of hope.

"Let's make the call," Clive said, stringing the phone to the seating area. He had the operator dial the number and handed it to Rose. "Dax is expecting you to call."

She sat on the coffee table, facing the others, and loosely held the earpiece end of the handset so Jules and May could listen. The call connected.

"Hello?" The man's voice was surprising.

"I'm looking for Dax Xander. She left a message to reach her at this number."

"Hold on," the man said.

"He sounds familiar." May narrowed her brow, digging deep into her memory.

"Hello?" Dax's voice was a soothing salve, wiping away every worry.

"Dax. It's Rose. Are you okay?"

"I'm fine. I found Hank and Charlie at Logan's old house earlier this morning." She further explained about Wilkes's men, the nail-biting car chase, and the harrowing launch onto the ferry. "Once I figured out we were in Alameda, I went to the only place I could think of."

"Papa's house," May said.

"Was that May?" Dax asked.

"Yes, it's me, Dax. I'm glad you're okay. Can I talk to Hank?" May and Hank exchanged several tender words, as did Jules and Charlie when it was their turn to talk. When Dax returned to the phone, Rose filled her in on Grace's meeting with the governor tomorrow morning and her call with Phillip Gandy to put a halt to the story.

"Please tell Grace I'm sorry. I hadn't fully considered the impact the media attention might have on her. I was thinking about how I could help Hank and Charlie."

"Grace knows and doesn't blame you."

Grace mouthed to Rose that she would send Clive to Dax as soon as they hung up.

"She's sending Clive to Alameda to retrieve the evidence against Roy Wilkes, so she'll have it for her meeting with Governor Rolph."

"Tell him to be careful. Wilkes's men followed me from Half Moon Bay today. I'm sure they're staking out the Foster House." Following her confirming reply, Dax asked, "Can anyone else hear me?"

"No, just me now. Why?"

"I don't want May to hear this, but Hank is in bad shape. I think he might have a few broken ribs. Can you ask Jules what I can do to make him more comfortable?"

Clive caught Rose's attention and mouthed, "I'll leave in fifteen minutes." She acknowledged, mouthing the timeframe back.

"I'll ask and have her pass along instructions to Clive. He'll leave in a few minutes, so expect him soon. Everyone agrees. You and the others should stay there. It's a safe place to hide out."

Following an emotional goodbye and Dax's promise to call the Foster House at eight in the morning, Rose cornered Jules across the room and explained Dax's concern. "What can she do?"

Jules replied, "I'll grab some supplies."

"That's a great idea. Clive can treat him until he can see a doctor."

"You don't understand. I'm going with him." Jules waved Clive over and explained. "If you drive me to the clinic, I can pick up everything I need to treat Hank."

"It's too dangerous," Clive said. "I might have to lose a tail if Wilkes's men follow us."

"I don't care." Jules stood firm. "I'm going."

Rose didn't argue. She knew there would be no talking Jules out of going. After informing May, and Clive and Jules left, she walked May home for the night and promised to call if there was any change.

"I'll be back to start breakfast before Grace has to leave to meet with the governor," May said.

"That would be wonderful." Rose left, knowing she could not talk May out of cooking. Her way of helping always involved food. She had a knack for choosing the perfect meal or snack to make everyone feel better.

Once back at the Foster House, Rose sat beside Grace on the couch, keeping enough distance between them to not send the wrong message after last week's unexpected kiss at the Seaside Club. Though, if she were backed against a wall and forced to admit it, she would have to say she'd pulled back too slowly from the kiss, and, for a brief second, it felt too familiar than it should have. It didn't rouse her like Grace's kisses once did, but it was comfortable, nonetheless. However, the uneasiness it caused didn't negate the friendship she still felt for Grace, nor her concern.

Rose shifted on one hip to better look her in the eye. "Something is wrong, isn't it? You've been acting strange for a week. The kiss. We can't reach you for days. You nearly faint coming upstairs. And now you and Jules are thick as thieves in your room." Rose softened her expression and grazed her hand. "Please, tell me what's going on."

Grace's smile looked forced. "And I thought nothing got past Jules. She has nothing on you."

"What is it?"

"Breast cancer."

Sensing her heart skip a beat, Rose gasped and threw a hand over her mouth. The thought of Grace being sick was incomprehensible. She was a larger-than-life force of nature. The idea of something invisible besting her was unimaginable. When her head stopped spinning, Rose finally asked, "How bad?"

"We caught it early. The doctor removed the lump on Friday, and I spent the weekend recovering from the surgery. Doctor Shapiro thinks he got the entire tumor."

Rose felt horrible for thinking Grace had picked the worst time to be absent. She didn't pick it. The time had picked her. "So, is that it? You're going to be better?"

"He wants me to undergo radium treatment after I heal to lessen the chance of the cancer returning, but I'm holding off to weigh my options. The side effects are frightening."

"Who knows besides Clive and Jules?" Rose asked.

"Greta found out on her own." Grace didn't have to explain. It was crystal clear. Greta had discovered the tumor during a moment of intimacy.

"Ah." Rose nodded. "How are things between you and her? Is she supporting you through this?"

"She wants to."

"But you're going back into your shell." Rose had seen firsthand how Grace protected her heart from further destruction. Never talking of passion beyond the physical. Never sharing experiences beyond the bedroom. She treated her "distractions" with kindness and grace but never opened herself to more than disappointment for a missed liaison.

Until, Rose thought. A memory of the night Grace let her go after Dax appeared in town came to the forefront, something which might explain last week's kiss. She remembered her saying something about Rose's hope of finding Dax had made her think she'd been the fool. Grace's vulnerability that night should have set off giant warning bells that Rose was more than a distraction, but it was setting off different bells now. It was why she would not let Greta in when she needed the most comfort.

"You know me so well, Rose."

"Which is why I'm saying this now. You need to let her be there for you. I know you love Clive, but you also need to be reminded that you are a desirable woman, not someone to pity and look after."

"How is it you know precisely what I need?"

Rose lifted Grace's hand and drew it to her heart. "Because you'll always live in here. I'm grateful for the time we shared. You helped me fine-tune my passion for singing and prepared me for Dax, for which I'll always love you." Rose formed a nose-scrunching smile, recalling a fond memory after Dax returned to her life. "You once told me I'd taught you love could be a winning proposition. It still can be. I hurt you and will always regret doing so. But please, don't give up on having love in your life."

"I love Clive."

"But you don't have passion. You need both. I know Greta loves you. Let yourself love her back."

"I'm sure she—"

"Don't say it, Grace Parsons. Don't say she doesn't love you. I see it every time you two are in the same room together. She can't take her eyes off you and finds every reason to be with you."

"That's lust."

"It's both. If Greta only wanted sex from you, she would have run for the hills after learning of your diagnosis, but she offered to see you at your worst and get you through this. If that isn't love, I don't know what is."

"Perhaps you're right." The slight smile forming on Grace's lips suggested Rose was getting through. She'd planted the seed and could do no more now than watch it grow.

CHAPTER TWENTY-EIGHT

Dax's father stepped through the front door, carrying a paper sack full of takeout boxes from the diner down the street. When Dax lived here, a trip to the Hobnob was a rare treat, occurring only if her father made more than expected from a carpentry job. Based on the lack of food in the house, the restaurant now was likely his daily retreat. He placed three boxes and a dollar on the coffee table. "Your change," he said to Dax. "I paid for my own."

"Thank you. We really appreciate you picking these up." She didn't want to argue with him but left the dollar on the table when she grabbed her meal.

"Like I said. I was heading there anyway." He adjusted his grip on the to-go sack and walked to the kitchen, where the family used to eat all their meals.

Dax distributed the boxes and utensils she'd gathered from the kitchen. She considered sitting with Hank and Charlie, but Charlie still appeared uncomfortable around her. Dax's options were an awkward meal with her former best friend, with the father who turned her out at sixteen, or alone. Taking the easy way out was attractive, but this might be her only opportunity to get answers from her father.

"If you two don't mind, I'll eat in the kitchen."

Charlie answered with a nod.

Hank grimaced while pushing himself upright and opening his food container. He was in pain but was finally getting some color back. "By all means, Dax. We'll be fine."

Joining her father in the kitchen stirred memories of regular family meals at this table. He was in his traditional chair closest to the wall and farthest from the stove and counter, where he was of no help during meals if something needed fetching.

"Mind if I join you?" Dax waited for his nod. She was no longer a child and didn't want to feel like one, so she didn't consider sitting in her customary childhood seat. Instead, she took May's old chair, signaling times had changed.

He continued to eat and drink his water without saying a word. The tension was so thick she would need her sharpest saw to cut through it. She would start by acknowledging at least one elephant in the room. "How have you been getting along since Mama died last year?"

Her father held his fork tightly. His piercing stare made her think he might have plunged it into her if Hank and Charlie weren't in the other room. "You couldn't bring yourself to attend the funeral, so how I'm getting along is of no business of yours."

"You really didn't expect me to come. She humiliated Rose and me, sent me away, and then tried to send me to a cousin's farm in Kansas after May's accident."

He shook his head in dismay. "May said you had become a loving, caring, responsible woman, but she was wrong. The woman was your mother. No matter the bad blood between you two, you should have shown your respect for her giving you life."

Dax's lips trembled at the harsh truth—she had disappointed herself. "You're right. I'm sorry." She would regret not being the bigger person.

"That was the most hurtful thing you could have done to me." He returned his focus to his food.

"It wasn't my intention, Papa."

"I guess it's my fault." He played with his food some, fluffing the mashed potatoes. "I taught you many things but failed to teach you about funerals. They're about the dead but are for the living. It's a time to say goodbye and say your final piece. I hope you learn the lesson before it's too late."

"Too late for what?"

"Before I join your mother."

Dax assessed her father's appearance, looking for signs of an underlying health problem, but saw none. "Are you sick, Papa?"

"Don't get your hopes up."

"Why would you say such a horrible thing? I hate what you did to me, but I don't hate *you*. I don't wish you ill will."

"We did what we thought was best for you. People were starting to ask questions about you and that girl."

"That's because Mama made a public spectacle of dragging Rose down the street. Of course, people would ask questions. What did she expect? And don't tell me she sent me away for my own good. She did it for herself. The whispers made it impossible for her to hold her head high in church or at the neighborhood market. Out of sight, out of mind. It was easier to get rid of me than to understand me."

"It's not true."

"But it was how it felt. Since we're talking about hurtful things, I can tell you Mama hurt me, but you cut me to the bone. After all the time we spent together. After you taught me your life's work, I expected more from you. I expected you to stand up for me."

"How could I? What you did was wrong." He shook his head.

"Wrong? You liked it when I worked and dressed like a man. You encouraged it. But as soon as I loved like one, suddenly I was immoral. I needed you to do anything but turn your back on me. I loved you, Papa, and you did nothing to keep me here when Rose and I did nothing wrong. How could love between two consenting people be wrong?"

"You were kids. It wasn't love. It was a sin. The Hamiltons blamed you. We blamed her. We all agreed to separate you two for good but not on who should go. Sending you both away was the only solution."

"Well, it didn't work because we found each other. Some would say it was luck, but I believe we were destined to find each other again. So does May. We may have been kids then, but Rose and I are grown women now. Our relationship is more loving than anything you and Mama ever had."

He popped his head up. His eyes were wide with shock. "So you found her, and May let you carry on with that woman?"

"Not only did she let me, but she also invited Rose to live with us. May and her husband don't care about us being women. They care about our happiness. I wish you could see how happy Rose makes me. I will love her all my life."

He buried his face in his hands as if the idea of his daughter loving a woman was worse than never having a relationship with his daughters again. Worse than living and dying a sad, lonely man.

"Suit yourself, Papa." Dax scooped up her dinner box. "Thank you for letting us stay here. We'll be out of your hair tomorrow." She stepped away but stopped before exiting the room and glanced over her shoulder. "If you want to see how we're all getting along, you can be my guest at the Seaside Hotel in Half Moon Bay. I'm the manager. You might like to know I'm overseeing the crew remodeling it for the reopening on the Fourth of July. I'm making good use of everything you taught me."

Dax left the kitchen feeling worse than when she arrived. She had hoped his feelings might have changed, and they could have reconnected as father-daughter again. Unfortunately, some people never change, especially someone as stubborn as him. However, he had changed her tonight. When he died, she would be at his funeral and speak about the good memories she had of him. The living and the dead deserved as much.

As Dax entered the sitting room, two headlights shone through the gap between the drapes covering the window facing the street. Placing her food on the table, she retrieved the pistol tucked into the waistband at the small of her back, went to the window, and peeked through. A familiar-looking Packard backed into the driveway and disappeared around the side of the house, making her relax.

"Clive is here," she said to Charlie and Hank. Charlie picked up their food containers and followed Dax into the kitchen. She stuffed the gun into her coat pocket. Her father was still at the table. His eyes looked misty as if he'd been crying.

"Papa, another friend is here to pick up something I have. He won't stay long. Is it okay to invite him inside?"

"Sure." His voice cracked with emotion.

When Dax passed him, she briefly touched his shoulder and said softly, "Thank you."

She wrapped her hand around the butt of her pistol, keeping it inside her pocket where her father would not see it. The car's lights went out, and two figures, each carrying bags, exited the Packard, putting Dax on alert. She'd expected only Clive. Two people might mean something was wrong, so she hit the light switch by the door, casting the kitchen into darkness.

"What the heck?" her father said.

"It's okay, Papa. I need to see a little better to make sure it's my friend." There was no sense in alarming him. Nonetheless, Dax pulled out her pistol and held it close to her chest. While her eyes adjusted to the dark, she focused on the people walking toward the back door. One was an average-sized man, and the other was shorter, thin, and—Jules. "What the heck is she doing here?"

"Who is she?" her father asked, lacing his question with an accusatory tone, one Dax didn't like.

"Another friend." Dax stepped to the side, using the wall as protection, opened the door, and waved them in. Clive and Jules quickened their pace. Dax shut the door and turned on the lights after they stepped inside.

Charlie's eyes lit with recognition. She rushed to Jules, pulling her in for a tight, emotional embrace. No words were needed to feel the relief in both women. "What are you doing here?" Charlie asked. "It's too dangerous for you to be here."

"Dax mentioned Hank needed medical attention and asked for advice," Jules said, dangling a leather satchel from a hand.

Charlie gave Dax the side-eye. Dax would have come too if the situation had been reversed. She offered Jules an impish smile. "I only wanted to know how we could make Hank more comfortable. You didn't have to come."

"I thought coming would make it easier to assess his injuries and give him the right treatment. Where is he?"

"I'll show you." Charlie led her to the next room.

Her father looked between her and Clive with questioning eyes.

Dax said, "Clive, this is my father, Harmon Xander." Neither offered to shake hands under the awkward circumstance but acknowledged each other with silent nods. She turned to her father. "The woman was Jules. She's a nurse and is here to help Hank." Dax got right to business, redirecting her attention to Clive. "I have the pictures in the other room. Follow me."

She led Clive to the sitting room and stopped at a small end table. She picked up and handed him the folder containing the photographs to show the governor. "This is everything Grace will need to convince the governor that Roy Wilkes is a corrupt jerk and should be investigated for murder."

"This should help." Clive set his focus on Hank as Jules examined him. His eyes narrowed in concern. "How bad is he?"

"He said it looks worse than it feels, but I'm not buying it. He favors his left side and limps like he's in a lot of pain."

"Thanks for looking out for him. He's like a brother to me." Clive opened his bag on the coffee table closer to where Jules worked on Hank.

"He's family, and so are you." Dax inspected the bag contents, discovering he'd brought handguns and sawed-off shotguns with extra bullets and shells. She didn't need to ask questions to know the items were their last line of defense. "Hopefully, we won't need to use these."

Jules wrapped Hank's torso with a bandage roll and gave him a pill. "This is a mild narcotic. It will help with the pain from those ribs. I know it's counterintuitive, but moving around and taking deep breaths will help, but don't overdo it. You need to keep those lungs working to prevent pneumonia."

"Moving around won't be a problem," Hank said. "We shouldn't stay here."

"Stay put until we call about Grace's meeting with the governor," Clive said. "We should know something before noon." Hank looked relieved. "We should go before the neighbors get curious about the growing number of cars in the driveway."

Jules positioned Hank at an incline on the couch. "Sleep propped up like this. The angle will let you sleep better and put less pressure on those ribs."

Jules and Clive said their goodbyes to Dax and Charlie in the kitchen and exited through the back door. Once their car rolled down the driveway, Dax's father eyed Charlie. "You're like her, aren't you?" His question was more of an accusation than a statement.

Charlie stood tall. "If you're asking whether I'm in love with the woman who just left, the answer is yes."

Dax stepped forward. "Jules is an amazing nurse and would make an incredible doctor if she had the money for medical school. And Charlie is a top-notch mechanic. She can fix anything with an engine or wheels. We're like everyone else. We love differently, but it's still love. She and Jules have been a couple for over a decade. They're a shining example of what any couple could and should be—faithful and loving."

Her father's sour expression softened some. She likely didn't turn him into an ally like May and Hank, but perhaps their talking made a dent in his wall of disdain for odd people like her and Charlie.

Charlie met Dax's eyes, lacing her nod with appreciation. "I should look at the truck and make sure it's ready to use in the morning."

"Do you still have your tools in the garage, Papa?" Dax asked.

He nodded. "I haven't used them in years. I haven't even driven that old Model T since it stopped working. There's no need. I don't go anywhere."

"You stopped doing carpentry work?"

"Not for a year." He lifted his hands, palms inward. "Arthritis. It hurts too much."

The thought of her father no longer working as a carpenter saddened her. It defined him, and she was sure he was lost without being able to do it. She wondered what he did for money but didn't want to pry. "Could she use them to check my truck?"

"Makes no difference to me." He shrugged. "Flashlights are in the same drawer."

Dax retrieved two flashlights from the utility drawer and asked Charlie, "Need an extra pair of hands to hold the light?"

"Sure. It would be a big help."

Dax and Charlie went outside, walking side by side like old friends. The tension between them for the last three years had dissipated some. Dax hoped the trend would continue.

Charlie kept her head low and stared forward. "Thanks for what you said in there."

"I meant every word. You and Jules are amazing people. I look at how you care for one another and want to do the same for Rose."

"You do, and Rose does the same for you. You're good for each other."

"Then why aren't you and I good for each other?" Dax lifted the garage door and pulled the string to turn on the overhead light.

"I guess it's more about me than you." Charlie located the tools she needed to inspect the truck.

"I'd like to help you work things out so we can be friends again."

Charlie met Dax's stare. "Maybe."

"Maybe" was the most Dax had gotten from Charlie in three years. She took it as an excellent sign.

Over the next hour, they worked together as a team, with Dax fetching tools and holding the flashlight and Charlie tightening things here and there and adding grease she'd found in the garage. Except for discussing the task at hand, they didn't talk. Nonetheless, it felt like they'd turned from being estranged to something else.

"She's about as good as she's gonna get without replacing a few things," Charlie said.

"Will she work if we have to get away in a hurry?"

"I suppose so, but I don't know for how long." Charlie rubbed the back of her neck, focusing on Dax's truck. "That crazy landing onto the ferry deck weakened the front axle."

"It was pretty crazy, wasn't it?"

"But it worked. You did some fancy driving in town, too. How did you learn to do that?"

"I don't know. I went by instinct." Dax shifted her stare to the Model T sitting in the garage. Based on the layers of dust on it, Dax figured it hadn't been used since last summer. Then it dawned on her. Her father had lost his wife and livelihood both in the same year. No wonder he didn't get the car fixed. He had no desire or money. She had to do something to help. "Hey, Charlie. Do you think you could take a look at my pop's car? Maybe figure out what's wrong with it?"

"I'd need the key to it."

"He used to keep it in the glove box." Dax slipped inside the vehicle and opened the compartment. Some things never changed. "Got it."

"Give her a go," Charlie said.

Dax put the gear into neutral, pressed the brakes, and inserted and turned the key. The engine tried to start but made sputtering noises.

"It sounds like the carburetor. Maybe the spark plugs. I'll give the parts a good cleaning and see if it helps. If not, I'll write down what your pops will need to keep her going."

"Thanks, Charlie. I really appreciate this."

"It's the least I can do since he's opened his home to us." Charlie spent the next hour taking out, inspecting, and cleaning various engine parts. She also crawled beneath and greased all the joints. When she came up, wiping her hands with an old rag, she said, "Give her another try."

Dax turned the key again, pressing the gas a little, and the engine started right up, bringing a smile to her lips. Fixing the car would not fix what was wrong with her father's life, but it might make things easier. "You're a genius, Charlie."

"Give her a little more gas and less choke. I want to hear the engine at higher RPMs."

Dax manipulated the pedal and lever and revved the engine higher. It sounded great to her.

"It needs a little adjusting." Charlie disappeared under the hood. A moment later, the engine sounded smoother. She appeared again, signaling Dax to kill the engine. "She's ready to drive, but a few things are worn out and should be replaced soon. I'll make him a list so the mechanic won't try to take him for a few extra bucks."

Dax returned the key to the glove box, exited the car, and pulled Charlie in for a tight embrace. "You're a good person, Charlie. You're going to make my pops very happy."

Charlie wrapped her arms around Dax, holding her tight. "This is what friends do for each other."

Dax released her grasp, holding Charlie in her gaze. They had some cleanup to do, but they had weathered the storm. She smiled and said, "Yes, they do."

CHAPTER TWENTY-NINE

With Dax keeping late hours at the Beacon Club for the last three years, Rose was no stranger to falling asleep alone, but she always woke next to Dax. This morning's empty side of the bed was a harsh reminder that the people she loved were still in danger. She ran a hand across the cold sheets, wondering if Dax and the others were safe or if Wilkes's men had tracked them down during the night. It was too early to grow concerned, so she pushed back the urge to call the Xander house out of fear of riling up Mr. Xander.

Dax only spoke of her father when a memory popped up while she had to use her carpentry tools. She'd get a distant look in her eyes, giving the impression that losing contact with him was her one regret. Rose wondered what it was like to reconnect with him and be in her childhood home again after all these years.

A memory of the last time she and Dax were in her Alameda bedroom flashed in her head. She'd never been more nervous and excited in her life. She recalled splashing on a dash of the perfume Dax had said she really, really liked before walking to her house for their first intimate experience. The choice was intentional to titillate Dax's senses and evoke the response she'd received that day—a carnal hunger.

Rose ran a finger down the gap between her breasts, trying to replicate the exhilarating, beyond-belief feeling of being touched for the first time. However, nothing she did to herself could come close to recreating what Dax had drawn out of her. Not even when Grace took her virginity could she recreate the feeling of simultaneous awakening between two women. The overwhelming mutual nervousness rooted in naivete had since created an unbreakable bond, connecting her to Dax.

After getting dressed, Rose opened her bedroom door as Grace and Clive stepped from the room across the hallway. A strong sense of confidence began to grow. She knew everyone would soon be home safe—because Grace Parsons could move mountains and stop the rains to get what she wanted. And helping her family was top on her list.

"I thought you would have been gone by now," Rose said.

"I could lie and say we didn't set the alarm clock," Grace said, "but I needed the extra sleep. If we leave now, we should still make it to the governor's home before he arrives."

"You're not planning to skip breakfast, are you?" Rose turned to Clive. "Please force her to eat before you leave."

"This is precisely why I didn't say anything until last night." Grace rolled her eyes. "Clive doting over me is one thing, but two against one is an unfair advantage."

"Make it three against one." Jules exited her room. Brutus romped down the hallway ahead of her. "I'm glad you shared things with Rose. The more support you have during the first year after cancer surgery, the better. We're all here for you, Grace."

"Then let's eat." Grace offered Rose her arm. Halfway down, the smell of coffee and freshly cooked bacon filled the stairwell. The lights were on in the dining room, and May was preparing breakfast when the group entered the kitchen.

"I'll have the food plated in a few minutes," May said. "Rose, I could use help with the toast and juice."

"I'm on it." Rose went to work.

"This looks lovely," Grace said, wrapping an arm around May's back. "We're running a little later than I'd prefer today. Would it be possible to pack this to go so Clive and I can eat in the car?"

"Absolutely. I can make a breakfast sandwich from the bacon, eggs, and toast and place some potatoes in a small box for you to share. Coffee, orange juice, or both?"

"Coffee for the driver and juice for me would be wonderful. I can't thank you enough."

"Working to bring Hank home to me is thanks enough." May cupped Grace's hand. "Please do what you do best."

"And what is that?"

"Make people bend over backward to give you what you want when you enter a room."

"I will do my best. Charlie and Hank are family."

After Grace and Clive took off with their to-go meals, a car followed them down the highway. It was likely someone working for Roy Wilkes. The rest of the group went to the dining room to eat. Rose wanted to ask Jules about Grace's prognosis but not in front of May. She would never violate Grace's trust and privacy.

After the meal, May, Jules, and Rose did the dishes and returned to play gin while waiting for Dax to call. Well, Rose watched while May and Jules played. After an hour, Rose grew concerned. Dax had promised to reach out by eight this morning, but it was half past. Waiting was not the strong suit of anyone in the room. Each glanced at the phone by the register frequently, willing it to ring.

"Gin." May threw down her cards, but the satisfaction of winning yet another game against Jules was gone. So was Jules's frustration of losing for the eighth consecutive time.

"Maybe Dax overslept. I should call," Rose said. Without waiting for concurrence, she went to the register. She raised the operator. "Good morning, Holly. I need to reach a number in Alameda."

"Is it the number Dax gave me yesterday?"

"Yes, she's late calling me back."

"Happy to help. Hold, please." The call went silent for several moments before Holly returned. "I'm sorry, Rose. The signal tells me the phone is off the hook. If you know a neighbor's number, I can ring them to check on Dax."

"I'm afraid we don't. Thanks for trying, Holly." Rose hung up the phone. Her mind jumped to the obvious conclusion— Wilkes's men had found them and stormed the house, knocking over the phone. The only question was whether they were all dead or had been captured.

She explained the situation to May and Jules, leaving out her horrifying assumptions. "What do we do? Do we wait?"

"We've already waited four days," Jules said. "They may be in trouble."

"Whatever happened overnight to Dax, Charlie, and Hank may have also happened to my father," May said. "We need to go there now."

"I don't disagree," Rose said, "but one of us should stay here in case Dax calls or sneaks in."

"I'll go, but I'll have to lose whoever follows me." Jules scratched her head. "I remember what Clive did last night and could duplicate it, but I'm not sure if I remember the directions to the Xander house. You'll have to write them down."

"I know how to get there, but I'd likely slow you down if you had to make a run for it," May said. "You should go, Rose. You also know Alameda like the back of your hand. Take the Seaside truck."

Rose was relieved that May had bowed out. She hadn't wanted to be the one to state the obvious or deny her the choice of searching for her husband. "Thank you, May."

"I have an idea to help you shake Wilkes's men staking out the front of the Foster House." While May prepared her diversion, Jules and Rose hopped into the pickup.

"I'm glad Charlie gave you driving lessons, Jules," Rose said. "Is it hard?"

"Not really, but it takes practice."

"Hmmmm." Maybe Rose should learn. She didn't like relying on Dax or Hank whenever she needed to go somewhere not within walking distance.

Jules drove along the paved area behind the Foster House and the other businesses until they reached the Seaside Hotel. She then inched the truck to the mouth of the entrance to peek down the sidewalk at the Foster House. May was at the driver's window of a sedan that had been parked across the street since last night. She knocked on the window, raising the breakfast tray enough for the driver to see.

Jules's cue came when he rolled down the window. She slowly pulled out to not draw attention and drove north on the main highway. A check of the side mirrors confirmed the car hadn't followed them. When the Foster House was finally out of sight, both women let out weighty sighs.

"I think we lost them," Jules said.

Rose glanced over her shoulder out the back window frequently until they reached the end of town to make sure they weren't followed. "I think you're right. May is a genius."

If things went right, they should reach San Francisco in an hour, be on the ferry in another thirty minutes, and be at the Xander house another half hour after that. They would get answers in two hours, but Rose could not get past the disturbing vision of Dax, Hank, and Charlie lying dead on the floor. She had the feeling this would be the longest drive of her life.

CHAPTER THIRTY

The breakfast May had packed was delicious and filling. It was no wonder the Foster House was the most popular eatery in Half Moon Bay. If Grace thought May would be open to the idea, she would suggest opening a Foster House in San Francisco or Los Angeles. Even in a sluggish economy, people had to eat, and her cooking style and affordable prices made for a winning combination in the current climate.

An hour after leaving the Foster House, Clive pulled up to the palatial Rolph estate in San Francisco's Presidio Heights neighborhood. It far surpassed Grace's property in scale and lavishness, starting with the ornate iron gate. The intricate design with flourishes and a giant R on both panels spoke to wealth as much as vanity.

Clive stopped at the shack guarding the gate and rolled down his window, letting in the cool morning air. An armed, uniformed state police officer stepped out. "How may I help you?" he asked. A second officer on the other end of the gate approached the Packard, peering through the back windows.

"This is my wife, Grace Parsons." Clive leaned back so the guard could see her clearly. "She arranged for a meeting with the governor through Sara."

The officer tipped his eight-point cap with the state police emblem pinned front and center. "Yes, Mr. Parsons. We've been expecting you. Please park near the main entrance." He retreated into his guard shack and pressed a button, retracting the heavy iron fence panels.

Clive issued a two-finger salute and drove through the gate. An army of landscapers was out taming each bush, shrub, and expanse of grass on both sides of the curved driveway into a perfectly manicured scenery. He followed the brick pavers to the main house, passing the dramatic entrance marked by Greek columns and wide sweeping steps before parking.

Grace ascended the steps, holding Clive's arm more firmly than usual. Her strength was returning, but not as quickly as she had hoped. The door opened when she reached the top.

Sara appeared at the opening. "Good morning, Mrs. Parsons. I trust the drive was comfortable."

"Very."

"May I take your coat? I've arranged for you to wait in the sunroom."

"If it's not too much trouble, I'd prefer the patio. I was cooped up inside for days and would welcome the fresh morning air."

"It's no trouble at all. I'll have refreshments and blankets brought out."

Grace and Clive followed Sara through the plush, immaculate home to the patio. The back garden was even more extensive than the front, thick with colorful flowers. "My, this is beautiful," Grace said. "I've never seen it in full bloom. Please tell the gardeners their work is impeccable."

"I'll pass along the sentiment, ma'am," Sara said. "I received word from the security detail. Governor Rolph and his entourage are on the ferry. He should be here shortly."

"Thank you."

Minutes later, a butler delivered a tray of ice-cold water, coffee, muffins, and a blanket for Grace's lap. She thanked him before he scurried off. After Clive poured her some water, she ruminated on the reason for her urgent meeting. In her thirty-five years, she had encountered only two people who could spark in her a burning need to take dire action, and both men had the last name of Wilkes.

Frankie Wilkes, her supposedly trustworthy business partner, was involved in the murder of May's father-in-law and had fired Rose to cover his tracks. Those acts had angered her to the point of tunnel vision. She saw nothing but the need for revenge. Roy Wilkes had turned the tables: retaliation was his game, something Grace was intimately familiar with. He would not stop until everyone in his sight was destroyed or dead. However, she had something he didn't—Governor Rolph's admiration and friendship. Being his primary campaign contributor and having rallied the vote of the upper crust to put him into office strengthened their bond but did not form its basis. They had been friends long before he became a politician.

Twenty minutes passed before the patio door opened again. Clive stood when the governor and Sara stepped outside, remaining by the door while he approached. Her old friend appeared worn down from weeks of travel. His receding thin gray hair and subtle matching mustache made him seem more distinguished than when Fatty Arbuckle first had introduced them at a Hollywood party more than a decade ago. He'd dabbled in documentaries and comedy shorts before turning his interest to the shipping industry and politics.

Grace came to her feet, greeting the governor of the fastest-growing and sixth-largest state in the country. Only the governors from New York, Pennsylvania, Illinois, Ohio, and Texas held more influence based on population. However, when this man made a decision, things happened instantly, not gradually.

"James, it's so good to see you. Thank you for agreeing to meet with me so soon after your trip."

"I never turn down the opportunity to chat with my dear friend." Rolph gestured toward the chairs. "Let's sit and discuss what has you concerned."

Once seated, Grace opened with, "You know of my history with Frank and Roy Wilkes."

"Yes, of course. It's a shame greed and revenge too often motivate men."

"No truth better told. Roy Wilkes was elected sheriff of San Mateo County during a special election. He took office a few days ago and is already wreaking havoc on my businesses, family, and friends in Half Moon Bay. He arrested and badly beat a dear friend on questionable morals charges and my husband's cousin, who runs my club, on a Volstead Act violation. You met Hank at my home several times."

"Yes, Hank. He's a good man. I didn't connect the names earlier today when my assistant briefed me this morning. Are you telling me Hank is one of the two fugitives who escaped custody and killed two San Mateo deputies?"

"I can say this with certainty. Charlene and Hank escaped custody, but they did not kill those men. Wilkes did." Grace slid a folder containing Dax's photographs of the evidence against Roy across the table. "While I don't have proof of his current crime, these pictures demonstrate his involvement in the murder of a Canadian national who went missing in Half Moon Bay eight years ago. The man's remains were found hidden in the wall of Frankie's office, and we have an eyewitness who placed Roy Wilkes with the deceased in the same office the day he went missing. The FBI was originally looking into the Wilkes brothers but backed off once the Prohibition agents on Frankie's payroll talked with them."

"I can see why you're concerned."

"I've spoken with Charlene and Hank. They are hiding at a house a short ferry ride from here. They told me Hank broke loose to prevent one of Wilkes's thugs from forcing himself on my dear friend in a vile sexual act. The attacker and the one who watched it happen deserved the beating they got, but Hank left them handcuffed and very much alive. I can't prove it, but Roy Wilkes's brutal history tells me he killed his own men for letting the prisoners escape and to make a convincing argument for shooting Charlene and Hank on sight."

"What do you need from me?"

"To bring them in safely until this can be sorted out and Wilkes can be investigated for his crimes and removed from his post."

Governor Rolph waved over his personal assistant. "Sara, please ask the chief of my security detail to join us on the patio."

"Of course, sir." Sara disappeared inside.

Rolph patted Grace's hand. "I'm happy to help. Mr. Wilkes has made a critical mistake by targeting you. I won't stand for corruption at any level in this state and have made my stance on Prohibition abundantly clear. I won't enforce the Volstead Act or support those officials who do. Mr. Wilkes has stirred a hornet's nest and is about to get stung."

"I appreciate anything you can do, James."

The patio door opened. A tall, muscular, uniformed officer in his forties emerged from the mansion and approached the table. "You wanted to see me, sir?"

"Yes. Sergeant Rawlins, this is Grace Parsons." The governor explained the highlights of the situation, including the false accusation of murdering the deputies. "Since I suspect law enforcement in the county is compromised with corruption, we must bring in the fugitives unharmed. They are not far from here. How many men can you send to bring them into custody?"

"Is there reason to suspect the sheriff's office might offer resistance?" Rawlins asked.

The governor glanced at Grace with questioning eyes. She replied, "Deputies know they took a ferry to Alameda Island. I'm sure they are scouring the area. In fact, someone followed us here today."

"It's the gray 1931 Ford Model A parked a block down the street," Clive said. "Two men in suits are inside."

"I'll have the duty guard check it out," Rawlins replied before turning his attention to the governor. "It looks like the deputies mean business if they have left their jurisdiction. I'd like to be prepared and bring the night shift team of eight men."

"Nine, if you'd like an extra gun," Clive said.

Rawlins inspected him with a critical eye. "This is a police matter, sir. We'll be fine."

The governor chuckled and turned his head to better look Rawlins in the eye. "You're talking to the Army's second most decorated sharpshooter during World War I, a man who was awarded the Distinguished Service Cross. The man you're about to bring in is his cousin, *the* most decorated sharpshooter in the war, also a recipient of that medal. These men are genuine American heroes. If your team enters a quagmire, you'd be a fool to turn down his help."

The officer looked at Clive with newfound respect in his eyes. "I'll keep it in mind."

"I know where they're hiding and can take you there."

"You can ride with me," Rawlins said. "Bring whatever firepower you think you might need."

Clive stood, replying with a firm nod before turning to the governor. "My wife isn't feeling well. May I trouble your staff to make her comfortable until I return?"

"She'll be pampered like the queen she is."

"Thank you, sir." Clive knelt at Grace's feet. "Please rest while I'm gone. I'll call as soon as I can."

Grace traced a finger down Clive's cheek. Loyalty and bravery had earned him stacks of medals on his military uniform. They also made Grace love him more with each passing year. He took on her fights, even when it put him in danger or might cost him dearly. Today, he offered the same for Hank and Charlie.

"I trust you will. I know you'll return with the people we love."

CHAPTER THIRTY-ONE

Dax had one word to describe waking in her old bedroom—bizarre. She was still a child the last time she woke up in this bed. And her only responsibilities were daily chores and homework. By noon, her mother had packed the things she allowed her to keep, left the twenty-five-cent ferry fare on the entry table, and turned her back when she walked out the door.

She considered herself an orphan that day, without parents to raise and care for her. It was the day she shed her childhood. Yes, she would go to live with May, but her tenure under that roof depended on Logan's goodwill. She refused to leave herself vulnerable to his whims by merely earning her keep with chores. Instinctively, she knew her construction skills and a tireless work ethic would be the core of her survival. It was a lesson she carried to this day, working long hours at carpentry jobs until she'd gotten things just right and at the Foster House, Beacon Club, and Seaside to ensure everything ran smoothly. She had become the one who others relied on for their survival.

Dax pushed the covers off and tossed her legs over the side of the bed. The room's bones—window, closet, wood slat floor, bed, and dresser—were as she remembered from her childhood. However, her mother had removed everything Dax had added—magazine clippings of woodwork she wanted to mimic, the bowl of marbles she'd collected from kids dropping them at school, and the ribbon Rose had once tied around her finger to stop a cut from bleeding. In their place were doilies, oil lamps, and framed photographs of great-grandparents.

Her mother had expunged Dax's existence from the room, but she could not erase her memories of her seminal childhood event. Memories of leading Rose up the stairs and to this bed flooded back. She even remembered the rose scent of her perfume and how it tickled her nose when she leaned in for their first kiss that day. *Rose for her Rose*, she thought.

Her heart had thumped so hard she thought it would explode from anticipation. Then, when her hand touched a breast for the first time, every nerve ending had sparked at once, sending tingles everywhere. She had never felt more alive, more connected to another person. And from that moment, she knew she and Rose would be connected for life.

After using the bathroom, Dax headed for the stairs. Unlike last night, the door to her parents' bedroom was open. Curiosity drew her toward it. She peeked inside. The room hadn't changed much since she saw it thirteen years ago, except for one minor addition to her father's nightstand—a framed photograph of her parents on their wedding day. Tears formed in her eyes when she imagined him looking at it every night while crying himself to sleep in his empty bed. He was alone every hour of every day.

Dax shook off her melancholy and went downstairs, discovering Hank asleep on the couch and Charlie sitting in the nearby armchair. Charlie raised an index finger to her lips, signaling Dax to remain quiet. Dax wished Charlie had taken her offer to rotate shifts sitting with Hank, but she had insisted on not leaving his side, saying, "We've been through too much together. I'm not about to leave him now."

Dax stepped closer and whispered, "Have you seen my father?"

"He went to pick up breakfast for everyone."

Dax focused on Hank. His scraggly whiskers made him look unkempt, a departure from his typically clean-shaven face. "How did he sleep?"

"He tossed and turned a lot but wasn't in pain."

"The medication Jules left must be helping."

"Definitely," Charlie said. "This is the most he'd slept in days, and I supposed this is the latest he'd slept in since taking over at the Foster House."

Dax glanced at the wall clock and gasped. It was almost nine o'clock. She'd promised to call Rose by eight. "I overslept too. I need to check in with everyone." She circled the couch where the phone was on the end table near Hank's feet, discovering the handset wasn't set on the cradle. "The phone is off the hook."

Hank stirred and pushed himself upright on the couch. "I'm sorry. I think I kicked it in the middle of the night."

"It's okay. We need to call our ladies." Dax picked up the phone handset, clicking the receiver several times to reconnect the line. Hearing the right tone, she had the operator dial the Foster House number. After the tenth ring, concern set in. Even on the busiest day at the restaurant, someone picked up by the fifth ring. Today was Tuesday, and the dining room was closed, but Rose, May, or Jules should have picked up by now, even if they were upstairs. She hung up and tried the number at May's house but received no answer. She tried the Foster House again, thinking they may have been out back or in the bathroom.

The call finally connected. "Foster House."

Dax recognized the voice. "May, sorry I overslept."

"Thank goodness."

"Charlie and I fixed up my truck last night, and we got to sleep late. I tried calling a few minutes ago, but no one answered."

"I was at the house hanging up some laundry. We tried calling earlier, but Holly said the phone was off the hook. I thought Wilkes's men had gotten to you."

"We're fine. Hank knocked over the phone in the middle of the night. Tell Jules the medication she gave him helped him sleep."

"She's not here. We were all worried, so Jules and Rose took the Seaside truck to check on you. They should be there soon."

"Here?" Dax's stomach churned what was left from last night's fried chicken. "They're coming here?" Her words came out too strong and likely came across as angry.

"There's no need to be cross. What were we supposed to do?" May sounded more hurt than defensive. "You hadn't called, and we couldn't ring the house. We thought you were dead or captured."

"I'm sorry, May. I didn't mean to upset you, but Wilkes's men likely followed them."

"Not a chance. I distracted them by bringing breakfast to their car so Jules could pull out from the Seaside." May laughed. "They were surprised but mighty thankful and didn't see a thing."

"That was very sneaky of you three. You'd make great cat burglars, but I'm still not sure their coming here is a good idea. It's dangerous."

"There was no stopping them if I wanted to. Frankly, I'd be with them if I didn't think I'd slow them down with this bum leg. But I'm glad I stayed. At least I know everyone is safe. How is it being around Papa again?"

"Awkward. We talked a bit. He wasn't happy to learn you were married to Hank when you came for the funeral and didn't say anything."

"Papa gave up the right to know how I was getting along after mentioning he'd read about Logan's death. He and Mama had no idea what kind of man he'd become and how I welcomed his death. As far as they knew, I was a grieving widow. I'll tell you why they didn't reach out. It was Mama. He always did as she said. She was still angry over my telling her where to stick it when she wanted to send you to Kansas. She also knew I didn't care about you and Rose being different and called me an abomination for allowing it. Papa should have stood up for us, but he didn't. I didn't want him to get excited about having another son-in-law."

Dax would have done the same thing. As May's father, he should have reached out to her despite his wife not approving of May's actions. "I'm sorry you went through that and for me letting the cat out of the bag."

"It's better this way. Now he knows how it feels to be cut off." Surprisingly, May sounded resolved, not hurt, which was sad. Their only surviving parent lived forty miles away, but he was so far apart from May and Dax he might as well have been on the other side of the country.

"He looks old and lonely," Dax said.

"As he should."

Their conversation had turned unexpectedly spiteful and needed a new direction. "Any word from Grace?"

"She called my number before I left the house and said the governor would help. He's sending several state police officers with Clive to take Hank and Charlie into protective custody until the California attorney general can sort things out."

"That's great news. I'll let them know." The front door opened, and Dax's father appeared around the corner with more to-go bags from the neighborhood café. "I gotta go, May. Papa came back with breakfast for everyone."

"I'll be darned." May's tone turned lighter than during their earlier discussion about their father. Maybe there was some room for reconciliation. "Please keep me posted."

"Will do." Dax hung up the phone and helped her father with the bags. "Thanks for the food, Papa. Let me give you some money for it."

Her father waved her off. "Charlie got the old Model T working. I thought that thing was a lost cause. Breakfast was the least I could do."

"It's much appreciated, Papa." Dax distributed the boxes. She expected her father to retreat to the kitchen to eat, but he sat in an armchair, placing his container on the coffee table. "Mind if I join you?"

Dax swallowed past the lump of emotion in her throat. "I'd like that."

After Dax told everyone about the possibility of Jules, Rose, Clive, and the state police coming, they ate in silence. Before they were half done with their meals, the sound of a car coasting down the driveway on the side of the house caught everyone's attention. Dax jumped to the window and peeked through the drapes but saw only a pickup's tailgate.

"It's a truck," Dax said. She and Hank drew their firearms from their waistbands, holding them at the ready.

"Guns?" her father said, recoiling. "What the hell are you doing with guns?"

Dax had never heard her father say a swear word until now. It sounded odd, but they'd rightly upset him. "I'm sorry, Papa, but those deputies nearly killed Hank and tried to rape Charlie. We won't give them a chance to try again."

He shook his head with disapproval. "I won't allow guns in this house."

"It's a little late for objections." Dax heard the truck park around back and turned to Hank. "You cover the front. I'll take the back."

While Charlie helped Hank off the couch, Dax darted from the sitting room and through the kitchen, stopping at the window at the door. She inched the curtain enough to peek through. Setting her focus on the passenger compartment, she saw two heads inside when the driver backed in, parking next to her truck. She tightened her grip around the butt of her pistol when the truck doors opened but relaxed when the people turned around.

"It's okay," she yelled loud enough to carry her voice to the front of the house. "It's Jules and Rose." She opened the back door. When she waved them inside, they picked up their pace. Jules darted in first, with Rose three steps behind. Dax closed the door, spun around, and pulled Rose into her arms. Their tight embrace spoke of profound relief for the other being safe.

Rose squeezed more firmly. "You're alive."

"You're safe." Dax pulled back, realizing Jules had disappeared deeper into the house. "You shouldn't have come."

"We thought you were dead."

"I know. I talked to May. She said the governor is sending the state police here with Clive. They should be here soon."

"Thank goodness. All of this will be over soon."

Dax's father appeared in the kitchen doorway, turning Rose's face ashen with fear. She withdrew her arms in a flash.

Dax placed a hand on Rose's back for reassurance. "It's okay, Rose." She turned to her father. "Papa, you remember Rose Hamilton." He acknowledged Rose silently with a nod, which was more than she expected. "They won't stay long. And like I said earlier, we should all be gone very soon."

"They were followed," Hank shouted from the sitting room. A second later, gunshots and the sound of breaking glass rang out.

"Get down!" Dax covered Rose with her body and fell to the floor with her. She craned her neck to locate her father. He was face down on the floor but wasn't moving. A sense of dread seeped in when she spotted a dark pool of blood growing near his head. He'd been shot. "Papa!"

The smell of smoke wafted in from the front part of the house and grew thicker as gunshots continued to pelt the building. Shouts and scuffling noises from the sitting room signaled the others were making their way toward the back.

"Stay down," Dax said to Rose. "I need to help my father." She crawled to him on her hands and knees. A closer inspection revealed a gunshot wound high on his shoulder on his back. Based on its location, the bullet likely missed his heart and lungs. She shook him. "Papa. Papa. Are you okay?"

He moved the arm on his uninjured side and moaned while turning his head.

"You've been shot. Try not to move."

Jules appeared in the doorway, carrying the duffle bag with the weapons and ammunition. Charlie was on her heels, supporting Hank with an arm over her shoulder.

"They're using incendiary bullets from the war to burn us out," Hank said. "The front of the house is on fire."

"We can't leave yet. My father was shot." Dax helped him to a sitting position. He was groggy but becoming more alert.

"We need to control his bleeding." Jules dropped the bag and removed his belt. "Grab me a bunch of dishtowels."

Dax dashed to the cabinet left of the sink, where her mother used to store the towels. Opening the second one from the top, she was relieved to see her father was a creature of habit. She grabbed a handful of towels. Jules pressed them against her father's wound and tightened the belt around his shoulder, crafting a makeshift tourniquet.

Hank dug into the bag, pulling out the shotguns. He kept one and tossed the other to Dax. "We have to get to the trucks and shoot our way out."

"Give me a gun," Rose said. "I'll help."

"Me too," Jules said. Charlie gave her a disapproving look, but there wasn't time to argue. Hank had trained the women on how to use a firearm properly. Dax and Rose had kept up with regular target practice at the dock, but Jules had only a few lessons in deference to Charlie's aversion to guns. Dax was an excellent shot and was comfortable with any type of firearm, but Rose and Jules had only practiced on pistols.

Hank handed them the two handguns Clive had dropped off. "They're loaded, but we're limited on bullets."

Both ladies nodded their understanding. Safety was paramount, but aiming small and pulling the trigger only twice in short bursts to conserve ammunition was the critical lesson to remember today.

Charlie and Dax pulled her father to his feet. "Can you walk, Papa?"

"I think so." His voice was weak, but his legs seemed steady.

"I have him," Charlie said, throwing his uninjured arm over her shoulder. "Let's get him into your truck."

"Not without Caroline's picture." Her father gripped Dax's arm and pleaded with his eyes. "It's the only thing I have left."

"I'll get her, Papa. I saw it on your nightstand this morning." Dax turned to Hank. "Get everyone outside. I'll be right behind you."

The smoke grew thicker, reinforcing the urgency. The sense this might not end well swept through Dax, driving her to pull Rose closer with her arm and kiss her with enough passion to last through eternity. Pulling back, Dax winked and said, "I'll be right back. You and me with my pops." Another volley of gunshots assaulted her childhood home. She handed the shotgun to Rose. "Go."

While the others went for the back door, Dax made her way toward the hallway leading to the stairs. From the corner of her eye she saw bright orange flames dancing toward the ceiling in the sitting room and curtains in the entry hall billowing from bullets passing through them. She dashed to the stairs, flinching as a round whizzed past her ear. The wisdom of risking her life for a picture of the mother she despised became questionable. However, her father was a broken man who clung to memories to get through the day. She had to do this for him.

She reached the top level in seconds, taking the stairs two at a time. Her father's room was the first on the left, but she ran first down the hallway to her old room. She took one last look at where her and Rose's bond first formed before grabbing the family pictures from the wall. Retracing her steps, she slipped into her father's room, snatched the frame from the nightstand, and flew down the stairs.

The flames and smoke had grown stronger, completely engulfing the front of the house. Fire would reduce her childhood home to ashes within the hour. Coughing through the rooms on the bottom floor, she bounded through the kitchen door to the backyard, clutching the only reminders of their family history.

Her father and Rose were waiting in Dax's truck. Charlie was boarding the driver's side of the Seaside pickup while Jules got in beside her, and Hank waited to climb in last next to the passenger door. Hank called out, "Windows down. Guns out."

Dax heard loud voices in the front of the house before jumping behind the wheel of her truck and placing her pistol on her lap for quick access. Her father was on the center of the bench seat, pressing a hand against his injured shoulder. Rose was sitting closest to the passenger door with the window down and the shotgun hanging out, ready to shoot their way out.

This was it. The next minute would determine whether they lived or died.

Dax started the engine and put the transmission into gear. A glance confirmed Charlie had done the same and rolled the Seaside truck closer. They were in this together to the very end.

Dax gave her a nod, pressed the gas, and prayed they would make it out alive. She turned onto the straight part of the driveway. Flames lapped from the house windows between them and the street. At least two cars blocked the end of the driveway.

Two men were behind the sedans with their guns pointed in their direction, but there had to be more. Roy Wilkes would not have come without an overwhelming force.

Dax positioned her foot to throttle the engine. A horrifying vision of Rose and her father dying in a hail of gunfire flashed in her head, making her hesitate. But what choice did she have? The house was burning. They were trapped and would die trying to escape or huddled in a corner.

She twisted her hands tightly around the steering wheel and asked, "What do we do?"

CHAPTER THIRTY-TWO

The bay wind whipped past the ferry's bow, chapping Clive's cheeks. Logic told him this was the fastest route to Alameda from the governor's private mansion, but standing at the deck railing, waiting while the boat took them to the eastern bay shoreline, made him feel like he wasn't doing enough. Every minute here was another minute Hank, Charlie, and Dax fell deeper into danger. When the ferry dock finally came into view, Clive returned to the back seat of Rawlins's state police vehicle. They were ten minutes away from bringing Hank and Charlie's nightmare to an end.

The sergeant craned his neck from the front passenger seat. His stern expression meant a lecture was coming. "Governor's pet or not, this is a police matter, and I'm in charge. If I need your expertise, I'll ask for it. Otherwise, you do as I say. Got it?"

Clive gave him a two-finger salute.

"You don't talk much, do you?" Rawlins eyed Clive like he was still sizing him up.

"No."

Clive's senses heightened once the ferry docked and the crew of dockhands buzzed around securing the lines. They would be at the Xander home in five minutes, hopefully beating Roy Wilkes in his high-stakes game. He double-checked the sniper's rifle he had brought. It was his preferred weapon—the one with which he had racked up the bulk of his kills during the war. He feared if his skills were needed, he would need every advantage.

He knew every aspect of the M1917 Enfield rifle and 1916 Aldis scope. The weapon weighed a little over nine pounds unloaded. The scope added another pound. The gun was forty-six inches long with a twenty-six-inch-long barrel. It had an effective firing range of six hundred yards, meaning he could hit his target as far as a third of a mile away. He'd tested that range only once years ago and, surprisingly, hit his mark. The center-mounted scope was one of the few with a micro-adjustable elevation dial, which came in handy at longer distances and would create the advantage he might need today.

The ramp extended from the dock and fell into place with a loud clank. A worker lowered the rail and chains guarding the aft. Rawlins's driver eased their police vehicle off the boat, and the other three cars followed.

Clive glanced at the horizon in the direction of the Xander home and saw a large plume of dark, billowing smoke rising in the sky. He had a sinking feeling it was a sign they were too late. He leaned forward on his seat to peer over the front bench and provided directions to the driver. The caravan sped down the streets of Alameda with the sirens blaring, parting the late-morning traffic with ease.

The thought of not getting there in time made his heart race. Things could end in disaster if Clive didn't counter its rise. Nerves and adrenaline were a sniper's worst enemy. Moving his hands a fraction of an inch or inhaling at the wrong moment could send his bullet off course by several feet, depending on the distance. He closed his eyes for a moment and put out of his mind the thought of lives hanging in the balance, the noise from the siren, and the movement of the banking car. Instead, he concentrated on taking slow, steady breaths.

"Holy hell," Rawlins said when the vehicle completed a turn. The increase in his pitch meant something was desperately wrong.

Clive sprang his eyes open, discovering he was too late. Wilkes had found them. The Xander home, six buildings down, was engulfed in flames. Four sedans were parked in front, blocking the street. Eight men, four wearing civilian clothes and four dressed in police uniforms, were using the vehicles as cover while firing their weapons at the house.

This was tricky. Despite the certainty of corruption driving the situation, the presence of uniformed officers meant the state police could not take on the attacking force without first determining the circumstances. That was unless Wilkes's men turned their weapons on Rawlins and his team.

The driver skidded to a stop three houses away, turning off the siren and angling the car to use it as a barricade. The other vehicles did the same.

A tall man dressed in a suit stuck out like a sore thumb. "It's him," Clive said. "That's Wilkes."

"Which means they're out of their jurisdiction." Rawlins exited their vehicle with a megaphone and took cover behind a fender. His driver followed, as did the officers from the other three cars behind them, drawing pistols, shotguns, and one force-multiplying tommy gun.

Clive leaped out with two pistols in twin shoulder holsters beneath his jacket and his trusty rifle in both hands. He approached the sergeant. "I can skirt the houses across the street and come up behind them if your men draw their attention."

"Get in position, but wait. We don't know what this is yet. You're my last resort." Rawlins lifted his megaphone toward the men firing at the house. "This is the state police. Cease fire."

Clive didn't wait to see what type of greeting Wilkes would give Rawlins and his men and took off to get into position. The properties had large front yards with houses set deep on the lot. Trees and shrubs in each yard provided excellent concealment as he dashed from one home to the next, carrying his rifle at the ready position.

The gunfire came to a slow stop after Rawlins repeated his command twice. The sergeant raised his megaphone again. "This is Sergeant Rawlins of the California State Police. I'm under orders from the governor to take the fugitives into state custody."

Wilkes shouted back, "I'm San Mateo County Sheriff Wilkes in pursuit of fugitives who killed my deputies. I'm ending this today."

"You were not in hot pursuit and have no jurisdiction in Alameda County, but I do. I will not repeat this order again. Lower your weapons and let my officers approach."

"They killed my brother," Wilkes shouted.

Clive took a position behind an old poplar tree, giving him a clear view of the burning house and Wilkes. Its trunk would provide excellent cover and a sturdy brace. Unfortunately, he was mildly out of breath and would need fifteen seconds to get it under control. Until he did, he could not trust his aim.

Five men lowered their weapons, but Wilkes and the other two remained steadfast. It was crystal clear, despite the lack of jurisdiction and orders of the state police, Roy would not let anyone in the house leave alive.

Hank was more like a brother than a cousin to Clive. Losing him would hit him hard, but at least he would go down fighting like a true soldier. Like Clive, he'd faced death so many times he no longer feared it. However, Charlie, Dax, and her father weren't conditioned to be so callous about danger and being trapped. Cornered animals feared the worst and made terrible choices. Clive felt most for Jules, Rose, May, and the others they would leave behind. The senseless loss would devastate them for years.

Rawlins's men moved forward with their guns drawn. The other two men lowered their weapons, leaving only Wilkes as the last holdout. He shifted position to shield himself from the approaching state officers but kept his pistol pointed toward the house. Then, Dax's truck appeared in the long driveway along the side of the house and crept toward the street. Wilkes raised his pistol to cock back the hammer. This was it. Clive was their only hope. Screw waiting. He would face the consequences after the dust settled.

His breathing settled. His surroundings faded quickly into white noise. He leveled his rifle, placed his right cheek against the American walnut butt, and lined up his eye with the scope lens. Angling the barrel, he aligned the heavy vertical post of the crosshairs with his target and lowered it until the finer horizontal bar was even with his aiming point—the center jacket seam between the shoulder blades.

After his first kill during the war, Clive learned to stop thinking of his target as a living, breathing human being. For his subsequent seventy-four kills, it became an inanimate object. A challenge to hit the button dead center at two hundred yards. He didn't consider the button was on a man's chest, fastening the uniform of someone's son, husband, or father. Today, however, his target had a name. Roy Wilkes had to die before he killed those Clive cared about most in the world.

He adjusted the brass elevation dial atop the center-mounted scope to account for the estimated fifty-yard distance. When Wilkes redirected his aim at the truck's windshield, Clive squeezed the trigger with slow, steady pressure in order to not jerk the rifle, sending the thirty-aught-six Springfield bullet down range at two thousand eight hundred feet per second. A half second later, it pierced his target dead center on the jacket seam.

Clive lifted his head to see the man, not the target. Wilkes jerked, stiffening his posture, before dropping to his knees. His pistol tumbled to the pavement a second before he fell face down. There was no chance of survival. Hank and Charlie's nightmare was finally over, but the footsteps approaching his own position rapidly meant his was about to start.

Clive raised his weapon and free hand to show he was no longer a threat. He'd taken the shot contrary to Rawlins's order to wait, but he'd seen too many times how waiting for the first shot ended in disaster. He stood by his decision.

Rawlins reached him while his men rounded up the others. His flaring nostrils suggested he was mad enough to toss a right cross at Clive's face. Instead, he gathered his anger with a deep breath and snatched the rifle. "I told you to wait."

Clive stared him directly in the eye. It was hard to tell if Rawlins was angrier at Clive for taking the shot or himself for losing control of the crime scene. "Things were happening fast. We both saw he was about to shoot. I did the right thing, and you know it. If you need someone to blame, point the finger at me. I would rather sit in jail than attend my cousin's funeral."

"You better hope one of those deputies backs up your wife's assumption about Wilkes. Otherwise, you'll face a murder charge."

"Then let's flip one." Clive shifted his focus to the Xander house when a clanging fire truck's bell announced that help to put out the fire was seconds away. Unfortunately, the house was a total loss. The doors to Dax's truck opened, giving Clive a heart-stopping surprise. Rose stepped down from the passenger side and helped Dax's father out. Dax rushed to his side. A second truck appeared in the driveway. Charlie and Hank exited, and Jules followed.

Clive took a deep breath of relief. If he hadn't taken the shot, Rose could have been killed, and the cataclysmic event would have destroyed Grace. While the group joined up near Dax's truck, he jogged across the street to meet them. Dax's father appeared to have been shot, but Jules was tending to him.

"Is everyone safe?" Clive asked.

"Thanks to you, cousin," Hank said, patting him on the arm.

A fire truck, two local police cars, and an ambulance converged on the street. The personnel buzzed around in a hectic fashion. Rawlins took command of the scene.

Hank divided his attention between Clive and the state police herding Wilkes's deputies and thugs to their vehicles. "Wait a minute. I have a score to settle." He marched to the group of uniformed deputies, flipped one around, and threw the most brutal punch of his life onto the man's face. "That's payback for the shiner you gave me."

A chaotic scuffle ensued while the state police officers held back the other deputies to prevent a free-for-all in the street.

Rawlins stepped into the middle of it. "Settle down." Once tempers cooled down, he lined up the men. "Are all of you San Mateo deputies?" Following affirming nods, he said, "Wilkes has been under investigation for murder and setting up the fugitives for killing those deputies. All of you are now under investigation, too. The first to tell us what we want to know will get a pass. Any takers?"

CHAPTER THIRTY-THREE

The last time Dax was in a hospital, she had been waiting for someone to tell her about May's condition following the leg-crippling traffic accident in San Francisco. Hours of not knowing if she would walk again, let alone survive, overshadowed her memory of that place. Twelve years later in Oakland, waiting for news on her father, she concluded all hospitals were the same. Providence Hospital was newer with more modern conveniences than Saint Mary's, where the ambulance had taken May years ago, but both had the same antiseptic smell, white walls, linoleum floor, overworked staff, and worried family members. The only difference was not being alone this time.

Dax's friends and family had taken over one side of the waiting hallway. Clive kept the state police guarding Charlie and Hank in check while they waited to be examined and treated. Jules served as the mover and shaker, translating doctorese and getting updates from the real people in the know—who turned out to be her former classmates from nursing school. Rose had fetched coffee and water from the hospital cafeteria for the group and distributed the cups before returning to Dax's side. The group remained quiet, adding to the tension of not knowing the outcome of her father's surgery.

"You should drink something." Rose offered her some water.

"Thank you." Glancing at the staff and other visitors in the hallway, Dax grazed a pinky against her hand while accepting the paper cup. She wanted to lace their fingers or link arms, but the public space didn't allow for more.

When they first arrived in the waiting area, a man sitting in a chair along the opposite wall had slung his arm around the shoulder of the worried woman next to him and regularly showed her affection. If Jules and Charlie or Dax and Rose had done the same for one another, they would have drawn stares, inviting the police officers a few yards away to haul them away for disturbing the peace. It wasn't fair, but it was the world they lived in. The harsh truth made their life at the Foster House unique and blissful.

Dax sipped the water and returned to her vigil, splitting her attention between the double doors on both ends of the corridor. The one to her left led to the surgical area, where the doctors were working on her father. The one to her right led to the hospital's main entrance, where visitors would arrive from.

Motion to her right caught Dax's attention. The doors swung open. Henry held the door open, and May stepped through, taking solid and urgent strides in her brace. Her limp was barely noticeable.

Dax placed her cup beneath her chair and stood, greeting her with a tight embrace. Their matching deep sighs spoke to their mutual worry.

May pulled back. "Any word on Papa yet?"

"We haven't heard anything officially from the doctors, but the nurses have kept Jules informed. Things were looking good, and he should be out of surgery soon."

May scanned the chairs lining both sides of the hallway. "Where's my husband?"

"In the bathroom."

May stepped to Charlie, pulling her up for a hug. "Hank told me a bit of what you two went through. Thank you for keeping him safe."

"We looked out for one another." Charlie dipped her head to hide a frown, clearly struggling with the events of the last five days.

May turned her attention to Jules, giving her an equally tight embrace. "You are a true nightingale. Thank you for tending to my husband and father. They might not have survived if you hadn't stepped in."

"You're welcome. I'll go bug the nurses again for an update." Jules turned to go down the opposite end of the corridor but bumped into Hank before taking a single step. Thankfully, they collided on his right side.

"Whoa. Trying to put me back in the treatment room?" Hank quipped.

"Drumming up patients? Now that's a thought." Jules laughed before heading down the hallway.

Dax glanced at May to catch her reaction. She saw her gasp and throw a hand over her mouth. Hank's bruises were in full bloom, but thankfully the swelling had receded from its peak. May might have fainted if she'd seen him when he could not open his left eye. She appeared unsure how to greet him. Dax would have, too, considering how he favored his left side and the swollen cut lip. A hug or kiss might spike his pain.

May's hand trembled when she rubbed his right arm. "I'm so relieved you're safe."

Hank gently pulled her head to his chest. "The worst has passed, but it's not over yet."

"When should we hear something?"

"It depends on how long Wilkes's deputies hold out. Until then"—he glanced at the two state police officers close by— "Charlie, Clive, and I are in their custody."

"At least Wilkes can't bother us again." May waved Clive up and also hugged him. "Thank you for saving everyone. I can't thank you enough."

"You're welcome, May," Clive said. "I'm relieved I got there in time, but the house was a total loss."

"The house doesn't matter. What's important is that everyone made it out alive."

Once everyone chose seats, the double doors to Dax's right swung open again. Sergeant Rawlins appeared. His expression was as unreadable as it had been on the street in Alameda.

Hank, Charlie, and Clive stood silently as if rising in court to receive the verdict.

Rawlins stopped a yard away and focused on Hank. "The one you gave a shiner flipped. He was there when Wilkes killed his own men for letting you get the jump on them."

"That's what I figured." Hank blew out a loud breath. "What about our initial arrests and escaping custody?"

"Once you were cleared of the murders, the governor had the attorney general drop the charges." Rawlins shifted his attention to Clive. "You're off the hook, too. Every one of the deputies confirmed the story. Wilkes wasn't going to leave until he killed everyone in that house. You're all free to go."

The group mumbled, "Thank goodness." "What a relief." "Finally."

Dax, however, thought of the lives almost lost today. She, Rose, Charlie, Jules, Hank, and her father. The new life May had built in Half Moon Bay would have been over. Dax imagined how her life might have turned out. She supposed Grace and Clive would have taken care of her, so a place to live and food on the table would not have been an issue, but loneliness would have. Everyone she held dear would have been lost, making Dax wonder how long she would have been able to go on.

Following a round of handshakes, the officers left. The group fell into comfortable conversation, adding a lightness to the air. The only unknown remaining was Dax's father, but Jules's smile when she walked through the double doors suggested their long nightmare might finally be over. Conversations came to a slow stop. Everyone focused on Jules for news. Dax and May clutched hands.

"He's out of surgery and is almost out of recovery," Jules said. "The bullet caused only tissue damage, so he should fully recover in a month."

Dax squeezed May's hand. "When can we see him?"

"I can walk you back now. His nurse is an old classmate of mine. She's given me full run of the place, but I had to promise to limit him to two visitors at a time."

May turned to Hank and Dax to Rose. Both squeezed the other's hand, but Hank added a barely there kiss on the cheek to not irritate his cuts. Dax wanted to do the same to Rose, but the couple across the hallway was looking on. "We'll be back soon," she said.

Dax and May followed Jules through the doors into the restricted area. Orderlies wheeled patients in gurneys. Nurses pushed wheelchairs. Several rooms were open, revealing sad, heartbreaking sights of patients wrapped in bandages, legs in traction, and one appearing to be at death's door with a mechanical breathing apparatus.

Jules entered the last door on the left, went directly to the foot of the bed, lifted a clipboard from a hook, and flipped through the attached papers. The room had the same white walls, linoleum, and sterile feel as the other parts of the hospital they had passed through. Their father was asleep on the bed, covered by white sheets and a gray wool blanket. His chest was exposed, and his shoulder was wrapped in white bandages.

"How is he?" May asked.

"His vitals look good." Jules returned the clipboard to its hook. "He was groggy in recovery but could answer questions and move his limbs. Other than the gunshot wound, he appears healthy as a horse."

"Thank goodness." May's shoulders slumped in relief.

Dax's knees nearly buckled. She'd hated what he had done but still loved him deep down.

Jules positioned two armless chairs bedside, close to her father's uninjured arm. "Take as much time as you need." She left quietly and closed the door.

Dax and May sat in the chairs. Dax touched their father's forearm while May held his hand. Fear. Worry. Sadness. Grief. Every heartbreaking emotion flowed between the sisters.

"I know he'll be okay, but I can't stop thinking how close he came to dying. I'm not prepared to lose him, too." May's voice cracked.

"Me neither." Tears fell from Dax's eyes. The last twenty-four hours had given her hope of opening a new chapter in their relationship. She wasn't foolish to think it would be perfect but hopeful enough to believe it would be an improvement. Even if it was merely being cordial on holidays, something would be better than nothing.

Her father stirred and his eyes fluttered open.

May stood, bending over him slightly. "It's May, Papa. Darlene and I are here."

"You're going to be okay, Papa." Dax rubbed his arm until he turned his gaze on her.

"Any word on the house?" he asked.

Dax dreaded telling him the only house he'd lived in since marrying her mother forty years ago no longer existed, but his dispirited tone suggested he knew the answer. "It's gone, Papa. The only things left are the garage, your Model T, and Mama's photo. I saved that."

His jaw muscles rippled. "What's done is done. Maybe I can live in the back of the truck until I figure out how I'm going to pay for the hospital bill."

"Don't worry about the money, Papa," Dax said. "I'll take care of it."

"And don't worry about a place to live," May said. "You can live with Hank and me. We have plenty of room."

His eyes turned misty. "I can't take your charity."

"It's not charity." May squeezed his hand. "We're family and need to stick together."

Dax cupped their hands with hers. "Yes, we stick together."

CHAPTER THIRTY-FOUR

December 5, 1933

Despite the arrests, shootouts, storm damage, and Grace's health scare, the Seaside Hotel and Club opened on time for the Fourth of July weekend, the traditional start of Half Moon Bay's tourist season. The hotel sold out the entire summer, attracting the elite from Hollywood, San Francisco, and Sacramento, and Rose's grand return to the Seaside Club made headlines from San Francisco to New York. The town was booming, and Frankie Wilkes must have been rolling in his grave because by the summer's end Half Moon Bay had finally become the West Coast's answer to Atlantic City.

Now, on the eve of a sea change for the country, Dax waited for her regular shipment at the top of the ramp in the chilly predawn air. The four men from the Beacon and Seaside Clubs and others from the nearby speakeasies, having a distaste for the cold, waited in their pickups. She enjoyed this time of night when the only noise was from the rhythmic waves lapping into the bay. The mesmerizing surroundings let her put regrets of the past and worries about the future aside and soak in the moment of being near the water. The ocean was mighty, standing the test of time. It was here long before her and would remain long after she was gone.

It was Tuesday, the day harkening her back to her first arrangement with the smuggler. Captain Burch had rotated the schedule following Roy Wilkes's death to keep the Prohibition agents guessing. The Foster House and Seaside Club were closed for the Half Moon Bay weekend, leaving only the hotel open with a skeleton staff to accommodate the offseason guests so she could sleep in after accepting their delivery.

The sound of engines grew louder as the Canadian motorboats approached the Foster House dock in the darkness. Six crafts pulled into the slips in a well-practiced formation. The crewmen unloaded the cargo in an assembly line. Five boats cleared out, but one, strangely, remained behind. While Dax descended the ramp, one man remained on the dock. Halfway down, she recognized his distinctive uniform and gray beard.

"Captain Burch, it's a pleasure seeing you again. To what do I owe the pleasure?"

"If today goes as expected, I wanted to be the one to deliver your last barrel."

Like Dax, he clearly sensed the end of an era on the horizon with the Twenty-first Amendment on the verge of ratification. When it passed, the production and sale of liquor would be legal again in the United States, effectively putting Burch's smuggling route out of business.

"That's very kind of you, Captain. I have a good feeling about today."

"As do I." His voice wasn't filled with sadness but with a resolve to accept the inevitable.

Dax had read the paper every day since the Seaside reopened. When Illinois and Iowa ratified, and Connecticut and New Hampshire did so the following day, it had become clear the amendment had momentum with other states voting and passing and calling for conventions. After Thanksgiving, Texas and Kentucky became the thirty-second and thirty-third states to vote for repeal. Yesterday's rejection in South Carolina was expected, but the conventions in three states today should guarantee passage unless state delegates went rogue.

"What do you plan to do after it passes?" Dax asked.

"I've been planning for months." A proud smile grew on his lips. "Once you and my other customers have secured legal deliveries, I'm retiring in Victoria. I bought a charming place on Harling Point where I can watch the shipping lanes instead of navigating them."

"I'm sure your wife will be happy to have you home more."

"If she's like every sailor's wife, she'll tire of me within a month and insist I find a hobby outside the house."

Dax laughed. "Try woodworking. It's very satisfying."

"Only if you agree to give me lessons during our summer visits."

"It would be my pleasure."

After bidding the captain a fond goodbye and overseeing her staff to store her last illegal barrel of whiskey, Dax slid into bed with Rose in their upstairs Foster House room. She had difficulty falling asleep. Her thoughts kept drifting to the transformation about to sweep through the country. Her business wouldn't change, but the way she conducted it would.

She'd negotiated deals with two bottling distributors in the Bay Area who were already gearing up for the end of Prohibition. Expecting that demand would outstrip supply at the beginning when more bars popped up, she'd built up a three-month supply of liquor in anticipation of a supply disruption. She was more concerned with how her clientele would change. What new kind of customers would her clubs attract? Would business drop off with the addition of competitors? Her one leg up was Rose Hamilton. Not a single club within two hundred miles had a star attraction of her caliber.

When the first signs of light broke through the window, Rose wiggled her bottom more firmly against Dax and adjusted the blanket to cover more of their shoulders to combat the chill in the room. Mornings in bed with Rose were Dax's favorite part of the day. They were rested and often sated from the night before. The quiet in the house before the restaurant opened made it seem like they were the only two people in the world. Except for the sound of running water in the pipes when Jules or Charlie used the bathroom, nothing would invade their private cocoon until they opened the bedroom door. Not prejudices. Not the law. And not their pasts. The only thing that mattered was the woman next to her.

Dax craned her neck to check the time on Big Ben, deciding eight o'clock was late enough for a possibly momentous day. "I think I'll get up. Pennsylvania and Ohio should convene at ten."

"Anxious?" Rose's voice was unexpectedly clear for just having woken, suggesting she might have been awake for some time.

"Aren't you?"

Rose flipped over to face Dax and traced a finger down her cheek. "Once it passes, you and the others won't be in danger of being arrested." Her hopeful eyes suggested all her worry would be assuaged once the thirty-sixth state ratified the amendment.

Dax scooted closer, placing a hand on Rose's hip. "I know the articles in the *Chronicle* about Wilkes's death spooked you, but you heard what the governor said when Grace introduced us. No one in the state will harass our businesses."

"But it doesn't mean federal agents won't come knocking today."

"True, but it won't be an issue in a few hours," Dax said.

Rose sighed. "At least Phillip Gandy left Grace's name out of the stories. She was worried about being connected to the clubs and it tainting her reputation with the public."

Dax fought back a grin but failed. "I can't believe you threatened to expose him as a cross-dresser." She giggled. "Remind me to never get on your bad side."

An hour later, Dax and Rose were showered and dressed. Dax's eyes burned from the lack of sleep, but she wanted to be awake for the broadcasts of the constitutional conventions being held today. Likely half the country would be listening, so she'd left instructions for the hotel clerk to turn on the radio in the lobby for the guests to listen. If things turned out as expected, passage of the Twenty-first Amendment would be the most impactful change the nation had seen since the 1929 stock market crash that still had the country in financial ruin.

They went downstairs and discovered Charlie and Jules at the center table in the dining room. They were also showered and dressed, which explained the water Dax had heard earlier. Brutus waddled over from Charlie's chair, greeting Rose first. That dog naturally gravitated toward her whenever they were in the same room, an instinct Dax understood. Resisting Rose's pull was impossible.

"Good morning, you two," Jules said before focusing on Dax. "The window in my room is sticking again."

Jules had moved in after the events in Alameda, and Dax had fixed her window twice since then. She suspected it had something to do with the frequent visits of Charlie and Brutus. Jules kept a storage chest under the window, and the claw marks on the sill said Brutus liked jumping up there to peer outside. Dax was surprised he hadn't broken the glass yet but held back saying something to Charlie. She was too damn happy having her back in her life.

Her dear friend was here four or five nights a week, staying overnight in her garage residence only when she had a large repair job requiring more time than expected. Dax understood why Jules hadn't moved into the Foster House sooner in deference to Charlie while she and Dax were on the outs. But with the bad blood behind them gone, she wondered why Charlie hadn't made it official and simply moved in.

"I'll get to it soon," Dax said. "Today should be a crazy day." She turned on the radio in the corner, tuning it to the San Francisco station carrying live information about the conventions, and returned to the center table.

The swing door to the kitchen opened, and May and Hank stepped through carrying trays of breakfast plates. May's eyes widened. "You're up this early on a delivery day?"

"I couldn't sleep."

"I left yours and Rose's plates under the warmer."

"Thanks. I'll get them." Dax held May's gaze for a few extra beats. Of all the changes in her past, May had been the one delightful constant since childhood. Through bad times and good. Through poverty and riches. Their bond was enduring and unbreakable, and seeing how happy Hank made her filled her with endless joy.

Dax squinted before turning and entering the kitchen. Her father was sitting at the center chopping block, eating breakfast. His face lit up when they locked eyes. "Good morning, Papa."

"Isn't it delivery day? I thought you'd be asleep for hours."

"It is, but I wanted to listen to the conventions."

"I think everyone will be by a radio today."

Dax picked up hers and Rose's plates. "Would you like to join us?"

His lips appeared to tremble. "I'd like that."

Since moving in with May and Hank, her father had taken most of his meals at the Foster House alone. His acceptance of her relationship with Rose and Charlie's with Jules had been steady. He'd taken a shine to Jules after the doctor told him whoever tended to his gunshot wound initially had likely saved his life. His gratitude for being alive was the wedge needed to slowly erode his bigotry. They were a long way off from Dax and Rose kissing in front of him, but yesterday he'd walked in when they were holding hands and didn't say anything. Joining them for breakfast was progress.

He grabbed his plate and drink and followed Dax into the dining room.

"Hey, Charlie," Dax started, alerting everyone to her father's presence.

Charlie jumped from her seat before she could say more, grabbed an extra chair from a neighboring table, and positioned it between Dax and May. "Right here, Mr. Xander."

"Harm. Please call me Harm."

Wow, Dax thought. He rarely allowed people to call him by his first name, not even Logan after he married May. A few friends from years back and Hank were the only exceptions.

"That goes for you too, Jules and Rose. We're all family, virtually living together, so we best be on first names."

"Will miracles never cease?" May mumbled before taking another bite of her potatoes.

Laughter broke out around the table, earning a smile from her father. They fell into a light conversation until someone called out from the kitchen. The muffled voice sounded familiar.

"In the dining room," Hank shouted. When Clive and Grace stepped through the door, he stood. "You're early. We weren't expecting you until this evening."

"We wanted to join you for the listening party." Grace greeted him with a hug before doing the same with the others around the table. Clive mixed it up with hugs and handshakes.

Dax was shocked when Rose told her about Grace's bout with breast cancer. But the poise she displayed while undergoing a week of radium treatment made Dax respect her even more. Grace looked stronger each time she visited. The cancer, thankfully, hadn't returned.

When Grace got to Rose, Rose's brow narrowed in concern. "How are you? Where's Greta?"

"I'm my old, old self." Grace winked. "She's filming and will join us on Thursday." She didn't have to explain. Dax had seen an incredible change in Grace after Greta joined her for the monthly visit to Half Moon Bay. She'd finally let go of the past and was living in the present.

After the dishes were cleared and coffee served, everyone listened in somber silence while the radio announcer relayed the near-simultaneous happenings at the Ohio and Pennsylvania conventions. When he announced both states had ratified the amendment, excitement buzzed in the room, with everyone recognizing the momentous event they were living through. The country needed only one more state's concurrence, and the Utah convention would convene within a half hour at eleven o'clock their time.

"I know it's early," Grace said, "but I think the next vote calls for champagne."

"I have something else in mind," Dax said. "Can you give me a hand, Charlie?"

"Sure." Charlie followed Dax downstairs to the Beacon Club bar.

Dax stopped to take in her surroundings, recalling the day she and Charlie had found the stray whiskey barrel at Gray Whale Cove and brought it here. "Do you remember the day we brought that first barrel here?"

"How could I forget?" Charlie grinned. "We sat in this room and hatched an idea to build our own speakeasy to sell it by the glass to pay for May's new leg brace and a little extra spending money."

"But our plan fell to pieces when Riley King busted up the place."

"And my head." Charlie ran a hand through her hair. Dax recalled watching Riley push her back, sending her tumbling down the stairs. She was terrified he might have killed her.

"Well, it was the start of a whole new life for all of us." Dax placed her hand on the ten-gallon whiskey barrel Captain Burch had personally delivered. "I thought it would be fitting if we all toast passage of repeal from the last barrel."

They carried the vessel upstairs, into the dining room, and placed it on the beverage counter. The head waitress, Ruth, had said the counter used to be the Foster House bar before Prohibition. Dax thought there was no better location for it. She tapped the barrel and poured seven glasses while listening to the Utah convention. At precisely 11:32, the announcer said, "…the amendment is ratified." Everyone cheered. By the end of the day, making and selling liquor would be legal.

Grace raised her glass. "What's old is new again. Thank you to everyone around this table for joining me on this journey. It has been the ride of a lifetime."

"Hear, hear!" everyone replied, drinking their shot in one gulp.

The phone rang by the register. Dax dashed across the room and picked it up. "Foster House."

"Miss Xander, it's Oliver." The desk clerk from the Seaside knew to call on her day off only if it was necessary. "You won't believe the line outside the club. It stretches up the stairs and out the lobby."

"Did you tell them we open at three for the celebration?"

"I did. Everyone is in a good mood, but they won't leave."

Dax peeked out the front window of the Foster House. A similar line had formed for the Beacon Club at the side of the building, making her laugh. "I'll be damned. The whole town wants to celebrate. Call everyone in early. We'll open both clubs within the hour."

The parties in the Beacon and the Seaside clubs lasted well into the night. Patrons drove in from as far as fifty miles to celebrate the repeal of Prohibition in Half Moon Bay. The staff was exhausted but in good spirits. Rose bounced between clubs, performing half-hour sets of upbeat songs with Lester every few hours to keep the energy high.

Around midnight, Dax took Rose by the hand, pulled her outside, and walked her to the Foster House pier. They went down the ramp to the end of the dock Dax had repaired years ago and stood at the railing, staring toward the dark horizon over the Pacific Ocean. This was home. Half Moon Bay with Rose would always be home for Dax.

A few stragglers from the Beacon were in the parking lot several yards away, so Dax resisted the urge to take Rose into her arms. However, when the clouds began releasing a light rain, she removed her jacket, draped it over their heads, and moved closer until their bodies touched.

"This reminds me of our first kiss under the poplar trees," Rose said.

"I burned that jacket." Dax remembered finding Rose in the poplar grove and throwing her school uniform jacket over her to shield them from the rain. The cocoon it formed had given Dax the courage to take a giant leap of faith and kiss Rose for the first time.

Rose gasped. "Why?"

"My mother wanted to sell it back to the school. I couldn't bear the thought of someone else wearing it, so I destroyed it."

"Oddly, that's one of the nicest things you've said to me." Rose giggled.

Dax chuckled. "You set the bar pretty low."

"I'm with you, aren't I?" Rose slapped her on the bottom.

"Forever, I hope." Dax kissed her, letting it linger. The sea didn't care if two women kissed, nor who they loved. Time would march on. She and Rose would leave more change in their wake, and years from now, their final kiss would be for all to see. And like the sea, no one would care because it would be commonplace. As it should be.

More Titles from Bella Books

Hunter's Revenge – Gerri Hill
978-1-64247-447-3 | 276 pgs | paperback: $18.95 | eBook: $9.99
Tori Hunter is back! Don't miss this final chapter in the acclaimed Tori Hunter series.

Integrity – E. J. Noyes
978-1-64247-465-7 | 28 pgs | paperback: $19.95 | eBook: $9.99
It was supposed to be an ordinary workday...

The Order – TJ O'Shea
978-1-64247-378-0 | 396 pgs | paperback: $19.95 | eBook: $9.99
For two women the battle between new love and old loyalty may prove more dangerous than the war they're trying to survive.

Under the Stars with You – Jaime Clevenger
978-1-64247-439-8 | 302 pgs | paperback: $19.95 | eBook: $9.99
Sometimes believing in love is the first step. And sometimes it's all about trusting the stars.

The Missing Piece – Kat Jackson
978-1-64247-445-9 | 250 pgs | paperback: $18.95 | eBook: $9.99
Renee's world collides with possibility and the past, setting off a tidal wave of changes she could have never predicted.

An Acquired Taste – Cheri Ritz
978-1-64247-462-6 | 206 pgs | paperback: $17.95 | eBook: $9.99
Can Elle and Ashley stand the heat in the *Celebrity Cook Off* kitchen?

Printed in the USA
CPSIA information can be obtained
at www.ICGtesting.com
JSHW082318140224
57425JS00001B/2